What readers are saying about Brooke Magnanti

'**Hugely impressive** . . . Brooke writes the kind of women we want to see in crime fiction'   Russel D. McLean

'One of the most **compulsively readable** crime novels of 2017 – 5*'   Amazon reader

'**Lively** and **entertaining**. When her victims are laid out on that slab, her unspeakably detailed descriptions are good enough to put the wind up Patricia Cornwell'   *The Times*

'**Whip-smart** thriller with surprises – 5*'   Amazon reader

'A helter-skelter of a book'   *Guardian*

'She uses her professional know-how to detail shockingly gruesome scenes . . . spins a web of real-life strands of political chicanery, greed and lies galore'
                                        Peterborough Evening Telegraph

'**Powerful** . . . constructively controversial'
                                        Hannah Betts, *Telegraph*

'A **clever**, satirical thriller'   *Daily Express*

'Twists which keep the reader engaged and the pages turning . . . **rewarding** and **engaging**'   *Huffington Post*

'**A thriller that steps outside the genre**'   Amazon reader

Brooke Magnanti received a Ph.D. in Forensic Pathology from the University of Sheffield, where she studied in the Medico Legal Centre and specialised in the identification of decomposed human remains. She later worked for the NHS in child health research and cancer epidemiology, before being revealed in 2009 as the anonymous author of the award-winning blog Belle de Jour and bestselling *Secret Diary of a Call Girl* series of books. She lives on the West Coast of Scotland with her husband and hardly ever sees dead people any more.

To find out more, visit her website at www.brookemagnanti.com, or follow her on Twitter @belledejour_uk

Also by Brooke Magnanti

The Sex Myth: Why Everything We're Told is Wrong
The Turning Tide

As Belle de Jour

The Intimate Adventures of a London Call Girl
The Further Adventures of a London Call Girl
Playing the Game
Belle de Jour's Guide to Men
Belle's Best Bits

YOU DON'T KNOW ME

BROOKE MAGNANTI

ORION

An Orion paperback

First published in Great Britain in 2017
by Orion Books
This paperback edition published in 2018
by Orion Books,
an imprint of The Orion Publishing Group Ltd,
Carmelite House, 50 Victoria Embankment
London EC4Y 0DZ

An Hachette UK company

1 3 5 7 9 10 8 6 4 2

A CIP catalogue record for this book
is available from the British Library.

ISBN 978 1 4091 6574 3

Typeset by Input Data Services Ltd, Somerset

Printed and bound in Great Britain
by Clays Ltd, St Ives plc

www.orionbooks.co.uk

For Mitali, Rosy, Emma, and Shilu.
For those nights in Newcastle,
and for the mornings after.

'Those who have inspected many bodies have at least learnt to doubt; while others who are ignorant of anatomy and do not take the trouble to attend it are in no doubt at all.'

Giovanni Battista Morgagni

: 1 :

'Fuck me, that's pure rancid,' Alastair Maclean said, and lit a cigarette. The sharp tang of smoke disguised some of the smell, but only a little.

In some places the first day of spring was sweet with the promise of life's renewal. In Cameron Bridge on the west coast of Scotland, the first day of spring smelled of slack tides and uncollected rubbish.

Police inspector Fiona Kennedy had other things on her mind. Namely the corpse on the ground in front of them. She looked askance at Alastair. He was the Area Commander and her boss, but he rarely acted that way. 'You think maybe you should have a smoke outside the tape?' she said. He shrugged, but did step closer to the edge of the scene.

The call had come in around dusk; a dead body behind the Yachtsman's Arms. No one had turned up to help them secure the scene, and the two witnesses, visibly shaken by the find, were still giving their statements inside. 'Davie's been ages with those kids.' She looked back at the pub. 'You reckon everything is OK?'

'Oh aye,' Alastair said and tapped his ash. The police had white plastic suits on over their clothes that crinkled every time they moved. Fiona wondered if his cigarette wasn't a fire hazard. 'The fella's one of the Bowden boys. Sheep farmers, that lot. He'll have seen worse.'

Fiona had grown up on a farm herself. Tales of delivering dead lambs by cutting their heads off first were typical gross-out-young-farmer stories. But this was different. This was a human. 'What about the girl?'

'Sarah?' Alastair said. 'Huh.' He paused to think about the implications of teenagers on a date finding a dead body by a skip. 'Nah, she'll be fine.'

Fiona dared not object. She had transferred down to Cameron Bridge from Inverness only a month before and was still feeling her way around this new town. Getting on the wrong side of her boss early on was not a good idea. Especially given how small the department was.

Davie Kennedy jogged over from the back door of the Yachtie. 'Got the statements.' Davie waved his notepad. 'Apparently they came out to check on the Bowden lad's dog . . .'

Alastair snorted. 'For a snog, you mean,' he said.

'He let the staffie off the lead, that's when they found it. Or rather the dog did. Jacky says Bingo was digging in the rubbish and he was trying to pull him out.' Davie grimaced. 'Hand came off in the dog's mouth.'

'I know.' Fiona had bagged the dry and blackened severed hand. The rest of the body wasn't fresh, but she couldn't guess at a time of death any more precise than 'a long time.' Now they were waiting on the forensic pathologist to turn up before moving the rest of the body.

'Amazed the dog could sniff out anything in this.' Alastair puffed on his smoke. 'When was the last time these bins were collected?'

'Two weeks, maybe more,' Davie said. 'Council halved the pickups over winter. You only notice now the weather's warming up.'

'Christ.' Fiona looked around. The headlights of the service cars had started to attract seagulls to the rubbish pile. After taking photos of the remains – brown and black mostly, half-wrapped in a cheap duvet – she had thrown some plastic sheeting over the scene. It was a makeshift effort and the birds were sure to start in on the mess if they waited much longer. She gave Davie a pointed look, hoping he would show some initiative and chase the gulls away, but he didn't take the hint.

Sited at the head of a sea loch, Cameron Bridge once marked

the border of a great Celtic kingdom that stretched from Ireland through the Hebrides and all the way up to the highest mountains in Scotland. Once Camerone Bridge had been a name that meant something. Now the town was just another coach tour stop chock-full of B&Bs with a high street selling tartan tat.

'Stupid place to dump a body,' Davie said. Alistair raised an eyebrow in his direction. 'I mean, you know, if I did someone in, I'd do it out in the country. Where they wouldn't be found.'

'You'd be surprised,' Fiona said. 'There's always a man with a dog. We had all sorts in Inverness. Weed growers dumping their spent plants in Culbin Forest, as if that didn't make it more suspicious.' Davie wasn't listening, though, he was checking his phone. 'Anyone in the pub see anything?' Fiona asked him.

'One or two, nothing detailed,' he said. 'Mind, it's Saturday and the auld boys have been propping up the bar since midday. They'd tell you they saw the ghost of Bonnie Prince Charlie dancing a jig on the bins if they thought there was a drink in it for them.' Davie looked at his watch. 'Where's the professor anyway? She's not usually this long.'

'What, you have somewhere better to be?' Alastair said. Davie reddened and looked away. 'Ah, night out is it? Saturday night picking up randoms at the Maryburgh?'

'Nah, nothing like that,' Davie said. 'I told someone I'd meet them for a drink, and . . .'

Alastair chuckled. 'I'm having you on, son,' he said. 'You go. Me and the skirt can hang around.'

Fiona gritted her teeth, and watched Davie disappear into the pub. Bit off for Alastair to assume she had nothing better to do that night. Not that she was the sort of person to desert an emergency call in favour of other plans. But the fact that MacLean didn't ask told her a lot.

'You tried Hitchin again?' Alastair said. A weekend call to the mortuary probably wouldn't be answered – the staff numbered only two – but the pathologist not picking up her mobile was unusual.

'Six times,' she said. 'Going through to voicemail.' Fiona had said it was an emergency, no specifics apart from the address, but what other kind of emergency did anyone ring a pathologist about? She spent the first hour expecting Harriet Hitchin to turn up, and the second hour concerned that something bad had happened to the professor herself. Now she was getting angry. This was surely taking the piss.

'You tried her house?'

Fiona nodded; there had been no answer there either. 'I could pop down the high street, try to find—'

'No, no.' Alastair waved his hand. 'No point chasing her down. Two of us have to stay on the scene at all times, that's policy. Anyway I'm tired of waiting. Go ahead and phone Iain, he'll bag it up. If Divisional Command have a problem later tell them it was my decision.'

Fiona scrolled through her phone contacts to find the mortuary assistant's number. She was not impressed that the only pathologist in Cameron Bridge was ignoring her mobile at a time like this. Alastair had a point: if Harriet Hitchin couldn't be bothered to show, then Fiona couldn't be bothered to go fetch her. Some things were more important than a Saturday night.

: **2** :

'Denise . . . Denise . . .'

The room was bright, too bright. The ceiling came into focus slowly. It was not the ceiling Denise had been dreaming of a moment ago. The last image imprinted on her mind was a rippling white cotton sheet, a fort made by two small children. Her and her brother's laughter dancing like motes of dust in sunlight.

This ceiling was different.

'Denise Ang? Miss Ang, are you awake?'

Now she remembered being carried through hospital hallways, the people who loaded her onto a bed and put on an oxygen mask.

A doctor stood by the blue privacy curtain. 'Hi. I'm Dr Deypurkaystha. How are you feeling?'

A hospital gown hung off Denise's thin shoulders. 'Fine, I think. Better than earlier.' Someone had removed her clothes, folded them, and laid the lanyard with the NHS identification card and office keys on top. She didn't remember being undressed. Denise adjusted the gown to try to regain some measure of dignity, but there was no point. The fabric was as thin as tissue.

She did not recognise the doctor, but that wouldn't have been difficult: the only doctors Denise usually saw at work were oncologists in the research unit. Newcastle's Royal Victoria Infirmary was connected to the medical school as well. There were hundreds, if not thousands, of people working there that Denise would never have recognised.

'Good, good.' The doctor waved a folder. 'We have some test results. But I'd like to talk to you first.' The doctor swept a plait of hair over her shoulder and perched on the edge of a chair. 'According to a witness, you were delirious, saying something about someone named Archie and a gun. Who's Archie?'

'Archie is . . .' Denise paused. After seven years together *boyfriend* sounded childish and insubstantial, but they were not married and he was not her fiancé. 'Archie is my partner. We live together.' Sort of. They sort of lived together. He was there almost as many weekends as not, anyway.

'I see,' Dr Deypurkaystha said. 'And something about your partner and a gun?'

Denise gulped. 'I don't remember,' she said.

'No, I thought not,' the doctor said. 'Anyway. You are not pregnant. We ruled out a heart attack. Everything in your ECG looks normal.' Dr Deypurkaystha's finger grazed over the sheet of test results. Lines showing Denise's heart activity scratched across the page in regular peaks and furrows. 'As a healthy woman – non-smoking, I hope? – we wouldn't expect your risk factors to be raised while you are still menstruating.' Dr Deypurkaystha looked over the top of her glasses. Denise nodded; she was only thirty. But there were layers to the question. She knew that. Her sharp shoulders and visible collarbones invited comment from random strangers, never mind what a doctor would think. 'Your blood work is normal and cholesterol within acceptable limits. Any family history of heart disease?'

'No,' Denise said. She picked at the edge of an electrode still stuck to her upper chest from the ECG examination.

'X-rays are back from radiology as well . . .' The doctor's eyes rested briefly on the bruise covering Denise's shoulder. It was weeks old now and fading, but the sunset of yellow and purple staining her skin would have been hard to miss. 'I know it wasn't what you were brought in for but . . . anyway. No harm in being thorough when someone presents with chest pains, is there? In case something is broken. A rib perhaps.'

'Was it?' Denise tugged at the hospital gown and looked

away. The bruise undoubtedly looked worse than it was.

'No bones broken,' Dr Deypurkaystha said. 'Do you mind if I ask what happened to cause that?'

'I . . . fell,' Denise said. 'I tripped and fell over.' Not technically a lie. It wasn't a good excuse, but she knew that people were grateful to accept even bad ones.

'It must have been quite a fall. To produce such extensive bruising. We would expect to see something like that from – oh, loads of things – falling down a flight of stairs. Or a severe beating.'

The last few syllables hung in the air over Denise. A dense cloud of black words that could fall on her, come crashing over her head and swallow her life if she dared look up, dared acknowledge them. 'No,' she said. 'None of those have happened. So what was it?'

The doctor set down the folder on the side of the bed. 'I see people with these symptoms every day. In all likelihood, you had a panic attack,' she said. 'Generally preceded by hyperventilation. Then pain, the shortness of breath, the collapse . . .'

Denise nodded. Maybe the doctor would keep talking about this, and forget about the other thing. 'Will it happen again?'

'Difficult to say,' the doctor said. 'Some people experience it once or twice in a lifetime. For others, it becomes a debilitating condition. What's happened is your body has gone into a fight-or-flight response triggered by something, probably stress. It dumps a load of epinephrine – adrenaline, as you probably know it – into your system. Your heart rate shoots up, respiration increases, and so on. Because it's being triggered in the wrong circumstances all that adrenaline has nowhere to go.' The doctor's eyes returned to Denise's bruises. 'Have you been under unusual amounts of stress lately?'

The black threads hovering over them started drawing down now, grazing the edge of Denise's hair. They were close enough that if she breathed they would shake some of their cold dust onto her. She exhaled in tiny puffs and tried not to disturb the air around her that now felt suffocating.

She could remember the moments before in stark detail. Most days Denise brought her lunch and ate it at her desk while she worked – she had her meals planned down to the last macronutrient, down to the last calorie – but there hadn't been time to pack one last night or this morning. So she had been stuck with the hospital canteen. The cheese salad, no. The chips, no. None of the stale, mouth-lacerating baguettes. She had walked past the hot line, its mystery meat swimming in pools of grey gravy, dished up by a girl with her bleached hair loosely held in a hairnet. She was laughing with a colleague, a diamond engagement ring bulging under her thin food-service gloves.

That was when it happened. The searing light of the hospital fluorescents, the smell of the refrigerated sandwiches by the till punched Denise in the face. Her heart thrummed. There was a sensation like a ratcheting of a belt over her chest, tighter and tighter. She collapsed on the floor. Denise tried to get up, to say she was OK really, but her limbs were heavy and her voice had disappeared somewhere in her stomach. The air conditioning pumped out cold air and the smell of meat grew stronger, cloyingly sweet.

A trickle of sweat popped up at remembering it, ran down her inside arm, under the hospital gown. She was aware that she smelled the same way as she did after a long run: like dirty dishes, like chicken soup. 'Once you sign the discharge papers here you're free to go,' the doctor said. 'But please, make an appointment to see your GP as soon as possible.'

Denise stretched her neck slightly to see what else was in the folder lying open on the bed. A white printed sticker with her name, her date of birth, a bar code. Her address in Wallsend – her and Archie's address, she reminded herself. 'I'll do that,' Denise said.

Dr Deypurkaystha looked over her glasses again. Her voice was more stern now. 'You should speak frankly to them and consider all of the options. If there are underlying issues, there are places where you could go if you feel in danger.'

'Danger?' Denise said. A dry feeling in her throat. Prickly. Danger.

'You might consider . . .' Dr Deypurkaystha paused. 'There are shelters. We can get you in a safe place, tonight. You wouldn't have to talk to the police if you don't want to.'

Denise tried to bring herself to a more upright position, aware that her efforts were slow and awkward. But she needed to move now, move before her inaction caused something to happen, something she would not be able to take back, hide, or explain away. 'Don't be silly. I need to get dressed and go back to work,' she said.

'I spoke to your supervisor. He's not expecting you back in the department today,' she said. 'Go home early. Rest.' A pause. The doctor reached out and touched her arm, a familiar gesture, as a mother or a friend would do. 'If you don't want to go home, there is help available . . .' Denise scowled and the doctor withdrew her hand.

'Really, all I'd like is some kind of sleeping pill. Not a long prescription,' Denise said. 'For a few days. I think it will help.' That was it, offer her something. Offer a compromise, then slip out of the door.

'Right, OK,' Dr Deypurkaystha said. 'But only three days' worth.' Her small hand fluttered out, but did not touch Denise this time. 'Consider what I said. The resources are stretched, but in cases like yours? I want you to know they are there. If you want them.'

Sunlight cut shafts in the gaps between buildings. Denise headed towards Haymarket. How to get home. The Metro? She wrinkled her nose. Too small, claustrophobic, and smelled of piss. The bus? But it was lunchtime, and swarms of people were going in and out of the station. She could already imagine their greasy pasties, the strong smell of lard and onions. No.

The black threads still crackled on the periphery of her vision. She blinked and blinked but they were still there no matter what she did.

She turned back in the direction of Jesmond. She could walk home, cross the bridge over Jesmond Dene, through the cemetery to the path that ran parallel to the Coast Road. It went practically to her front door.

Once past Jesmond Dene there was no one to be seen apart from a few children playing on the Waggonways, paths converted from the railway lines that used to join one pit to another. Gravel crunched under her feet. The doctor's words had unnerved her, almost as much as the collapse itself had done. She should have spoken up, said something. She should have set the record straight. Defended Archie. The doctor might think she could tell something from what she saw, but she didn't know the whole story.

Archie was always distraught by what he did. Appalled. He had no clue how it happened. Where it came from. It was against everything he stood for, everything he was. Maybe it was because of his ex? Being with her had changed him. And he was getting better, he really was, but it would take time to undo the damage Josie had done. It was almost eight years, now, that Denise had been with him.

She always forgave him, she told herself, because he loved her so much. He said so and it must have been true. He loved her so much that sometimes he couldn't control himself.

In the garden next door to Denise her elderly neighbour, Judy, rummaged by the gate with a clutch of garden tools. Judy's King Charles spaniel trotted out in front of her with a pair of gloves clamped in his little jaw.

She had bought a house at Archie's insistence, furnished it with a basic bed, sofa, desk, television. But it still looked as sparse as the day she moved in. Her work outfits hung in the closet, the gaps between them on the rail failing to disguise the unoccupied space. Black dress, grey dress, two pairs of trousers. Grey cardigan, green jumper, three button-down shirts.

She was the only person on her street who was not from Wallsend. Born in London, to the disappointment of people who asked where she was 'really from' Single, no children. Conspicuously not white. Neighbours were polite to her face. The locals were famed for their friendliness but Denise found over the years that it was all surface: that the charm and smiles extended only as far as their front doors.

Judy's dog was her constant companion since the stroke. Before retiring, Judy had worked for a small publishing house. Now she had no words left. Judy could only say a few things – mostly 'he' and 'no' and 'that'.

Archie could not imagine a worse fate, trapped inside your own head. 'I would sooner top myself,' he had said to Denise. It was of utmost importance that strangers and casual acquaintances never thought ill of him. Denise didn't argue even though she suspected she disagreed. Was Judy's world the living death sentence Archie thought it was? Judy could understand what was said, and on quiet nights, when Archie was away and Denise sat in the lounge reading, she could hear her television through the shared wall downstairs.

Judy nodded at Denise and smiled. Denise raised her hand and waved before going into her house.

Not my house, our house, she reminded herself. It was exactly that kind of carelessness, that self-centred habit of not thinking about *us* that Archie hated so much. It was what kept him from committing to her. She knew that. She turned her key in the lock and stooped to pick up the post from behind the door.

'You're home early,' a voice said.

Denise froze. Her chest felt tight. 'Archie? What a nice surprise. I didn't see your car.'

She had been good, very good, while he was away. She had only tried to ring him once. He didn't like it when she did that. It reminded him too much of Josie the bunny boiler. It had rung a few times before going to answerphone. The ring sounded odd, foreign, but of course that couldn't have been the case. He wasn't abroad. He had told her where he was going to be: Nottingham, or near there. As a tax investigator, he worked all over the country looking for counterfeit goods being smuggled through car boot sales.

'I parked at the office and walked back in the glorious fresh air.' He tucked his blond hair behind his ears. He looked flushed as if caught in the middle of something. 'I have decided to start parking elsewhere. You know how bad the crime is in this neighbourhood, Kitty-Cat.'

His generous girth filled up the entryway. Denise waited for an indication of what kind of a mood he was in. There was a pause, then he leaned forward and pecked her on the cheek. His broad hand with its shortish fingers patted her hair, smoothing it as he might a child's.

'I suppose you're right,' she said. It wouldn't do to argue. Even though the local statistics for home break-ins and theft were no worse in their part of Wallsend than they were in any other area bordering Newcastle.

If she mentioned the stats she knew what he would say. The same thing he said every time he introduced her to friends, or to any group of people. 'You know the saying, there's lies, damn lies, and statistics,' he would crow. 'And Denise, she works in statistics.' She hated the way it made her work sound made-up and suspect, but it seemed to get a laugh out of everyone else.

'I will never know why you insisted we move here!' he laughed. But it was lighter than usual, and only wounded her a little. 'I say, here's an idea.' She braced herself; his voice suggested a forced conviviality, that anything he was about to suggest would be something she could not easily refuse. 'Since I'm home early and you are too, why don't we go for an afternoon drive up the coast? We can frolic about on the beach, get a cone of chips. Enjoy the afternoon.'

Denise waited while he went to fetch the car. She hadn't expected to eat chips today, and hadn't budgeted for the extra calories. The food in the fridge could wait. She could put in some extra work on her run tomorrow. If there was one thing she had learned in their years together, it was that Archie could never be talked out of a drive to the beach. Or anything else for that matter.

In spite of that she was grateful. He had saved her from losing everything. She had been in a downward spiral those first few years after her brother died. It was seven, almost eight years ago she met Archie and he changed everything. If not for him, who knew where she would be now?

That was what she told herself. It was what she had told herself for so long that whether or not it was true hardly mattered any more.

: 3 :

The music in the morgue was so loud it shook chips of paint off the shuttered ambulance entrance. The mortuary building was up at the far end of a glen outside of Cameron Bridge, on a dead-end road, and had no close neighbours. A small flock of birds scattered from branches outside into the cool air, startled by the noise.

Inside, Dr Harriet Hitchin was trying – and failing – to hear herself think. The latest addition to her mortuary assistant's CD collection was a thrash metal album featuring Denmark's ten loudest bands. 'Would you turn that down?'

No response.

'Iain? Iain, would you turn that down?'

Still no reply. Iain bobbed his head to the thrash of guitars from a stereo. Every time the bass thrummed, steel instruments lined up on the tray vibrated in sympathy. 'FUCK'S SAKE, IAIN, TURN THAT OFF NOW!'

Iain turned, the handle of a PM-40 scalpel in his hand. He pushed the spatter guard up and away from his face. 'Is the music too loud?' he said.

'I've only been shouting for ten minutes,' Harriet said.

'Apologies, Professor.' Iain loped across the morgue to the CD player and turned it off.

Harriet wondered if Iain set out to wind her up, or if it came naturally to him. Today he was wearing a t-shirt with a picture of a severed head that read, 'Days Since Last Accident – 0'. His wiry arms were covered in faded army tattoos from wrist to shoulder. If not for the white welly boots and plastic apron,

14

he could have passed for a middle-aged rocker on his way to a gig. Or a crazed serial killer on his way back from the scene of a crime. Possibly both. It was not a look that inspired confidence.

'Sorry.' Harriet wandered to where Fiona Kennedy stood. 'Iain has . . . a very particular way of working.' She smoothed a wisp of straw-coloured hair out of her eyes.

'You're all right,' Fi brushed her off. She fidgeted in her uniform, having turned down the offer of scrubs and an apron. The policewoman's eyes flitted from the fluorescent lights, to the linoleum floor, to the bowl of steel instruments from earlier autopsies, still dripping with gore.

Iain tied up the internal organs of the body he was working on in a black bin liner and pushed them down into the corpse's chest cavity. He popped the middle of the ribcage over the top of the black bag. A pastry lid on a meat pie. A long line of running stitches closed the abdomen from neck to crotch – the body was finished, ready to be collected by the funeral director.

This was not what Fiona had come to see. The body she was here for was next. 'Alastair decided this morning wasn't worth his while, did he?' Harriet asked.

'He had other things on,' Fiona said. 'Getting us moved into the new station and all that.'

'The shoebox of Blair Mhor,' Iain quipped. He put on a fresh pair of gloves. 'How are you getting on over there?' he asked.

'Fine. Yes.' Fiona wrinkled her nose. It was no secret that the shift to single services could have gone smoother. With all of Scotland's police forces being run from the central belt instead of a Highlands service centred in Inverness, decisions were made that did not always map well with what departments needed. Especially in the Highlands.

The new station had been built at great expense off a roundabout outside of Cameron Bridge. In the original plans, it would have been metres away from a shopping complex. But when the supermarket that started the development pulled out, the station building went ahead anyway. It now sat, gleaming white, on the edge of a muddy rectangle that was meant to have been a 200-capacity car park. Instead of a police hub at a reinvigorated end of the high street, the Cameron Bridge police looked out on a forlorn scrap of undeveloped land.

'Feels like an airline terminal most of the time,' Fiona said. 'Suppose at least it gives us something to grow into.'

Harriet frowned. 'Could have used the money in other ways,' she said. The building they were standing in was over fifty years old. It had been a replacement for a Victorian hospital mortuary when it was built, but now had serious structural problems and was in need of new equipment throughout.

'I'll mention it to Alastair, if you like,' Fiona said coolly. 'Seeing as you're so busy here . . .'

Harriet detected the sarcasm but did not bite. 'Won't make a bit of difference, I know,' she said. 'I'm only blowing off steam.'

Iain snapped the wrist of one latex glove. 'Ladies, if you're ready . . .' he said.

Much of the work in the facility was routine: people who died suddenly, outside the care of a GP or hospital, routed to the morgue for an autopsy even if their cause of death was obvious. Accidents also came their way, generated by the steep mountains behind Cameron Bridge, or traffic collisions out on the A-road that wound its way from Glasgow up the West Coast of Scotland. A few industrial accidents turned up as well – the logging, sawmill, and fishing industries had dwindled significantly but still produced their fair share of fatalities.

This body was not any of those.

Iain opened the stainless steel door. He pulled out a trolley and guided it to the middle of the room, where he slid the white body bag onto an autopsy station.

He unzipped the bag around the remains. 'So, this was the Lochside body,' Harriet started. 'We performed the initial post-mortem yesterday.'

Fi nodded. 'Mummified, aye. I was at the scene,' she said, and cut her eyes in Harriet's direction. 'Unlike some.'

'No such thing as an emergency when the patient's already

dead, isn't that right, Professor?' Iain said. 'As Monty so often put it.'

'Mmm.' Harriet's predecessor Professor Moncreiff, or Monty to almost everyone, had been at Cameron Bridge from the 1970s until he keeled over in a bowl of cock-a-leekie some four decades later. They said Monty could pop into the morgue, finish a full evisceration in fifteen minutes, and leave without getting even a drop of blood on his shirt. Impressive stuff, Harriet supposed, but he had also been the sort of swivel-eyed sexist who would have touched her up in her student days.

Fiona and Harriet looked over the scene photos. Davie had taken them, and not done too bad a job of it. A dark brown head and part of an arm sticking out from a thin, cheap duvet. The hand was missing from the arm, found by the man's dog. Now the slightly chewed extremity lay next to the body on the slab. The small bed covering was folded, bagged and sat alongside the remains as well.

Harriet slipped the pictures into an envelope. 'How is the police end progressing?'

'No solid leads,' Fiona said. 'A few calls but no pointers to who this is, no way to ken when the body was dumped. Bins were industrial recycling, it could have been there for weeks.' She sighed. 'Alastair dumped a pile of CCTV tapes on my desk. Unhelpfully, most of the security cameras in the estate point at doors, not at bins.'

'How about the petrol station on the roundabout? They'll have CCTV,' Harriet suggested.

'Sure, but if we can avoid it I'd like to. Take ruddy ages.' Fiona stepped closer to the body. 'The individual was dead longer than a month, right?' she said.

Harriet nodded. The body's tissues had lost moisture as it mummified, making the corpse feather-light. The skin was tight and brown like a drum, stretched over the sharp bones of the skeleton. A line of vertebrae poked out of the back. The flesh of the limbs was so desiccated that the knees and elbows bulged in comparison.

'Aye, if it was only a month old, I'm Princess Diana,' Iain agreed. 'This one could be Di for all we know. Looks about the same vintage, anyway.'

Harriet rolled her eyes. 'Dead for a year beforehand,' she said. 'Possibly longer. Once a body has mummified like this it's difficult to give an exact date. I would say a year as a minimum. Ten max.'

'That's not even a little bit helpful.' Fiona shook her head. 'Any signs of overdose?'

'We're waiting on the toxicology,' Harriet said.

The first post-mortem had opened the abdominal cavity and removed most of what was left of the organs there, leaving a hollowed-out middle. Fiona glanced at the white containers alongside the remains that held the internal organs now. They looked uncannily like old ice cream tubs. 'Any injuries of note? Signs of attack, defence wounds?'

Iain shook his head. The post-mortem had found no lacerations, no cuts, no gunshot wound. No signs of chronic disease. 'We found this though,' he gestured at the neck. A slender spear of bone had been partly dissected out. 'See the sharp edges? Broken hyoid.' He noted Fiona's questioning look. 'It's like a chicken's wishbone, but for people. The only bone in the body that doesn't articulate with any other bones. Tough to tell if the break was perimortem or post-mortem. No healing on it, anyway.'

'Strangled?' Fiona asked.

'Or hanged,' Iain said. 'Soft tissue's gone too dark to see if there's a ligature mark. No fracture in the cervical vertebrae, but that isn't so unusual. A lot of people get the rope wrong and end up dying slow.'

Fiona shuddered. 'And then what?'

'What we do know is someone must have kept the body indoors before disposing of it. Too damp here to have been sitting outside for long.'

Fiona asked what she meant.

'It needs to be somewhere relatively dry to mummify. Sheltered,' Harriet said. 'Undisturbed.'

'And this.' Iain poked at the bedding. 'Dry as a popcorn fart inside. I've had Arbroath smokies that were less dry than this.'

'Thank you for that . . . *interesting* imagery, Iain,' Harriet said.

Fi nodded. 'So this was kept hidden first, then rewrapped for dumping.'

'Double bagged,' Iain said. The back of the body was flattened and compressed. He ran a gloved finger along a crease of what once was skin.

'A body this far gone would have leaked a large amount of fluid as it decomposed,' Harriet said. 'The body is over half water, by weight. It doesn't simply evaporate. This would have stained everything it came into contact with. Somewhere there will be fluid purged from the corpse over a period of weeks or longer. Or stains soaked up by carpet.'

'Possibly hoaching with maggots.' Iain ignored Harriet's sharp look of reproach.

Fiona scratched at her notepad. 'There should be more evidence to find, somewhere,' she said. 'I'll try the flooring contractors.' She tapped her teeth with the end of her pen. 'Maybe we can get storage units closest to the site to let us have a nosey round.'

'If it's even a local,' Harriet said. 'Which it might not be.'

'Cross that bridge when we come to it,' Fiona said. 'For now, I have to exhaust the possibility this was a home-grown crime. Lack of ID or a time since death is the limiting factor . . .'

Iain nodded. 'Didn't come with a wallet.' He paused. 'Might actually *be* a wallet, mind.' Harriet cleared her throat loudly and tapped one welly-booted foot.

Harriet gave Fiona an outline of what identifying details they could get from the body, but it wasn't much more than had been obvious at the scene. Female, race undetermined. 'But likely white,' Harriet said. 'From the hair.' The wavy strands were mid-brown with reddish glints. Harriet put an age estimate at late twenties to mid-thirties, height between five-foot-five and five-seven. No tattoos. 'Not much help, I know. As average as average could be.'

Fi looked at the hand in the plastic bag. When it had been found, the fingertips were dark and shrivelled, the skin black in patches and drawn so tight it was possible to see the outline of the phalange bones underneath. Now, pieces of flesh had been shaved away to try to recover fingerprints.

They needed a name for the deceased, at least. Or a photo. If they were going to jog witnesses' memories, they needed something to start with. Fingerprints were good, but they weren't always easy or fast to search.

Even DNA wasn't the lock everyone thought it was. Samples had already gone to a lab in Glasgow, but if the deceased had never been cautioned or arrested, chances of a match on police databases were slim. The samples might be used later on to confirm a family connection but to do that they needed a possible identity in the first place.

Harriet frowned. 'You know, this reminds me of a case I had in Leeds. It was a fire death and not a mummification, and it was found straight away . . .'

'Oh, here we go,' Iain said.

'What?' Harriet snapped.

'Don't mind her,' Iain said to Fi and waved his hand in the air. 'Old pathologists don't go into their dotage, they go into their anecdotage.' Fiona pulled her mouth to one side and tried to hide a smile.

'As if you aren't always on about Srebrenica this, Omagh that,' Harriet said. 'Right, well, I think she's seen enough.' She herded Fiona back to the changing room, waited while she retrieved her jacket out of the locker, and escorted her to the door. 'Keep us looped in if you and Alastair get anything useful.' She smiled. 'I want to see this wrapped up as much as you do. I mean . . . God, I'm starting to sound like Iain with his double entendres. I want whoever this is to get the closure they deserve.'

Fiona opened her mouth and looked as if she was about to

say something, then changed her mind. 'Thanks,' she said. 'I'll see you soon.'

'I'd like that,' Harriet said.

Harriet marched back into the autopsy suite. 'For pity's sake, Iain, can you not do that when someone is here?' she said.

Iain glanced up from the body. 'What now?'

'Make jokes all the time. Undermine me. Does everything have to be a punchline with you?' She crossed her arms over her chest.

Iain nodded. 'Listen, Professor—' he said, and caught her scowling. She wasn't a professor any more, not since she was forced to leave Leeds, and he used the title to poke fun at her. 'I mean, Dr Hitchin,' he said. 'I know you do things differently. But I've been working Cameron Bridge for ten years, and army and UN morgues years before that, and this much I know – you're a long time dead. Take the jokes where you can get them. If you can't have a laugh at the fact we're all just a bag of mince, what can you laugh at?'

Harriet took off her glasses, sighed, and dropped them in the front pocket of her scrubs top. She always looked a bit tired – the fluorescent lighting in the morgue did no one any favours – but today there was more to her face. A look of sadness, of resignation. 'I didn't mean to get at you. I'm not feeling myself today. It's just . . .'

'Stood up on a date the other night?' Iain asked.

'Stood up?' Harriet's head snapped up. 'Why? Are you spying on me?'

'Aw, a lucky guess,' Iain said. He didn't want to admit he had been looking at a dating website and when he clicked on local women he had seen her profile. The details were sparse and the photo old and blurry, but it was her. The usual wistful cliches were all there: *meet and see where it goes, friends or maybe more.* She had checked the box to say that she was looking for both men and women, friends only, but Iain knew that was a cover. True desperation never stated its needs up front.

Iain gave himself a mental slap. Fuck that. Other people's personal lives were none of his business. Harriet was in Cameron Bridge because she was not good at her job, but not bad enough to be struck off. No one credible wanted to work here – the post had been empty eighteen months before she arrived. Most of the time he was alone in the mortuary while Harriet was in her office, and when she did deign to show her face, her being there only doubled his workload. He wasn't her babysitter and he definitely wasn't her friend.

'I have somewhere to be this afternoon,' Harriet said. Her glasses were back on and she had recovered her brittle manner. 'You can put the body away.'

'Nae bother,' he said. *This one's not going anywhere fast*, he almost added, but did not. He checked his watch. Not even lunchtime yet, a new record. She was leaving earlier and earlier all the time. At least she was going out and drinking, rather than staying round here reeking of booze.

Maybe while she was out he could grab a sneaky nap in the flat in the morgue. The flat was a small, self-contained en-suite off the far side of the locker rooms. It had been designed for overnight shifts and a larger staff. Inside, it was last redecorated around the late 1980s, but Iain didn't mind. A clean single bed, a wee CRT television and a kettle were all he needed. The flat reminded him of caravan holidays when he was a wean.

Iain looked again at the remains, at the face so dried and shrivelled it might have belonged to an ancient mummy. Who was this? Whoever it was had been dead for some time. A year, maybe more. And if it was a murder, the murderer might even be thinking they had got away with it by now.

He thought of the bodies he had seen in the former Yugoslavia, pulled from mass graves when he worked in Srebrenica. The men had been rounded up, driven out to fields and killed in many cases by neighbours, by people who had grown up going to the same shops and schools that their victims had.

The forensic recovery team did what they could for the families so that they could get closure. Evidence was collected, remains identified if possible. High-profile leaders were tried in international courts, but who had pulled each trigger, dug every mass grave? The foot soldiers of genocide? They disappeared back into everyday life as if none of it had ever happened.

The front door slammed shut as Harriet left the building. Outside, her tyres squealed as she tore out of the car park.

Iain sighed and returned the remains to the fridge.

: 4 :

A lone bird chirped in the hedge outside the beige curtains. Denise opened her eyes. For a few moments, she was still in both worlds. There was anywhere. Here was nowhere.

The black threads had grown into vines around her body in the night. She took deep breaths, felt her chest rise and fall, until they snapped. She had to brush her teeth, wash the taste of sleep and of him out of her mouth. She had to put on clothes and go.

Archie was in the shower, whistling. A seesaw of breath through his teeth, aimless and tuneless. It was his third shower since last night. One for each time they had sex. Archie was away with work as many days as he was in Wallsend. This meant being pawed by him constantly when he was home, the look in his eyes imploring her to give in, not to make him force her again.

She felt no different when she let him from those times when he hadn't given her a choice. Giving in was simply easier and over faster. She would stare at a spot over his shoulder, stroke his arms over and over. After a few minutes it felt as if she wasn't even there. He would be hunched over her inert body, thrusting at her through the thick, rubbery barrier of her indifference. Her real face hovered about a centimetre behind the face that he could see. That way it wasn't her that he was doing this to, but a doll. If she thought about moving an arm or leg a split second would pass before the limb responded. Then it would be over.

'Running to the coast. Back in two hours,' she called through the bathroom door. The whistling paused. She tensed, waiting to find out which way it would go.

'Are you getting the bus back?' Archie said.

'Yes,' she lied. There were three of them going on a training run, Denise and two men from the club. The less Archie knew, the easier it would be.

'Have you had breakfast already?' he said.

'Yes.' Another lie.

Her supervisor had said she was fine to take the rest of the week off, insisted on it even. She was so relieved not to have to rehash the circumstances of her collapse that she agreed. It meant more time with Archie though. And the possibility he would find out what happened, interrogate her about it. She needed time, time to process all of it. So she had told him she was taking work from home days.

Three lies, but manageable ones. For now.

'Great. See you later.' He started whistling again on the other side of the door. She exhaled, grateful.

Denise plugged a pair of headphones into her mobile and pushed the earbuds deep. She warmed up slowly, stretching her elbows above her head as she jogged past semis that stretched from her end of the road to the other side of the housing estate.

Today her playlist was all country music. The kind of tunes she could stride into, heavy on Dwight Yoakam and Lucinda Williams, with a few classics from Buck Owens and George Jones. She turned the volume up high, so high anyone passing could have heard the music too.

As she ran, the last of the black threads started to withdraw. She had been on edge ever since Archie returned. It had been weeks since she saw the things she shouldn't have. A good thing and a bad thing. She didn't know what to do about either of them.

She had not been snooping – had not – only she left her work bag in his car one day. When she opened the boot she saw the bad thing. Shocked, she slammed it shut, her heart fluttering in her chest. *That's what you get for snooping,* a voice in her head scolded. *Your bag is in the back seat, not the boot.* That was when she saw the good thing. A crumpled piece of paper in the footwell on the driver's side. She picked it up. It was a receipt from a jeweller. A receipt for an engagement ring. She had dropped it as if it was on fire. But once she knew – once she saw it – it could not be unseen.

What did it mean? Was there a way to ask about one without admitting she had seen the other? He wouldn't believe it was an accident. No, better to pretend none of it had happened. A full untruth was easier to manage than half a lie.

A ring. A ring. A ring! No matter how she tried, she couldn't stop coming back to it. What did it look like? She wondered if he knew her ring size, or guessed. They had been together for seven years, and she was thirty. Maybe he felt she was finally ready. He was probably waiting for the right time to propose. But the longer he left it, the harder it would be for her to pretend to be surprised. The waiting made her anxious.

And the other thing. The bad thing. *That's what you get for snooping.*

The route to the coast took her from the suburbs of Newcastle to Whitley Bay. Visible signs of regeneration grew fewer as the salt smell in the air grew stronger; more and more houses were closed up, metal sheeting bolted over the windows to prevent vandals from entering.

Denise settled into her pace and let the run do its job. There was nothing else now, nothing but the music in her ears and the rhythm of her breath. In-in-in, out-out-out. It was a little chant her father used to do with her and her brother when they were young. He would stand on the edge of the leisure centre swimming pool, counting when they took their breaths, nodding with satisfaction every time she and her brother turned a lap.

Swim practice is daily for Denise. For Darwin it is twice a day. After the evening session they go back to the chip shop and

Dad sneaks them an ice lolly from the kitchen. Darwin turns the television over to a music channel and puts the volume up. He loves country music and anything American. Mum is preparing for the evening crowd, turning on fryers and stacking takeaway boxes. She rolls her eyes when the music comes on. But it is as much a part of the routine as going to the shop is, and Denise loves those moments, when it is just the family and she and Darwin can sit on the counter eating Orange Maids and watching Shania Twain videos until Mum shoos them off.

It is the version of them she likes best. The family still feels like a single unit. People are starting to come to the pool and watch Darwin from the bleachers, only a few at first, then more as reports spread. Soon enough the university recruiters come, 'college scouts' they call the American ones. Her own laps are a perfunctory warm up and warm down by then, and her father's post holding the stopwatch by the side of the pool has long since been taken over by coaches.

Darwin wraps a towel around himself while he talks to coaches, over one shoulder and under one armpit, like a toga. The sound bounces off the walls in the leisure centre and magnifies his voice. His eyes meet hers and he twitches his eyebrows. She twitches hers back, their old code for a hidden smile.

She used to love to watch him. The way he stretches his arms over his head. When he dives in his arms reach impossibly forward, out of love for the further shore.

When they swim together, which is rare enough at the end, she can tell he is holding back for the first few laps. He might try some crazy stroke, corkscrewing from front crawl to backstroke, or swimming underwater, legs only, holding his breath for the full length of the pool. This way they stay almost even. Then he switches into his warmup laps and the distance between them opens up. She has no chance. Every day he is a little further from her. One day, he is gone forever.

*

Denise never swam now. Not in the sea, where she could lose her footing, be swept away. Not in a pool either. Archie laughed at her for being afraid, picked her up and threatened to throw her in at the beach a few times for a joke. But even he knew not to cross that line.

Denise went to London twice a year to see her parents. Each time they asked when she was moving back, and why Archie hadn't come with her. She promised that she would soon and that he would next time. Two more lies. It was a well-rehearsed script, familiar to all participants. She could not be where Darwin wasn't, where his absence was felt the deepest.

They never said it. They never would have. Still she could not escape the feeling that everyone thought the wrong twin had died.

Denise dropped her eyelids, far enough to shut out the details of what was around her, and pictured the long muscles of her brother's body as his strokes became laps and his laps became a mile. The cadence of her steps shifted. It was like a video loop in her head, the way his catch hit the water, his narrow kick, a stroke rate that looked too vigorous to keep up over any distance past the first 50 metres, yet somehow he did. There was no pause and glide in his stroke and he never stopped moving. *He has something we haven't seen before*, she once overheard a scout say to her father.

If she let her thoughts unspool too far she would start thinking about what happened yesterday. About the collapse. About what the doctor had said. Things between her and Archie weren't perfect, she knew that. She would always manage in the little time they had together to disappoint him. 'I just wish you could see, there's a Good Denise you could be if you really tried,' he would say, sadly.

He appeared distracted by something this time, which made not being up front with him easier. When she told him the days off were so she could work from home, he seemed to buy that. It fit with his belief that her work was not 'real work' anyway. Not in the sense that his work was.

But it would be only a matter of time until he found out; he always did. She had given up locking her phone or changing her email password. If he couldn't get into her things he would try to crack it until she was blocked out of her own accounts. Then he would throw his net wider, contact the neighbours, her co-workers, and get information from them. He was good at that. He had the gift of the gab and an uncanny ability to get people on his side.

There was a glint of sunlight off the sea as the road sloped down on the approach to the promenade. The bright white dome of the Spanish City amusements rose above the houses. Here her route turned north again and skirted the wide pale beach of Whitley Bay. The wind had picked up a bit and she narrowed her eyes against sand blown over the pavement.

Denise stopped at the cafe that was their meeting point. She panted, leaning on her knees, and looked around. No sign of the others yet. It was unlikely she would beat the men of the club outright, unless they were lost. She checked her GPS watch. Distance, bang on eight miles. Her splits had been below an eight-minute mile. A decent time, for her.

Denise went into a corner shop and bought a pint of skimmed milk and a local paper while she waited. She flipped through the first three pages: police callouts and shopping centre closures. The usual. She was about to put it in the bin when a headline on an inside page caught her eye.

Northeast Woman Found Dead In Highlands

Her steps slowed to a standstill as she read. *Miriam Rachel Goldstein, 33, originally of Gateshead.* The body had been found on an industrial estate in Cameron Bridge. There was a date for a service listed. The piece was otherwise light on substance, apart from the cause of death being unknown and a 'no possibility is being excluded' statement from Police Scotland. There was no photo.

It could be another Miriam Goldstein, Denise told herself. Of the same age. From the same place. It was a common enough name, and the Jewish community in Gateshead was large. A filament of black thread wound itself around her heart and made her chest squeeze. It was not someone else, and she knew it instinctively. Of course it was her Miri.

Denise hadn't heard from Miri in years. She had not even known whether she was living in Newcastle any more. She had seen her, briefly, some time ago. Denise walked out of Starbucks with a coffee (skinny latte, half a pump of sugar-free vanilla syrup, extra shot) on her way to work. She heard a familiar laugh and looked up to see a flounce of Titian hair. Miri was walking along the cobbles of Haymarket with a black woman. Miri bent and whispered into the woman's ear, no doubt sharing plots and secrets the way she used to with Denise. When was that? A year ago at least. Around the time of the Great North Run before last. Eighteen months, give or take.

Worse than the fact of Miri's death was where they had found her. *Cameron Bridge*. They had talked about going there together someday, planning a trip to Glencoe then hiking on to the Highlands town. The last third of the West Highland Way, the most rugged and isolated part. It was Miri who went with Denise to buy her first pair of hiking boots – '*proper* boots, not your city fashion boots,' she had said. They were packed away, good as new, in the cupboard under the stairs.

A silver Audi S8 pulled up on the other side of the road. A man got out and started waving. It was Archie. Denise stuffed the milk carton and paper into a bin.

'Kitty!' He bounded across the grass. 'I thought you would like a lift instead. Why get that filthy bus back. You hate it, right?'

She nodded. He threw a fleece at her. 'Thought you might need this.' He grinned widely but his eyes searched her face, gauging her precise amount of gratitude.

'Great, thank you.' Denise wrapped herself in the fleece, which was far too large and swamped her like a dress. He rested an arm on her shoulder and steered her back to the car.

She glanced over her shoulder as they walked. A skinny guy was stretching off a run in front of the cafe. It looked like Mark.

He raised a hand but didn't shout or come after them. The guys from the club would figure out what happened. It wasn't the first time she had to blank them in public. It probably wouldn't be the last.

: **5** :

Iain whistled as he lowered a basket of stainless steel instruments into the autoclave. It had been a good week. The fingertips he had excised from the mummy came up trumps. After soaking them in sodium carbonate solution he was able to take a full set of prints, and they scored a match in a missing persons database in England. Mitochondrial RNA from the body matched the missing woman's mother and sister.

He twirled the lid nuts until the machine was tightly closed. Scalpel handles, rib shears, and spreaders all went in; anything that could be cleaned at high pressure and used again. The scalpel blades and bread knives – for the ribs, when the bones were small or soft – he disposed of after every use.

A lot of the mortuary equipment was older than he was. The autoclave reminded him of the pressure cooker his mum used to make the Sunday roast and vegetables. Only it was a bit larger than hers and did not perpetually smell of old fat and cabbage.

After the autoclaving finished Iain locked up outside, checking the front door and the accordion shutter in the back. This was where ambulances and hearses came in or out, dropping off or collecting bodies into a concrete garage that opened onto the morgue.

A small grey hoolet launched itself from the low branches of a tree and coasted into the evening light like a ghost. Iain looked up, and when he did, noticed the motion sensor light was broken. He wriggled off the remains of the light cover, screwed out the base of a shattered bulb.

Might have been damage from a storm. Or maybe not. There had been a few problems reported in the area recently. Nothing serious, kids getting into unsecured sheds for the most part. He remembered what it was like to be that age and could sympathise. Young people bored senseless with waiting for something to happen.

It had been the same in other places where he had worked. Kids got pished and thought it would be a laugh to break into where they keep the dead bodies. The act itself was almost as much punishment as they needed. Youthful bravado was no match for the reality of realising you were alone in a building full of corpses. The ones it didn't put the fear of God into, well, those were the ones you had to watch out for. Nine out of ten neds were more bark than bite. The other one in ten? Proper sociopaths.

Iain chuckled. If he met himself now as he had been back then, he probably would have written himself off as that one in ten. Up to high doh on Buckie and footie and ready to pop at anyone who looked at him wrong. Time changes everything.

He decided to drop into a pub for a celebratory drink. His usual place was crowded with locals – karaoke night. The thought of supping an ale while well-oiled groups howled their way through 'Angels' and 'Caledonia' was off-putting, so he slipped into the quieter climbers' pub over the road.

The place was sedate, though no doubt a few of the karaoke crowd would stumble across in time. As soon as Easter came it would be heaving with visitors who liked to haul themselves up and down mountains for fun. Not that Iain disliked visitors, particularly – he himself had moved up from Glasgow years before. And not because he disliked mountains. But he was tired of having the same conversation with strangers, ones that ended as soon as someone asked him what he did for work. Not that he blamed them. Meeting the guy who was likely to cut open your body should a belay or harness fail halfway up the north side of the Ben would put a damper on anyone's holiday mood.

He looked in the mirror behind the bar while the barman fetched his change. The accumulated toll of forty-odd years on his face was softened by the dim lighting and greasy glass, but he still looked tired. The face of someone who spent too many hours indoors.

The mirror made the motley collection of tattoos on his arms appear even more faded than usual. An outline of Great Britain, filled in with the colours of the Union Flag. A skull in profile wearing a top hat. A crudely drawn hand giving the two fingers up, and below that blue-black letters spelling out the name of his first girlfriend. Mementoes of the terraces when he was a kid, and then the army. Why did he need the ink to remind him? There was a question. He could be back reliving the violence any time he wanted to. Some of it was still as fresh in his mind as if it was yesterday.

Harriet was fine, this was fine. She could handle meeting someone in a bar. She didn't have to drink simply because there was alcohol available. The compulsion was . . . well, it was manageable. Just about. Tonic and lime was enough for her. She made a mental note to suggest a coffee shop next time.

She looked up and recognised the man at the bar, then looked down again. Too late. He was heading over, pint of eighty shilling in hand. Iain stopped in front of her table. 'All right?' he asked.

'Iain, what a surprise.' She didn't try to hide the irritation in her voice.

He winced. 'I can shove off if you're, you know. Waiting on someone,' he said.

'No, it's fine,' she said. It wasn't fine, and she was waiting for someone, but she felt bad for snapping at him. 'They're not here yet anyway.'

'Running on Highlands time,' Iain said. He was shuffling now, the slow dance that suggested it was her turn to be polite, to invite him to sit down. 'Timings aren't so much written in stone as gentle suggestions.'

In spite of herself, Harriet smiled. 'Oh, I'm used to it,' she said. 'The way of the locals. Anyway it gives me an opportunity to catch up on the news.' She waved her smartphone.

'OK if I sit?' There were two glasses of tonic and lime already on the table. 'Is it a date?'

Harriet blushed slightly. Even after two years at the mortuary she still told Iain as little about her personal life as possible. She should never have agreed to a date at a pub on the high street. 'Um, sort of, yes,' she said. 'Although they're running a bit late. None of my messages are going through.'

'Well if they stood you up, that's their loss.'

Harriet coughed, surprised. Was he making fun of her? She took a sip from her glass. 'Mmm,' she said noncommittally and looked back at her phone.

If he had been a friend, she might have admitted this was a reschedule of a date she was meant to be at on the night the body was found. She had got to the meeting point on time, her date had been late, and feeling snubbed, she turned her phone off in a fit of pique. That had been a poor decision. How was she to know? Few if any out-of-hours calls came in that she was required to attend.

Iain fiddled with the corner of a damp beermat, picking the layers of card apart with his nail. 'So, anything interesting happening in the world?'

'Usual political bellyaching,' Harriet said. 'Rumours of a coup brewing in the Shadow Cabinet.'

'They've been printing that same story since the Scottish referendum.'

Harriet set her phone down. 'And the general election. And the EU referendum,' she said. 'What a palaver that was. Why anyone thinks it's a good idea to put serious decisions to the general public is beyond me.'

In spite of the fact he had been a vocal Yes supporter, she was surprised to see Iain nod. 'Always going to be a problem when the results are close,' he said. 'Whoever loses, they will want to see heads roll. Look at the Holyrood elections after the Scottish vote. Labour were destroyed. It almost doesn't matter which way the vote goes, someone has to pay.'

'I have the sinking feeling that when it comes to Brexit, we're the ones who will pay,' she said. 'Ironic to think we were on the same side for once.'

'Yeah. Even if it was for different reasons.' A silence passed between them. They had never had such a long conversation that wasn't work related before.

'Indeed,' Harriet said. 'Still, a good work week. You must be pleased. The mummy and all.'

'Cheers,' Iain said. 'You know what? We should celebrate. I'll get the next round in. What are you having?' He peered at her glass. 'Gin is it?'

'That's kind of you to offer, but no, thank you.'

Iain leaned forward over the small table. 'Listen. Maybe I'm being a bit forward . . .'

Harriet jumped up and waved as the pub door opened. 'Oh hallo!' she called to the newcomer. 'I was starting to think you'd changed your mind.'

A dark-haired woman heaved a bag off her shoulder and kissed Harriet on the cheek. 'So sorry,' she said. 'Alastair found a whole crate full of files at the station we hadn't unpacked yet, and my mobile was dead . . .' The woman looked down at Iain. It was the officer who had been to the morgue a few days before, Fiona Kennedy. 'Hey, fancy seeing you here,' she said.

Iain stumbled to a standing position. 'Sorry, I've taken your seat, haven't I?'

Fiona took a free chair from another table. 'No problem, there's plenty to go around.'

Iain looked back and forth between the two women. 'Are you two . . . ?' he said. 'Ah. I mean . . . ha, my fault. I thought Doctor Hitchin said she was waiting on a date. I must have misheard.'

Fi and Harriet exchanged a look. 'Yes,' Harriet said. 'Fiona is my date.'

'Sorry. Sorry.' Iain smacked his open palm on his forehead.

'Of course.' He grabbed his drink off the table. 'I'm an idiot. I'll leave you two in peace.'

'Don't be silly,' Fiona said. Harriet shot her a look but she patted the pathologist's hand and smiled at Iain. 'Finish your drink at least. I guess we have you to thank for the breakthrough on the Lochside mummy. I'm in the mood for a celebration.'

: 6 :

Denise glanced at Archie from the corner of her eye. He was watching a news panel show, talking back to the presenters as if they could hear him and elbowing her with a grin whenever someone made a point he agreed with.

Not a word about the ring yet. And nothing about Miri. But he seemed normal. Normal for him, at least. Maybe being a local story, the news about Miri hadn't hit any of the sites he read yet. She would need to be ready for when he found out. She would need to figure out the right reaction when he told her, the right thing to say. The right face to put on. A balance between shock and upset, but not too upset.

'How about dinner soon, Kitty?' he said.

Archie had stuffed the refrigerator with pasta ready meals, things she would never have bought for herself. Her hands were shaking as she cut open the packets. The pills from the hospital were in a white paper bag in her coat. One of those might take the edge off, but if she went for them now, he would notice. She pulled a bottle of wine from the rack. She had no appetite, but Archie would say something if she ate less than usual. She grabbed two long-stemmed glasses from the shelf and put them on the table, paused, then added a second bottle of wine.

'She's unbelievable, that Scottish woman,' Archie fumed as Denise dished up. He speared a piece of pasta with his fork, jabbing the air as he spoke. 'First she campaigned against Brexit. Now she's on all the shows. It's political correctness gone mad is what it is.'

Denise chewed her food slowly. She carefully cultivated

having no particular opinion on politics. Though she did like Morag Munro well enough. She had always struck Denise as someone with unmovable inner steel.

'She's another one of those social justice warriors complaining about not enough women at the top,' Archie continued. A blob of food rotated around in his mouth like laundry in a washing machine. Denise unfocused her eyes a little so the sight of it wouldn't make her gag. 'How many do we flipping need? They'll be demanding we have black lesbian handicapped single mothers on every ballot next. I'm sick of the sight of her. Sick!'

Denise pulled her mouth into a smile and swallowed her food. A healthy glug of wine chased it down.

Archie followed political news hungrily, gobbling up every right-wing columnist and magazine he could lay his paws on. She did not understand the appeal. He howled about political correctness this and British values that. He seemed to have swallowed the prevailing political message wholesale. That there were skivers and there were strivers, and to be on the winning team, the peacocking and the privileged, was a way of proving you were a striver. And Archie was one of those, he was a striver, investigating counterfeit goods on behalf of Customs and Excise, bringing down criminal gangs that would make a mockery of Britain's borders and use their ill-gotten gains to fund terrorism and trafficking worldwide.

'I *said*, why do you think she even bothers after the Scottish Referendum, and all you can do is shrug?' Archie paused to drink his wine. When he smacked his lips his teeth were purple. 'God, Kitty, aren't you interested in what goes on in the world?'

Denise raised a shoulder as apology.

'I can't wait to get back to work where at least there are people who are interested in things outside their own pathetic lives,' Archie said and threw his fork down on his plate. 'You're supposed to be some kind of scientist and you can't even have a real intellectual conversation. I get more stimulation online than I do at home . . .'

Denise supposed, at some point now long in the past, she

had enjoyed the odd bout of verbal sparring with other people. She and Darwin argued almost constantly in their early teens, but it was never serious. Things changed when she met Archie. He was less interested in being challenged on his thoughts than in hearing the sound of his own voice. So she weighed up the cost of being thought argumentative or being thought dull, and chose dull.

Denise opened the second bottle of wine and refilled both glasses. Another drink would make it easier to put a barrier between her head and her body when he took her to bed that night. She reminded herself to take one of those sleeping pills, too, when Archie was out of the room. She had a feeling that tonight she was going to need more help than usual.

Archie was away the next morning, mumbling something about a car boot in Rothbury. In the shower she caught her reflection in the mirror. The bruises on her chest that the doctor noticed had almost gone. But she felt a pain inside, a familiar deep ache. The first time, he put in three fingers alongside his cock, up to the last knuckle, and it felt like he was tearing her in half. Each time it was more and with less warning. She reached between her legs and was relieved to find she was not bleeding this time.

She sat at the kitchen table with her breakfast. On the days when Archie was away, it was the same thing every day. Frozen fruit, bran sticks, flax seeds and fat-free yoghurt for breakfast. Vegetarian sausages, carrot sticks and hummus for lunch. A slice of toast and Marmite if she had a long run later. Stir-fried vegetables and scrambled eggs for dinner. One square of dark chocolate. One small glass of red wine, preferably pinot noir. After the two bottles last night she would have to offset yesterday's calories against today's.

The calculations of what she ate, how much, happened almost without her wanting them to. It started after Darwin died. She could not have stopped it now if she tried. Archie disliked how she was around food, found her habits unattractive. 'It's a mental health problem, that much is obvious,' he said. 'There's something wrong with you. Eating disorder most likely. Or autistic. I have never met a woman so unfeeling as you. It isn't natural, you know that, don't you?'

Yet he would have been the first to say something if her weight increased at all. Her diet didn't bother her, far from it: it was a comforting blip of predictability, like her training runs. Like filling in spreadsheets at work.

Routine. Mindfulness. It helped to keep the snarled, black threads at bay. So she counted the calories, the running steps, the data cells of spreadsheets.

She signed into her work email. There was a note from one of the nurses hoping she got well soon. Denise scrolled through news websites on her computer. Maybe she should rethink not paying attention to politics. Maybe that was why he had yet to mention the ring. Good Denise should be able to hold an interesting conversation. Good Denise would care about the things he cared about. She needed at least to try.

That was when she saw it. She nearly choked when she spotted the headline. *Scottish Mummy is Three Hundred Quid Call Girl*, read a headline on one site. Below that, explicit photos. Of Miri.

> *Sources suggest that Miriam Goldstein, whose mummified body was discovered dumped in a skip in Scotland, was working as a call girl shortly before she died. According to Punterweb. com, Miriam – or 'Lamia' as she was known to her clients – commanded prices as high as three hundred pounds an hour for services that ranged from a 'girlfriend experience' to 'kinky domination fantasies'. Goldstein, whose family are prominent in the Orthodox Jewish community in Gateshead, was not previously known to police for any solicitation offences. Calls to her family for comment were not returned . . .*

Denise scrolled up and down, clicked away from the site, and clicked back again. Was this a joke? No, it was real. The tiny item in the local paper, the one she was not yet sure Archie had seen, was now breaking into national news. For all the wrong reasons.

Denise felt a tingling at the base of her neck and her heart started to beat harder. The pictures were difficult to look at. Miri in a wrap dress splayed on a leopard-print spread bed. Her face was blurred out but it was her. A thousand comments below the line on every news site and growing. Denise's chest squeezed. A warm drop fell on her hands, and she realised she was crying.

: 7 :

It was dreich outside. No other word for it.

Harriet was unlikely ever to pick up more than a few words of the local lingo, but that one suited Cameron Bridge down to the ground. Grey, drizzly and sombre. A gloomy lull following the stormy season before the biting midges came back with a vengeance. Welcome to the West Coast in spring.

She sighed. There had been two routine post-mortems that morning, both men who died at home of a sudden heart attack. She was conscientious about completing the reports in a timely manner – she could hardly afford not to be, after Leeds – but they were far from stimulating. People ate too much, drank too much, let themselves become estranged from family and friends. When they did die it was sometimes a couple of days before anyone noticed them missing. That the modern world was isolating was not a question in her mind. But then, if she suddenly failed to turn up at work, who would bother to come round looking for her?

Sudden death was the least of her worries, though. If things went on the way they were, it was possible she would not have a job soon regardless of how diligently she filled in paperwork. Last year someone on the council suggested moving the forensic service over to one of the local funeral homes. 'There aren't many cases of police interest,' Councillor Margaret Douglas reasoned. 'Why not eliminate the staff, and call experts from Dundee on an as-needed basis?'

They rejected it in the end. The facility might have earned a temporary reprieve but that didn't mean their jobs were safe.

She knew, for example, that Iain's position was set to be advertised anew. This time with a lower pay grade and no benefits. The qualifications required were embarrassingly sparse. 'Restructuring', they called it. She knew what it really meant. They were counting on him being so insulted that he would walk, or at least refuse to apply. He didn't know about this yet, and she didn't want to be the one to tell him. But if not her then who?

Harriet typed with one hand and cradled a cup of tea with the other. She liked her tea strong enough to trot a mouse across it. Sometimes it was the only good thing about her work day.

Her mobile phone buzzed. She fished it out of her pocket and swiped the screen. 'Hallo, it's a nice surprise to hear from you,' she said.

'This is not a social call,' Fiona said on the other end. 'There's something happening over here you need to know about. It's your case. The mummy one. Miriam Goldstein.'

'Well, it's not really my case as such, now that Newcastle—'

'Doesn't matter,' Fiona interrupted. 'You're about to get slammed with public attention. As in, start writing a press release kind of attention.'

Harriet shifted in the office chair. She had had her fair share of press over the years, with the odd celebrity death that she worked on, the tribunal after her evidence was contested for the Bulgarian nanny case in Leeds. As far as she was concerned, the less said to the media, the better. 'Go on,' she said.

'Some website has broken the story that the victim was a prostitute.'

'Saw it this morning. Don't worry. No one's going to care where she was autopsied.'

'There's more,' Fiona said. 'It turns out she was not just any prostitute, but linked to serious names. They're saying Labour Party leadership.'

'No,' Harriet said. 'Lionel Brant?'

'Courtesan to the great and good, or what have you. No names yet, but it's only a matter of time. Our switchboard has been lighting up like Stonehaven Hogmanay.'

'Fuck.' Harriet squeezed the mug handle. That was all she needed, a media firestorm over a fact she could not confirm in a case she was no longer handling. 'Is it possible this is a wind-up?'

'Might be, might not. Have you ever heard of the website Rome Must Burn? Some kind of clearinghouse for Westminster rumours and gossip. They broke it, and it's getting picked up everywhere,' Fiona said. 'Have a look.'

Harriet clicked into a web browser. Finally she saw the story. The headline was bad enough – *Scottish Corpse is Labour Favourite Hooker* – but the story was even worse.

> *Reports on punter review website suggest Miriam Goldstein, a 'sex worker' whose body was found in Scotland last week, may have been on better than first-name terms with grandees of the Labour Party. Dates for reviews last year seem to match with the Saturday night following the keynote speeches. Was the prostitute known as 'Lamia' – whose services were offered at an eye-watering £300 per hour, surely putting her out of reach of the rank and file membership – getting it on with MPs . . . or perhaps even party leadership? No one seems to know for certain and calls to the party offices went unanswered, but rest assured Commodus is on the trail of what surely will prove to be a 'stimulating' story . . .*

The photo below the headline showed a topless woman wearing black lace knickers and high boots, reclining on a chaise longue. Her face was blurred out; her long reddish hair fell in waves over one shoulder. According to the site, the call girl was called Lamia. Well of course, they never used their real names, did they?

Other pictures showed her sitting on faux-fur spreads on a bed, in a black-painted room with silver candelabras lit on either side. The kind of thing, she supposed, you could find on any escort website.

'Have you found it yet?' Fiona said.

'Blimey. Yes.' No names yet, but as Fiona had said, with a story like this it wouldn't be long. 'Is it really her?'

'They're saying it is, and to be honest it doesn't matter. You can't shut a story like this down. It's impossible to libel the dead,' Fiona said. 'I guess with all the rumblings about a coup in the Shadow Cabinet, someone has finally found the material to do it with.'

Harriet sighed. What was the old saying about how to end a politician's career? Get caught with a dead girl or a live boy.

She had heard the rumour that Cameron Bridge's MP, Morag Munro, was tipped to be the next leader of the opposition when – if – Lionel Brant ever stepped down. It was about time the party had a woman, and anyway Morag was, if not the most exciting candidate for the job, the one with the requisite experience. A safe pair of hands. But his party's loss in the general election hadn't managed to dislodge Brant, who went from PM to leader of the opposition. Nor had the Brexit debates that made him look like the embarrassing bit of old wood he was. So it was only a matter of time until someone went looking for something really damaging.

'Thanks for the call,' Harriet said. She paused. 'Are we still on for dinner at yours tonight?' She hoped so. She liked Fiona, a bit more than she wanted to admit. The hope inside Harriet that had been lying dormant for years, ever since her partner walked out on her after the Leeds inquiry, was starting to wake up.

'I have a feeling we might both be very busy for the next few hours,' Fiona said. 'I'll grab a takeaway if this runs late. Let's meet up at mine. Ring you later?' Harriet agreed. Fiona's phone clicked off the line.

Harriet put her head in her hands. Cameron Bridge was meant to have been an easy job. Low population, none of the big-city crime that plagued metropolitan areas. Come in, tick off the hours, go home. A way to show other people in forensic science that she could handle herself. That she was more than a series of blundered reports and discredited research. A way, eventually, for her to bide her time until everyone forgot about what had happened in Leeds.

The electronic purr of the desk phone jolted Harriet from her thoughts. The three mortuary landlines lit up simultaneously. Whatever was about to happen was starting right now.

Harriet drained her tea. It wasn't enough. At a time like this, nothing short of gin would do. She looked at the mug and threw it against the bare block wall. It shattered in a spray of pieces.

: 8 :

Denise dithered about playlists before selecting a classic coun-try mix. George Jones, Buck Owens, things Darwin would have liked when they were kids. Her footsteps got faster and faster as her legs warmed up.

In the last couple of days it seemed like Miri's face was every-where. Every time she looked online it was worse. First, Miri was a hooker. Then stories started to pop up hinting that some of her clients were politicians. Where would it end? She still hadn't heard from Archie. He must have seen the news by now. His silence was starting to worry her.

At Jesmond Dene, Denise slowed to a walk. A tiled turret came into view, then the entire building.

The large Victorian house sat on a corner plot next to the park, at the end of a street of similarly large houses. It had an overgrowing rose garden, and the concrete lion in the corner was stained with moss and mildew. Above the door, a fanlight with delicate, glided letters spelled out *Lamia House* in ornate script. Men in boiler suits walked back and forth through the doorway, carrying boxes to a removals van. It was then she no-ticed the FOR SALE sign on the gate.

A middle-aged couple stood on the pavement. Her long silver-streaked hair was plaited neatly and hung to the middle of her back. The man had broad shoulders, his dark face creased, a few grey hairs among his tight curls. He leaned down to her ear and Denise heard him speak her name. Bella.

So these must be the owners, then. It gave Denise a small shock to realise that in all the years she had known the house

– even during the time when she stayed there more often than she had stayed at her own – she never met them.

The woman turned. 'No more reporters,' her voice rasped. The husband put a protective arm around his wife's shoulders.

'I'm not a reporter,' Denise said. 'I used to come here. Miri was my friend.' She could sense their scepticism. Miri was the caretaker of the house for absentee owners; of course they would have no idea who her friends had been. 'I'm not trying to get a photo,' she said. She closed her eyes. 'There's a guest room in the attic. It has skylight windows, there's no way to see into it from outside. In the room is an oak bookshelf with your travel books, and an acoustic guitar on a stand. It has an en suite, and the toilet is set too low, and the walls are papered in old circus flyers.'

The couple looked at each other. There was no way she could have known all that if she wasn't telling the truth. Denise offered her hand. 'I'm Denise Ang,' she said.

The woman shook it, but her grip was weak. 'I'm Bella Parata, this is my husband, Alan.' The tall man nodded. 'I'm sorry I snapped at you. We've been up to our neck in sorting out this house, and then this happens . . .'

'It was a hell of a shock,' he said, with an accent Denise supposed must have been from New Zealand. The couple invited her inside for a cup of tea. It would have been rude to refuse.

'This might sound strange,' Bella said as they entered, 'but would you know what happened to the chandelier that used to be here?' She gestured at the ceiling above the double-height entry. 'Pink-tinted carnival glass imported from Venice. It was original to the house, made specially in fact.'

Denise looked up. If there had been a chandelier, she couldn't picture it now. Certainly nothing like Bella described. 'No, I don't think so,' she said. 'It was always just those bare wires as far as I can remember.'

'Odd,' Bella said. 'She never mentioned something had happened to it.'

In the kitchen Alan put the kettle on and Bella retrieved a few mugs from a cardboard box where they had been packed away. The hanging racks that used to be cluttered with pots and pans were empty now, the cupboards bare. Bella had met Miri when she came into a shelter where Bella was working. 'After her family . . . you know, they kicked her out,' Bella said, 'she had no money to let student digs, and we were preparing to move ourselves. It seemed like the perfect fit.'

Denise nodded. What must Miri have been like then? Frightened and uncertain, adrift in a world she did not yet fit into? Or had she been preternaturally confident, always champing at the bit of her upbringing, ready to pounce on all that life had to offer?

'We last heard from her, I suppose, over a year ago,' Alan said. 'The last inventory she sent us before we decided to move back. When we arrived last month she was gone, but, I mean if you know Miri . . .'

'She had her ups and down,' Bella finished his sentence. 'But she had always come through before.'

'Maybe she had reconciled with her family,' Alan added. 'That was the only thing that made sense, disappearing like that, right? Why she would leave all of her things?'

'She left everything here?' Denise said. She blew on the surface of her tea, which Alan had added milk and sugar to without asking. Miri would have offered coffee, and she would have known that Denise liked it black.

Alan shifted uncomfortably. 'We came back because of Bella's MS. I guess we thought she would get in touch as and when. We had no idea Miri was really gone. We were so busy.'

Denise knew what they meant. There had been enough times when she had woken up in a random room of the house and found her way down to the kitchen, only to find Miri had stayed somewhere else that night. It was one of those things everyone accepted about her. Miriam Goldstein came and went as she pleased. Even in her own life.

'God, I can't wait to be out. I never liked this house,' Bella said. 'It was never a happy place.' She eased herself into a chair. 'My great-great-grandfather built it. Three of his wives died here. Two suicides. It wasn't . . .' Her voice broke down completely.

Alan squeezed his wife's shoulder. 'The police went through her things already, you know, to see if there was anything. Her parents are coming tomorrow to box up her personal items, but if you want to go upstairs and look, you can. If there's anything you want to keep.'

Denise went up the Persian-carpeted steps to the first floor. The adornments on the walls were much as she remembered them. Art prints, maps, covers from *Punch* magazines, heavily framed and screwed in place like pictures in a pub. The enormous brass gong on the first floor landing was still there.

One picture in particular caught her eye, a reproduction of a painting. The colourful daubs showed a woman in a turban and deep orange dress whose face was turned towards the viewer. Next to her, another woman, nude with wide-set glassy eyes, leaning her head on the first woman's shoulder. Denise's memory instantly supplied the name of the artist and the painting. *Die Freundinnen*, by Gustav Klimt. The picture made her catch her breath. She couldn't remember having seen it there before.

The door to Miri's room swung open on its hinge, dislodging traces of white fingerprint powder the police had dusted on the frame.

The room was a mess. It always had been. The police would have struggled to find the floor in here, much less anything else. Piles of clothes hung off the edge of furniture. A wardrobe was full to bursting with sequined mini dresses, slippery silks, and rugged outdoor wear shoved in together. The makeup pots and palettes scattered on the vanity table looked like someone just set them down and walked off: an enormous, old-fashioned tin of powder with a pink puff, the same brand of cheap liquid eyeliner Denise remembered Miri drawing in stark rings around her eyes. The effect was magnified by the four full-length mirrors in the room, one against each wall, making it look like an endless, jumbled dressing chamber.

A coloured shaft of light bounced from mirror to mirror and wall to wall, a deep red glint. Hanging off the bedside lamp was a long string of faceted garnets. Denise lifted the necklace off the lamp. Miri had been wearing that same necklace the first time they met. Denise fingered the oval beads. They were warm from the sun through the window, as if they had just been taken off a woman's neck. 'It's an heirloom, my grandmother's,' Miri had said.

Later Denise came to understand that was not necessarily true, that it was as likely to be from a charity shop or a mall. Miri wearing it had been what gave it the gloss, the timeless beauty.

The dark gems looked like clots of blood in Denise's hands. She looped the necklace over and over until it was wound snugly around her wrist. The clatter of the semiprecious beads as she went downstairs was like the sound of high heels on the floor in another room.

She scanned the wall for the Klimt picture, but couldn't find it now. Alan and Bella were still in the kitchen. She should at least let them know she was going.

She paused at the door and took a deep breath before going in. 'What have you done, Miri?' Denise whispered. She felt a squeeze in her chest, only perhaps half anxiety.

: **9** :

It is the second half of her master's course in Newcastle. Her first spring in the city, after a winter of freezing rain and baffling lectures. Denise's cheap coat, good enough for the London cold, is insufficient here and beginning to come apart at the seams.

She logs her hours in the computer lab, turns in every piece of work on time, and phones her parents twice a week whether they answer or not. Usually they do not. She waits for the answerphone, leaves a message as if everything is the same as it was before. Before she moved to Newcastle to start a master's course in genetic epidemiology. Before her brother died.

There is money in her account, far too much. One hundred and fifty thousand pounds. The number glares at her every time she has to use the cash point. She can't spend it and she doesn't want to keep it. But giving it away is no good either; it would be like giving away the last photograph of a loved one. It would be unthinkable.

Denise throws herself into her master's project. She analyses single nucleotide polymorphisms in genetic samples of families with a history of colon cancer. A text-based program calculates risk predictions for future generations in those families. She tweaks the code, pleased when she shaves microseconds off the runtime of each simulation. It is like the swimming practices she and Darwin did as teens. Working over weeks, months, even an entire season to prune down their personal bests.

One night Denise is at the bus stop when she sees some of her course mates in a pub. It looks warm inside, the bus is almost twenty minutes late, and she has five pounds in her pocket she forgot to spend on lunch. She crosses the rain-slicked road and goes in.

'Denise!' a man at the bar waves. 'I'm getting a round in. What are you having?'

'Hi, Jack.' Denise smiles. 'That's very kind, thank you. Diet coke and lemon, please.' Jack has blue eyes and wears his hair long but it suits him. His smile is kind and his eyes seek her out in lectures, exchanging a look that seems to indicate they are in on some kind of secret together.

He always seems so nice, at ease in any group, charming and smart. She realises she has probably had a crush on him for some time now.

A crush she can never act on. Because he has a girlfriend. This girlfriend is called Miriam. His eyes go soft whenever he mentions her, as if the sound of her name has a sort of power. Denise has never met this woman, but the others have, and they agree she is wonderful. She is not sure what to imagine. A petite and serious brunette, perhaps, the kind of studious woman who is primly perfect when she takes her glasses off? Or else a tight-bodied, hockey-playing blonde, the sort of country girl already settled into Jack's family, accompanying his parents on weekend trips to the garden centre?

The other students are dressed more formally than usual, a woman in a short purple satin frock, the men in trousers and jackets. Is there something on she has forgotten about?

'Didn't think you'd be out tonight.' The woman's teeth look dull yellow next to her lipstick. 'Or did you get a ticket in the end?'

Denise accepts a glass from Jack at the bar. 'A ticket to what?'

The group erupts in a peal of laughter. 'To the Medics Ball? At City Hall?' A hot redness blooms on her cheeks. The epidemiology students aren't medics even if they are in the medical school; why would it occur to her to go?

'I wouldn't worry about it,' Jack says. 'I went last year. It's not all that. Terrible meal. The disco is dire. You're not missing anything.'

'Are we ready or are we ready?' a voice calls out behind them. Denise follows the others' eyes as they look to the door.

'Miri!' Jack says. 'Finally.'

The woman in the green velvet dress enters the pub. It is a cold night, but she is wearing no coat. Probably local to the area, then – one of the first things Denise noticed about Newcastle was that the rumours were correct: true Geordies went out in all weather without jackets or hats. Her hair has the colour and movement of fire. The crushed velvet clings to her pear-shaped body and reveals plainly that she is wearing nothing underneath. A long string of garnets, dark as the shadows in her hair, is looped once around her neck and hangs almost to her waist. She is wearing the kind of strappy sandals Denise often looks at in shop windows but can never bring herself to buy: too impractical, too showy. But the black patent straps look just right around her narrow ankles, not too showy at all.

Her only concession to the cold is a pair of black satin gloves that come past her elbows. Denise looks away but not before she notices Miri slip an arm around Jack's neck and his twist to kiss her on the cheek.

'Who's this?' she asks, meaning Denise. 'I don't think we've met.' Miri's voice is smoky and deep, a surprising contrast to her pink cheeks and baby skin. She detaches her arm from where it is snaked around Jack to offer a hand. Denise mumbles her name, first and last. 'Are you coming?' Miri smiles. Her smile is a sweet tiny bow, the face of a Victorian valentine.

'I was on my way home,' Denise says. 'I don't have a ticket . . .'

Miri laughs, full throated like a goose. 'You shouldn't let a thing like that stop you!' she says. 'Come with me.' She grabs Denise's elbow and leads her to the toilets, shouting to the rest of the group to go on ahead, they will catch up.

Inside are two toilet stalls, one missing a door. Miri indicates for Denise to take off her coat, which she does. Miri folds it and stuffs it into Denise's bag. Suddenly Miri is peeling off her dress. 'You can wear mine,' she says. 'You can't walk in there dressed like that. Give me your clothes.'

Denise hesitates. As she suspected Miri is wearing nothing underneath. Miri tilts her head and smiles, slinky green fabric in her gloved hand. The dress looks smaller off her body, hardly more material than a swimsuit. 'Go on, it's stretch, it fits everyone,' she says. 'You're almost as flat up top as I am.'

'But what will you wear?'

Miri smiles. 'Your clothes, obviously. Don't worry. I know the doormen, it won't be a problem for me to walk in.'

Denise doesn't know what to do. It is impossible to look at the girl standing in front of her wearing nothing but gloves, a long necklace, and heels. It is almost as hard not to stare. Miri is slim up top and heavier below. She has the kind of seal-like limbs, smooth, that Denise often thinks of as boneless. Her legs taper from firm round thighs to tiny narrow ankles. It is not the type of body that is fashionable now, not the body celebrated in haute couture shows and women's magazines. But the way she is standing tells her that Miri is more comfortable in her skin than she with her angular limbs and narrow hips ever will be.

Denise doesn't want Miri to laugh at her for being a prude. She does not want to have to see Jack and the others later, tomorrow or the next day or next week, in the library or in an exam, and explain what happened. She closes her eyes and begins unbuttoning her shirt. The hands feel as if they belong to someone else, as if all of this is something she is watching in a film. Miri pulls the velvet dress over her head. To Denise's surprise the dress does indeed shrink and stretch in the right places to fit.

'Hair,' Miri says, and reaches forward, her arms encircling Denise's neck. Her eyes, which looked blue at a distance, are green and violet close up, flecked with yellow, the fire of opals in her pale face. The scent of her is sweet and sharp, sweat and vanilla. Miri's small hands untangle Denise's pigtail, arrange the strands over shoulders. 'Not bad,' she pronounces. 'Do you have makeup?' Denise shakes her head.

'That's OK, we'll make do.' Her face suddenly darts forward, and she plants a firm kiss on Denise's lips. She leans back and examines Denise's surprised face. 'Perfect,' she declares. 'Now you have some of my lippy.'

She tells Denise to look in the mirror. Denise's cheeks are flushed as if she has been running and her lips are a bright pink like Miri's. The ends of her hair graze her collarbones, now exposed by the low neckline of the dress. Denise stares at her reflection as if she is looking at someone else entirely, someone who resembles her but not quite. A close relative, perhaps. A twin. She had a twin once. Then her twin was lost and she has been alone ever since. If the mirror can be her twin, perhaps she isn't alone after all.

She glances down at her watch. 'We should hurry,' she says. 'We don't want to be too late.'

'Is being on time important to you?' Miri says.

'I guess so.' Denise hesitates. Wasn't being on time important to everyone? 'It's rude to be late, isn't it? Like, you would get in trouble if you were late for work—'

Miri's throaty laugh cuts her off. 'There are only two kinds of people who are paid to be on time,' she says. 'Train drivers and call girls. Anyway, what's the rush? Let's have a drink, get to know each other a little better. Jack tells me nothing about his friends. I want to find out more about you.'

'What's to find out? I'm very boring.' But Miri is standing there, expecting something. 'OK, my name is Denise Ang. My family is from Macau, I was born in London. My parents have a chip shop.' She is about to mention Darwin but stops herself. She looks at the mirror again, it is almost impossible not to. Twin-Denise moves her mouth when Denise does, but she is different somehow. Both her and not-her. She has a thrilling, guilty feeling of looking at herself for too long, as if someone has caught her staring at them. She clears her throat and looks away again. 'I have a degree in maths. So I guess I'm kind of a walking cliché.'

Miri tilts her head. 'How so?' she says.

Denise is confused. Is she taking the piss, or does she really not know? 'I'm very boring,' she repeats.

'Nonsense,' Miri says, and her reflection smiles at Denise's. 'In my experience, it's the quiet ones you have to watch out for.'

Everyone is well into their cups by the time Denise gets to City Hall. No one even checks the ticket she is clutching in her hand. Half-eaten plates of chocolate cake litter the tables and someone has thrown the contents of a fruit salad bowl over the floor, making it slippery with diced melon.

Miri, as promised, has found another way in. Denise spots her by the kitchen doors, her fingers tracing over the chest of a skinny waiter with a cigarette tucked behind his ear. She kept the gloves when they switched clothes, and the effect on Miri is odd yet beguiling, like a cross-dressing cabaret singer in a Weimar-era music hall. Her hand reaches up and takes the cigarette, taps the tobacco end against the waiter's chest. Denise is surprised Miri would openly flirt with someone else when Jack is in the room, but he doesn't seem to notice. He sits in the corner, drinking cheap white wine with the rest of their course mates.

'Oh my God, I love this song!' Miri appears next to Denise and drags her to the dance floor. Yellow and blue shafts of light bounce through the crowd, changing direction to the beat of the song. Denise shifts her weight from foot to foot and watches Miri close her eyes and raise her arms to the ceiling.

She had wondered why Miri would agree to put on her dowdy outfit, but now in the crowd of women in satin slip dresses and men in hired dinner jackets the effect is remarkable. In a jumper and jeans with the hems rolled high to show her strappy heels, Miri exudes androgynous cool. As if she planned it that way all along. Men dancing stiffly with their partners steal glances at them as Miri leads the way around the dance floor. The women stare too. When Miri spins round Denise notices the cigarette from the skinny waiter tucked behind her ear.

Denise looks to where Jack was sitting. He smiles and waves, and she raises a hand shyly back. He gets up and her heart starts beating faster, completely out of step with the music. He stops in front of her, smiles, and begins to match her steps, swaying back and forth as she does. His hand grazes her hip and then, a second later, presses against the small of her back. The small curls behind his ears are damp with sweat, glistening against his skin. She decides he really is quite perfect.

It doesn't last. Miri dances back to Denise and Jack and flings her arms over his shoulders. Jack grins and pulls Miri's hips snugly against his own. They look into each other's eyes as if they are the only people in the world. He has been reclaimed and Denise is alone, again. The flicker of envy she feels lasts only a moment. She dances nearby, in the shadows.

: 10 :

Denise picked up her phone, started to dial, then hung up before it connected. They needed to talk, but she was afraid to be the one who phoned him.

Archie was still in Northumberland she supposed, though according to the web, the next car boot sale in Rothbury wasn't until next weekend. The stories about Miri were out of control. Now they were claiming that textual analysis of her escort reviews proved who some of the clients were. There was no way Archie hadn't seen the news by now.

Brant accused of call girl dalliances . . .

Labour in turmoil . . .

More questions than answers . . .

There were too many things she had pushed aside over the years. Worried what Archie would do if she told him what she had seen and what she knew. And there was the bad thing, the thing she had seen in the car. They needed to clear the air. Sooner rather than later.

When Denise wakes up the night after the ball she does not know where she is. She stretches her arms and legs slowly, experimentally: a bed, then, but not her own. Alone. Naked apart from knickers. The ceiling is plastered in an old-fashioned repeating pattern like scallop shells. A brass lamp hangs down from the centre. She searches her memory of the previous night, but cannot even remember leaving City Hall.

The room looks like a home office and she is on a futon sofa pulled into the middle of the room. There is a desk in the corner with an old computer, a big grey tower, probably ten years old. In another corner a guitar rests upright on a stand. Next to it, a bookcase. Are these Miri's books? Jack's? Collections of sheet music, arrangements for classical guitar and mandolin. Travel guides to New Zealand, Japan, and Australia.

Denise pulls the curtain to face the North Sea fog that seems to perpetually hang over Newcastle. So she is on the second floor of wherever this is, then. The garden below her window is crowded with unkempt rose bushes. A cast-iron bench, wooden slats rotted through, stands near a concrete lion. Beyond the garden, a misty, sculpted parkland that might be Jesmond Dene.

The sound of spoons clattering against the sides of bowls filters up from two floors below. Denise slings her bag over one shoulder and, shoes in the other hand, tiptoes down the stairs.

The stairwell is wide with Persian carpet running down the middle of the steps. The walls are covered in framed vintage prints. One picture catches her eye, a painting of a red-haired woman kneeling in front of a man. There is something intimate about the pose, almost graphic, but the man is wearing a suit of armour and the woman is wearing a white dress. A snake is wrapped around her arm and waist. Denise leans to have a closer look, stumbles, and hits her shoulder on a gong hulking in the corner of the landing. The startling noise vibrates through the house.

'Are you finally up?' Miri calls.

Denise pauses. 'Yes,' she says. There is no getting out quietly. At the bottom of the stairs she glances up. Bare wires emerge from a ceiling rose. It looks as if there was a chandelier there, once.

The kitchen is showered in light from many windows, a perfect contrast to the dark stairwell. Jack is sitting at a table in a Victorian conservatory. His hair sticks up in all directions and his hands clutch a mug of coffee as if his life depends on it.

Miri flits about a kitchen island, piling scrambled eggs and sourdough toast high on a platter. Her hair hangs loose over her shoulders. Denise feels a pang of envy as she notices, again, that

Miri is beautiful. The way she flips her hair from one side to the other, combs her fingers through the strands. She is clearly the kind of woman who wears her looks as casually as an accessory.

A bright orange and blue patterned kimono is tied around her waist, and when she bends to refill Jack's mug, it exposes the edge of her pale nipple. Denise flushes. Somehow Miri's semi-nakedness now seems more of an exposure than seeing her stripped in the pub toilet the night before.

'Coffee?' she asks. 'How do you have it?'

'Black like my soul,' Denise says. She bites her lip. She doesn't know where that has come from, and it feels false in her mouth.

Miri hoots a laugh. 'Black like your soul! I love it, Jack, did you hear this one?' He nods sullenly.

Miri puts the platter down, and next to it a stack of mismatched, flower-sprigged plates. 'Breakfast!' she chirps. Jack mutters that he has to get home. Miri puts a hand on his shoulder but he shrugs it off.

Miri rolls her eyes and looks at Denise instead. 'You seemed to be enjoying yourself last night.'

'What I remember of it. It's been years since I had such a full on night out.' Her entire life, in fact.

'Welcome to the Miri Goldstein show,' Jack says. 'That's what it's like twenty-four hours a day, seven days a week.'

'Mistress of the fucking night, that's me.' Miri spears a forkful of eggs and waves it under his nose. 'If you can't keep up, I should find someone who can.' Jack pushes her hand away, knocking the fork to the floor. 'Oh, now what is it?' she says. Her voice has a sing-song note to it, a parent indulging a well-rehearsed tantrum.

'You seemed to be doing a good job of finding someone else last night.'

Denise stares at her plate. She has never known how to deal with people who have their arguments in public. 'This is an incredible house,' she says, trying to change the subject.

'Lamia House,' Jack says. 'AKA, Labia House. Don't let her lady of the manor act fool you. It's not hers.'

'Don't listen to Jack, he woke up on the wrong side of the bed this morning and decided to get upset over some meaningless flirting. He thinks playing the part of grumpy bear makes him more interesting. Little does he know, there is nothing he can do that will make him interesting.'

Jack jerks his thumb in Denise's direction. 'Go on, ask her. She saw it all.'

Denise's head snaps up. 'I don't remember anything,' she says. 'I really don't know most of what happened last night. I don't even know where I am.'

'Fine.' Jack stands up and almost knocks over his chair as he does so. 'Whatever. Get other people to cover for you, as usual.' He looks at Denise pointedly. 'Just so you know, she only stays interested in people if they have something she wants. As for me, I've had enough of this.'

'Well, you know where the bus stop is.' Miri shrugs. 'Out of the door, turn left, end of the street.'

Denise holds her breath. She keeps holding her breath until the front door slams. She exhales and Miri breaks into uncontrollable laughter. 'Holy smokes, is he always like that?' she asks Denise.

'I was going to ask you the same thing. Do you two always have bad fights?'

Miri holds up her hands. 'Wouldn't know. It hasn't happened until now.' The bright silk kimono falls back from her wrists, and there are small, raised scars on her forearms, white and long healed, criss-crossing the skin covered by the gloves the night before. Her fingernails are surprisingly dirty, bitten and short.

'Oh.' Denise isn't sure what to say. 'I'm sure he'll ring you and you two will make up soon.'

'I wouldn't expect so.' Miri shakes her head. 'It's not as if he's my boyfriend. That kind of possessiveness? I can't be doing with that.'

'He's not your boyfriend?' Denise says. 'I thought . . .'

'That he and I were an item?' Miri laughs again. 'He wishes.

No, he's been making the moves for a few months. I brought him home last week just because I was bored and he was convenient, and then there was the ball, so . . . Goes to show what a pity fuck will get you.'

Denise tries to look as if she knows what that means. 'You have a lovely house,' she says.

Yet again Miri laughs. 'This house? It's not mine. He was right about that. I'm only the housesitter.' The owners, she explains, are a married couple. The wife inherited the house. She met her husband in New Zealand; they planned to come back to Newcastle someday. 'And anyway, could you imagine getting rid of a place like this?' Miri says. Nothing in Lamia House is hers apart from her clothes, makeup, and a diploma for a degree in art history shoved in the top drawer of a desk. Twice a year the owners send a typed checklist of items to be inventoried which Miri ticks off item by item and posts back. There is nothing in it for her apart from having a place to live – but what a place.

Miri's eyes sparkle with amusement. 'Enough about that,' she proclaims, and starts stacking breakfast plates. 'What are you doing today?'

Denise shrugs. 'I have to work on my thesis . . .'

'But, hangover, right?' Miri says. Denise nods. 'Fab.' Miri stands up and dusts her hands on her hips, a movement Denise finds surprisingly incongruous, like a carpenter brushing wood shavings off their hands. 'I have an idea. Let's walk Hadrian's Wall. You'll love it.'

Denise snorts a small laugh. That is the last thing she expected Miri to say. 'I'm sorry, what? No, that's . . . that takes days, doesn't it?'

'Not all of it. Just a bit. Have you never been?' Denise admits she hasn't. Miri opens her mouth in exaggerated shock. 'Well, you can't come to the North East and not at least see the ruins at Steelrigg,' she says. 'Has to be done. Today. *Now*.'

'I wish I could. But I would need to go home, and get different clothes. I don't think . . .'

'Nonsense!' Miri waves her hand. 'There are loads of clothes upstairs. Come on.' Denise can see no other option but to give in to this dazzling and confusing woman.

'Morag.' Arjun put a hand on her elbow as she stood up from the committee table in Portcullis House. 'Delphine Barrett. Outside.' The parliamentary assistant's eyebrows were raised.

'Thank you, Arj.' The MP for Cameron Bridge gathered up her notes. Morag Munro had put herself forward for the All-Party Parliamentary Group on Disaster Response, counting on it to bolster her credibility as Shadow Home Secretary. With the live inquiries underway, however, it looked like another pointless slog. A year's worth of consultation that was destined to die, unimplemented, on the library shelf. 'Grab us a quiet meeting room, will you?' she said. 'Alone.' Arjun frowned and batted his eyes over the top of his tortoiseshell glasses, but did it anyway.

Morag smoothed her greying bob behind her ears and went from the Grimond Room into the hallway. She waited for her eyes to adjust to the gloom. The wood panelling and concrete ceilings of Portcullis House had been intended, she supposed, to make the most of the natural light. The only problem was, this being Britain, it meant the meeting rooms and hallways were permanently in shadow.

She spotted a woman loitering in the hallway. 'Delphine,' she said in her gentle Highlands accent. 'What a pleasure. How are things on Fleet Street? Shall we grab somewhere private?'

'No, the coffee corner is fine.' Delphine steered Morag into the waiting area at the end of the hall. As usual it was haunted by navy-suited interns scowling over their laptops. 'Fucking epic start,' Delphine sighed. 'I take it you've seen the latest about Brant.'

It was a misty morning in London, the County Hall and functional façade of St Thomas's Hospital visible over the river. Behind them, the blunted shaft of The Shard rose, its top floors shrouded in low clouds. 'Of course,' Morag said.

Arjun always briefed her on any overnight developments first thing. The rumours that Brant had been seeing a call girl were no longer rumours: a photo had surfaced of the man himself, naked but for a collar, on all fours at the end of a dog lead. The photo was blurry but it was undeniably the party leader.

Worse still: the call girl had been photographed wearing a Nazi uniform. With an SS cap at a rakish angle and an over-the-knee boot planted on Brant's backside. Between her Jewish background and the identity of her star client, the media was in meltdown.

'You worked as his press advisor until recently,' Morag said to Delphine. 'Did you know about this . . . this Nazi business?'

'It was as much a surprise to me as everyone else,' Delphine said. 'I had no idea this was coming.' She helped herself to a coffee from the machine, and offered one to Morag. 'I mean, we heard stories about him and prostitutes. Everyone does it. But this? Believe me, if there had been even a whiff of antisemitism when I was working for him, I would have walked out on the spot.'

Morag doubted that. Delphine had been a spin doctor, precisely as amoral as the job demanded. Delphine had spun everyone from embezzling Chancellors to double-dipping non-doms without a word of complaint. Once she latched on to Lionel Brant's team, she seemed to have found her perfect match. Anyone would have thought it would take a real catastrophe to separate them.

Granted, that loyalty hadn't saved her when the general election results came through and the party found themselves in a minority. Brant put Delphine's head on the chopping block instead of his own, hoping the voters hated unelected advisors more than they did politicians. No one was appeased, not the public, and certainly not his colleagues. Failing to step down had not gone over well.

Delphine licked her wounds and took a job as political diarist for the *Afternoon Standard*. With Brant alienating most of the party, it was only a matter of time before someone opened the vaults and released something truly damaging. Call girls were one thing. But a Nazi fetish? At a time when the party was already battling accusations of antisemitism? That was quite another. Six weeks ago it looked as if the man was never going to give up the leadership. Now he was an international laughing stock. He would be lucky to last the week.

The photo had appeared on a right-wing website first. A grubby little outfit, in Morag's opinion, appealing to the worst in online hate. But they had published the pictures when other media would not have dared, and for that she had to give them credit.

'So . . . the thinking is you'll be tipped to be interim leader until the party elects a new one,' Delphine said.

'Brant is still party leader, and speculation about what may or may not happen is inappropriate in the circumstances,' Morag said.

'But you will be standing in for him at the opposition dispatch box during Prime Minister's Questions this week. A vote of no confidence must be coming. Today? Tomorrow?'

'The party leader is on a leave of absence,' Morag recited. 'Come on, Delphine, you know all this already.' Morag drummed her fingers on her cup. 'Why are you really stalking me?'

'OK, no bull,' Delphine said. 'If he steps down, what next? Will you be running to replace Brant or won't you? It has to be tempting, right? Who cares about interim. Imagine it – Morag Munro, Leader of the Opposition. It's been a long time since the party looked outside London for its leadership. And they have never had a woman. It's your time, right? You'd be a fool not to go for it.'

As the MP for Cameron Bridge, her outsider bona fides would serve her well. She couldn't help the fact that she had once been one of 'Brant's Babes', a freshman MP swept into office during the last economic boom. But for once it looked like being a woman – and a Scot – was going to count in her favour.

Not that Delphine needed to be told any of this. 'Nice try, but no comment.' Morag made for the stairs. 'Flattery usually gets you everywhere. But not today.'

'Is it a constitutional crisis?'

Morag sighed. She wished that whichever journalist had first seized on that term – now used to describe anything from license fee hikes to local by-elections – would banish the phrase back to wherever it came from. 'No,' she said.

Delphine tottered along behind. 'After your support of the No campaign in Scotland paid off, you must have been disappointed with Shadow Home Sec instead of Shadow Chancellor, right? Everyone knows it's a chop shop for no-hopers . . .'

Morag paused. 'You know what I'm going to say. As of now we have a leader. In the event he does decide to go, no one can predict who will be nominated and how much support they will receive from the other MPs. Until something changes, I have no further comment.'

'I have a source that says that Vernon Coyle is already putting his team together,' Delphine pressed on. 'If he becomes leader, would you expect to be on his front bench?'

Morag paused. The Honourable Member from Maidenhead. Coyle was a youngish buck who had tried to get her drunk and put his honourable member in her hand at a party conference in 2009. He called her a cougar. She wasn't sure what offended her more: that he had tried it on with her, or that he thought implying she was old would get her into bed.

No doubt Delphine's 'source' on Coyle gunning for the leadership was Coyle himself. And no doubt he thought he was ready for the leadership because of his public school sense of entitlement. 'No comment,' she said.

'Will you be nominating anyone else for the position?' she asked.

'Delphine . . .'

'Come on, Morag. Throw me a bone.' She was canny, Morag had to give her that. Phone calls would be too easy to ignore; better to turn up and badger someone in person. 'Off the record. I can put it as "sources". We've known each other for years. Have I ever done wrong by you?'

Delphine had never done her any harm as such. But she had never given her much of a helping hand either. Like most people Morag had met in London over the years, she was out for one person: herself. Not to mention her new career in journalism. 'You and I both know that won't hold up,' Morag said. 'I'm saying nothing. Speak to the party if you want sources.'

'That is perfect,' Delphine trilled. 'I'll put you down as "refuses to comment". Cheers, hon!' She disappeared down the stairs, her kitten heels click-clicking on the floor.

Arjun poked his head out from a meeting room, spotted her, and scampered over. 'How did it go?' her personal secretary said, a fresh cup of coffee in his hand. Morag took a deep drink and sighed. He did know how to declaw her, always.

'Super.'

'So.' Arjun's dark eyes sparkled. 'What's the word on the street? Any clues as to who leaked the photo?'

Morag shook her head. They headed downstairs. 'Someone with a pretty fair knowledge of libel law, I should think,' she said. 'Otherwise why go to a rubbish little website?'

'Delphine?' Arjun suggested.

Morag considered the possibility. 'On balance, no,' she said. 'Not that it isn't the sort of thing she would do.'

'What was it they used to call her favourite tactic? "Throwing a dead cat on the table." Well, this Lamia person certainly is a cat that is no longer with the living.'

Delphine had been known for her strategy of putting around shocking, yet usually baseless, accusations about political opponents to set them on the back foot. It directed attention away from her clients. And it usually worked; anyone having to vigorously deny accusations of secret jihadist sympathies or ties to paedophile rings would find themselves the topic of conversation for days. It didn't matter what was true. It was an effective smokescreen.

'The way he dumped her from his inner circle has to sting,' Morag said. 'But I don't think so. She wouldn't be chasing down angles so hard today if she had been the source. She hasn't profited from this at all, which is unlike her.'

'You're probably right,' Arjun said. They strode out onto the pavement in the direction of her office. Arjun glanced at his hand, admiring the neatly manicured fingertips. He brushed the nails against the lapel of his tweed jacket. 'Still, what a mess. Must put the frighteners on anyone in here with skeletons in their closet. Which at last count is, like, everyone.'

'Yes,' Morag agreed. 'What do you think about that Commodus?'

'The Rome Must Burn fellow?' Arjun said. 'Are you asking what I think, or what I *think*?'

'Bit of both,' Morag said.

Arjun sniffed. 'His name is Harold Woad. I think we'll be hearing a lot more about him and his website in the weeks to come.'

'He's good?'

'He's the best at what he does, no question,' Arjun said. 'The only problem is, what he does is shite.'

'Nicely put,' Morag said. Arjun gave her the digested version: Woad had hung around Fleet Street for years trying to make his break. He achieved some notoriety in the early years of the web, raising funding for a tech gossip site that over-promised and underdelivered and folded suddenly, leaving contributors and investors out of pocket. Since then he had been funding new ventures and trying new schemes. He always closed out his limited companies before the first accounts came due – so no one knew what he earned or where his income came from. RMB was the latest. Woad claimed to be twenty-five, but thirty-five was nearer the mark. Standard practice. After all, it's tough to be the new kid on the block the further you get from being a kid.

'But,' Arjun said, 'this could be his career moment for real this time. If he plays the exposure well – the right news panels, broadsheet guest columns – there is no reason he couldn't become a permanent fixture of the commentariat. It is so obviously what he wants. Provided he distances himself from some of the – how shall I put it? – more extreme opinions on the website.'

'And the other thing?'

Arjun sighed, a ripple of irritation passing over his face. 'No, he's not gay.'

'Not even with that hair?' She waved a hand by her ear, indicating Woad's cropped blonde Afro.

Arjun shook his head. 'Not even with that hair. Fashions have changed. Cameron Bridge might be stuck in the sixties but the rest of us have moved on.'

Morag reddened. She felt silly for asking. Arjun was her only connection to the younger generation; she and her husband had no children. She desperately wanted to know what they thought, and more importantly, how they would react to a woman as leader. Instead she was pumping him for opinions of what some gossip columnist got up to in his private life. 'Remind me again why I do this job?'

'Good question . . . service to the community? The incredible perks? The adulation of millions?' Arjun pinched his staff pass out of his pocket and swiped the card reader of a side door at the Palace of Westminster. The security guards nodded and waved them through.

'Millions?' Morag grimaced. 'Dozens, at best.'

Arjun smiled, and she knew he had forgiven her clumsy questions. For now.

: **12** :

'Don't be such a buzzkill, Denise,' Darwin taunts. *Buzzkill* is his new favourite phrase. He picked it up from television, some American reality show.

Denise looks up to the ladder her brother pulled down from the ceiling of the leisure centre. He scampers into the rafters above the drained swimming pool. The asbestos ceiling tiles have been removed. A feeling of vertigo overcomes her as she tilts her head towards the cathedral-like space. She has often looked up at the ceiling when turning laps of backstroke, at the strings of bunting that mark the last few metres before the end of the lane. The cavernous emptiness without the tiles makes the bottom edge of the rafters look twice as high as normal.

She and Darwin aren't meant to be in here, not in this part of the building, which is being refurbished. He looks down to where she is standing, her hand hesitating on the lowest rung.

'I'm not sure I can pull myself up,' she says. A wave of fear runs over her.

'Quit stalling,' Darwin says. 'You're the strongest girl I know.' He turns away and his body tenses. One large step, almost a jump, and he is on the next rafter. 'Come on.'

It is always this way. Darwin jumping out ahead, Denise following whatever he does because she cannot think of any other way of doing things. The fact that she was born first was a temporary anomaly; he has been outstripping her every day since. She is good at swimming, he is being talked about as potentially world class. She is good at maths, he is better, but prefers novels and music 'over dry old numbers anyway'. He gets higher marks than her in spite of doing no revision that she can see. She is proud of him but also a little afraid. Afraid of losing him. She is also afraid of the small dark tangle in her heart that wants, just once, to see him fail.

'If you don't come down I'm going to . . .'

She does not finish the sentence, because it is an empty threat and they both know it. Yet again she is an unforgivable buzzkill.

Darwin laughs. The boyish cackle rattles around the space, cracking off the tiles of the pool like a chorus of ducks. 'Going to what? Call for help? Grass on me? No one's here.' Darwin turns away. His body dips at the knees, his hips thrust forward, he jumps again.

But something is wrong. His knees weren't right and he lands too soft this time. He wobbles, his balance gone. For an achingly long moment his body hovers on the edge of being on the rafter, and falling. One leg hanging out over the space, his foot pawing at the empty air.

Denise gasps and scrambles up the ladder. She plants both hands at shoulder width on the rafter and pulls her lower body over like a paratrooper scrambling over a wall. As she crawls out towards him Darwin tenses his muscles and brings his body upright. He pivots at the waist, looks at her and grins. 'See? I knew you could do it,' he says.

'You arsehole.' Denise is panting from the effort, her hands on her knees. He tricked her into coming up. 'You could have died.'

'Don't be so stupid,' he says. He jumps again and lands solidly this time. 'See, it's easy. Now your turn.'

Denise looks down. From here the swimming pool is tiny, dusty with construction debris. Broken pieces of ceiling and other rubbish have collected in the bottom. She can imagine what his body would look like down there, twisted at unnatural angles, blood bubbling out of his mouth. She closes her eyes, suddenly sick.

'Please stop.' Denise knows he won't come down until she

does it too, until she jumps. He won't stop until he gets her to start. He always wins, but to him it is no fun playing if she isn't playing too.

'Better hurry,' he calls back. He is five rafters ahead now, and still going. 'Last one to the end of the hall and back has to mop the shop tonight.'

The family found out how Darwin had died the same way everyone else did. It was breaking news on Boxing Day.

Not Darwin, not specifically. The tsunami. The moment she saw those first juddering seconds of mobile footage from Thailand on a twenty-four-hour news channel, Denise felt the black threads tighten around her heart. Her parents tried to ring his mobile but the lines were all down. There was nothing for it but to sit and wait.

The last time they heard from him was Christmas Eve. He rang before Midnight Mass. It had always been a magic night when they were kids, being allowed to stay up late and decorating the tree after coming home from church. And there was always Mum's cheese and onion bread pudding. She put it in the oven when they left for church so it was golden and fluffy by the time they came home.

Denise and her parents hung the long paper garlands they kept in a cardboard box in the attic. She and Darwin had made them the year they were ten, cutting and gluing loops of foiled paper together.

Forty-eight hours later the magic was drained from the holiday for ever. The gold and red chains sagged on the walls, ridiculously out of place now. White fairy lights on the tree blinked on and off at a grave tempo. She watched sombre heads of newsreaders repeat the same few facts they had been reiterating for hours. An earthquake measured over 9 on the Richter scale, centred off the coast of Indonesia, in the Indian Ocean. Governments and aid agencies responding. Families urged not to panic. Her parents sat on the sofa, side by side, hands on their knees. Her mother's knuckles were white. They said nothing, nothing. She could see they were trying their best to calm themselves until they heard whether their son was dead or alive. Denise, however, already knew.

Darwin had raved about the scuba diving when he phoned them. His American girlfriend Shelley's idea; she was certified. He took a crash course a couple of days after they landed. He had to learn to swim a different way, slowly so as not to scare the sea life, taking little sips of air so their tanks would last. They were taking a long-tailed boat to the local islands for the next few days to get closer to the shark reefs and some shipwrecks, he said. The dive instructors were wearing Santa Claus hats under the water all week. Thais weren't Christian, but they knew their tourist market.

It was the wrong twin.

The family faxed Darwin's dental records to Thailand before his remains could be flown back. There was a small service at the Catholic church. Friends and acquaintances who had once told the family how fortunate they were – so lucky, to have a boy and a girl twin – stood, sat, and knelt in the right places during Mass. Afterwards there was tea in the sacristy, the room with two sinks. A regular one and one with a pipe that ran straight into the earth. The second sink was for washing the vessels that held the blood of Our Lord, for returning the particles directly to the ground. Aunties and cousins touched the powder-blue sleeve of Mrs Ang's suit, murmured their condolences, and never met her eyes. Water to water, dirt to dirt.

Life as they knew it did not go on. How could it? It was another few months before they found out about the money. None of them had known Florida University had taken out life insurance on Darwin. Denise's parents wired a few thousand for the memorial service Shelley's family held in St Petersburg six months later.

Denise flew out to meet them. The humidity when she stepped off the plane hit her like a punch. She stayed at Shelley's family's house, a big new building on a small marshy lot. The sprawling city was dominated by chain shops and highways.

The kind of place where old guys drove pickup trucks and kids joined Scouts and tried out for cheerleading.

The service was crowded, overflowing. Denise stood by the lilies her parents sent and had stilted conversations with strangers who looked at the floor and jiggled paper cups of apple juice in their hands. Almost all of them, it seemed, had met her brother, or knew someone who lived in England, or had been to London. The sickly perfume of the lilies stuck in her nostrils. Everyone agreed the church was done out tastefully, and 'what they would have wanted'. Was it? Did Darwin ever think about death, much less what his funeral would be like?

She wondered if he ever found the America he was looking for. Because she wasn't sure this was it.

There were white candles everywhere and on the service programmes a photo of Darwin and Shelley. His arms were wrapped gingerly around her as they posed for a homecoming dance portrait. His face was so like Denise's own, long and angular. Younger pictures of Shelley filled the church. With braces on her teeth, pigtails, holding a softball bat. In baby pink cowboy boots at her Sweet Sixteen. Hugging friends as they sat on the bonnet of her white BMW.

Denise stood, almost without realising she was doing so, during a reading from Ecclesiastes

. . . neither shall there be any remembrance of things that are to come with those that shall come after . . . in much wisdom is much grief: and he that increaseth knowledge increaseth sorrow . . .

She walked to the front of the church to the space where a coffin would normally have been. Everyone, the American Legion vets, the soccer moms, the unflappably monotonic Baptist preacher, hushed. She took a pink-edged carnation from the largest flower arrangement and ate it. Petals, stem and all. The only sound for a minute or more was her jaw working through the bud and its bitter leaves.

It was the last time she ate something without thinking about it.

*

It took two more years to finish her degree. The chip shop shut, then reopened, though now her father always stayed in the front, her mother always stayed in the back. When Denise came in on evenings and weekends, she felt like a walkie-talkie relaying messages from one side of the wall to the other.

Denise framed a photo of her parents, herself and her brother. It was taken at the going-away party before he left for Gainesville where he had a full-ride athletics scholarship and plans to major in English Lit. She had felt, in that moment the camera snapped, that they had never been so happy. Looking at it now she was sure that was true. Her parents were greyer than she liked to think of them but smiling, her father's arm around her mother's shoulders. Denise was looking at Darwin and he was holding a glass of champagne. His eyes were closed and he grinned.

All other photographs, she hid. It was his eyes; she could not see them and not wonder what his face had looked like when he was found. His dark, mischievous eyes robbed of their glint. She imagined the bodies piled up in Ao Nang. Pulled from the wreckage of long-tail boats, laid out on the sand. What was it like? Was it like the rows of frozen fish that were delivered to the chip shop every week, their eyes cloudy and lifeless?

She boxed everything she could find and put it all deep into her parents' attic. His books, which no one else in the family would read. His old tapes and CDs she saved.

She scraped a 2:2, in the end. Then she started applying for master's degrees. She couldn't stay in London a moment longer. She was turned down over and over. Newcastle gave her a conditional yes. It was the best she was going to do, and she took it.

Her parents gave her most of the insurance money. It was too much, but if she'd had someone to give it away to, she would have tried to get rid of it too. Blood money, her gran in Macau would have called it, and Denise did indeed think it was tainted. She couldn't send it back. If she did that she would have nothing at all. And it was a ridiculous amount of money, life-changing; enough to buy a house if she wanted.

Every time she checked her bank balance, the zeroes looked up at her like blank, drowned eyes

: 13 :

Everything happens so quickly from the day after the ball. Denise tells Miri about Darwin. She doesn't want to, at first, but Miri is curious and keeps asking questions. *Then what? How did he do that?* Denise has a lifetime of answers. Sometimes it feels as if she can remember every moment of his life, not only because it was for the most part her life too. She was his twin sister but also it felt like his biggest fan.

'Do you wish you'd been there?' Miri says. 'With him. In Thailand.'

The question surprises Denise. 'I . . . I don't know. I try not to think about it.'

'Yeah,' Miri says. There is an odd look in her eyes, as if she is suddenly not there, but somewhere behind the surface. 'That makes sense. It would drive me crazy. What would you do to save the person you loved most in the world?'

Miri is a great talker but also, Denise discovers, an even better listener. Her wide green eyes drink up every detail. It doesn't occur to Denise to wonder why, because she has never had a friend like this before. She was born with a best friend. Making a new one is, she tells herself, a very different process. You have to teach each other. You have to learn.

The trip to Hadrian's Wall is a bus journey with two connections. Miri and Denise pass a can of Red Bull topped up with whisky back and forth as the Northumbrian countryside rolls past.

Miri's hands are cold, the fingers waxy. She has wrapped up

in waterproof trousers and a forest green coat but no gloves. Denise rubs her own hands together to try to build up heat, then wraps them around Miri's. It isn't enough.

Denise scoots along the bus seat until their thighs are touching. Miri jams her hands instead in the soft warm space between Denise's knees and her crotch. Denise, shocked, says nothing. Miri is still talking, about something else now, as if her hands aren't only inches from Denise's—no. Stop. She focuses, instead, on the thin tree branches scraping the sides of the bus as it careers around corners. On the low gentle voice talking about local history, about border raids and reivers. They ride that way the last half hour of the journey, longer.

The visitor centre has shut. The wall itself is free to view, but apart from the sad crumbling stone and a vast plain stretching north of them, there is little to see. 'Imagine being sent here,' Miri sighs. 'From Rome to here. And nothing to look at every day but acres of brown grass.'

They walk to a cheap B&B where the ancient proprietor tells them she won't stand for any 'lesbian antics'. Denise blushes but Miri only laughs. The room is a converted attic. Miri declares it perfect. They sit on the bed alternately swigging value lemonade and Pimm's from bottles and trying to find anything to watch on the room's ancient television. All of the channels are grey and snowy. Miri turns it off.

She kneels on the bed, opens the two small windows and leans the top half of her body out as far as she can. 'This is the real show,' she tells Denise. The lilac of the dusk sky fills with the calls of birds seeking their mates. She tilts her head and listens. 'Sedge warbler,' she says to a crickety chirrup interspersed with sharp peeps. 'Mistle thrush.' A sing-song whistle. She puts a hand to her ear, listens a while longer, then points out the window excitedly. 'Nightjar! A nightjar, very early for this far north.' Denise listens. The spooky chatter of its call sounds unearthly, mechanical.

'How do you know all those?'

Miri sits back on the bed. Sitting there she looks so plump

and alluring, like a Turkish odalisque. Her limbs splay out when she moves, unselfconsciously, and Denise can see why men are unable to resist her. 'When I was growing up, listening to the dawn and dusk chorus was all the entertainment I had from Friday to Saturday night.'

'Why?'

'I'm Jewish?' Miri's face crinkles at having to explain something so simple, and Denise feels silly for not having put it together before. Miriam. Goldstein. Obviously. 'We were not allowed to turn on a television or radio on the Sabbath. Couldn't even boil a kettle or flush the toilet.' A sly smile flickers over her face. 'Forbidden bird, the nightjar. We are not permitted to eat it, you know.'

'Forbidden?' Denise says. 'Does nightjar come up on a menu very often?' She doesn't even know what the bird looks like but it has a name like something her gran would eat. She once offered Denise a jellied duck's foot, but only once.

'Not really,' Miri says. 'But it made me wonder why we are so afraid of certain animals. Of the wilderness.' She tells Denise about Scotland, about a school trip she once took. She fell in love with the hills, and wants to go to Cameron Bridge someday to climb the country's highest mountain. It seems like a modest ambition to Denise.

'We'll go to Taynuilt,' she says. 'The haunted bothy.'

'What's a bothy?'

'They're free places to stay in the Highlands,' Miri explains. 'Little cottages, abandoned houses. Taynuilt was a deerstalker's cottage once.' Her voice drops. 'They say the stalker hanged himself there and no one has been able to spend a night in it without going mad ever since.'

'I don't believe in ghosts,' Denise says.

Miri nods. 'Probably a good thing. They say Lamia House is haunted too.'

Denise laughs. *Who does?* she thinks. 'No it isn't,' she says. The sounds in the roof at night, they are only the wind. The voices in the hallways, nothing but an overnight guest looking for a toilet. 'Anyway, Scotland isn't so far away. You can go any time you like.'

'You don't understand.' Miri rolls over on the flower-print counterpane that covers the narrow bed. She looks up at the ceiling. 'Women in my family don't do things like that. They don't do anything. They marry young and pump out kids. Going shopping in Gateshead is the highlight of the week. Of their *lives*.'

'You make it sound as if you were raised by religious . . .' She stops before she says it, but the unspoken word is in the room anyway. Religious freaks.

Miri's voice goes quiet. 'Sort of. Depends who you ask. My family are Hasidic. They arranged a marriage for me and I told them I couldn't do it. I wanted to go to university, see the world.'

Denise knows little about Orthodox Jews, though she has seen some from time to time in London. The women, dressed in heavy, frumpy clothes, with wigs covering their natural hair. The rumour at her school was they had shaved heads underneath, but surely that couldn't be true? The boys, with their skullcaps and sweetly curled ringlets at the sides of their heads. Like a people living in another century.

'What did you do?' Denise asks, but the answer is apparent. They would not be there, in this room, if Miri had agreed to the marriage.

Miri closes her eyes. 'I ran away. I thought, if I could show them how much it meant to me, how happy it would make me, they would change their minds. I was wrong. When I made that choice, they disowned me.' Miri's eyes open; they are brimming with tears. 'I saw a family friend a few years later, in town one day. She said my family sat shiva for me. As if I had died.'

'My God,' Denise whispers. 'So you never travelled?'

'Oh, I travelled.' A smile spreads across Miri's face. 'After the first year of my degree. I met a guy who was looking for someone to go around the world with. It was a free ticket, so I was like, why not? We started in India, trekking in Nepal, then all over Southeast Asia. By that time we had used up most of his money and only had a couple of days in the US, so we came back.'

'Wow,' Denise says. 'That must have been some boyfriend, to last going to all those places together. Being in each other's pockets for so long.'

'He wasn't a boyfriend, as such,' Miri says. 'More of an arrangement. He provided the money, I provided . . . other things.'

Denise is shocked. 'You mean – sex?' She knows Miri is wild, but it seems like a line that once crossed, could never be un-crossed. 'That's basically . . .' She can't bring herself to say the word.

'Prostitution?' Miri says. 'Not a lot different from marriage, in my opinion. Only with an end date. My parents had been ready to sell me off to the highest bidder. That's worse when you think about it.'

'I guess.' Denise isn't prepared to argue the point, and anyway, it won't change Miri's mind. Or indeed anything she has done in the past. 'If you've been to all those places, what's so special about Cameron Bridge?'

Miri shrugs again. 'Because it would be under my own steam. No one telling me where to go and what to do.' She lifts her head, grabs the remote, and starts searching for television reception again. 'Because it's our own backyard, and the people I grew up with act as if it's as far away as Patagonia.'

Denise doesn't know what to say. How can Miri stand being a stranger to her family, who live only a few miles away? Her own parents came halfway around the world to build a life in London. It was not easy but they had the support of their families. What happened to Miri seems the cruellest fate imaginable. Denise feels sorry for herself for losing her brother, but Miri has lost an entire family. An entire world.

'Weren't you afraid?' Denise says.

'Afraid of what?'

'Afraid of the man,' Denise says. 'Afraid that after doing something like that, you could never go home again.'

Miri laughs loudly. A flock of starlings take off from the tree outside. 'That,' she says, 'is the exact opposite of what I'm afraid of.'

From that day on Miri isn't simply a casual acquaintance; she is a friend. More than that. People start to refer to the two of them in the same phrase *MiriandDenise* as if they are sisters or a couple. When they are out clubbing with friends and the party continues back at Lamia House, it is 'to ours'. Not 'to hers'.

Denise is fascinated by her. She seems to be both of this time and not. Miri knows everything about events from hundreds or thousands of years ago but nothing of the recent past. When people make references to favourite childhood games or television programmes, she never contributes. She surrounds herself with people who talk about art and philosophy, but never politics. She is clearly English to Denise, but without any of the pop culture touchstones other people use to measure their place in society. It is as if she was raised in another time.

One morning Miri bursts into the room in her orange and blue kimono, and shoos out the man curled up at the foot end of the bed.

Denise's memory of the previous night is disjointed and technicolour. Like chopped-up parts of television programmes while changing channels. They went to World Headquarters, and it was crowded, warm. She danced and danced and it felt like oblivion. She doesn't remember this guy's name. Was it Robbie? Reggie? Something like that. It doesn't matter. When everyone came back to the house he talked for ages about Japanese film directors before putting a hand on her thigh and leading her away from the rest of the party. The kissing was just OK, the sex somewhat better. He had a ring in his penis and old-fashioned swallow tattoos on the crests of his hips. He put a finger in her bum and it was nicer than she expected. She does not tell him it is her first time and is relieved he does not seem to notice.

Something has been unlocked. A feeling that starts on the dance floor, spinning around, her shoulders and back rubbing up against strangers. The pulsating music in her ears, through the floor, in her bones, inducing a kind of euphoria. When she is around Miri, she feels unselfconscious enough to dance; when she is dancing, she feels able to talk to people; when she talks to them, all she can think about is what they would feel like in bed next to her body, what they would taste like.

They are in an attic bedroom. The space is crowded with framed prints leaning against the wall. At night it is cool and moonlit, latticed with the shadows of trees in the Dene. So far it is her favourite. Denise has woken up in three different bedrooms in the house now, all fully furnished even down to clothes in the closets, even though no one apart from Miri lives there. There had been a housemate, she says, an odd girl, French. But she left suddenly one day and Miri could not be bothered to find someone to replace her.

'The sun has got his hat on!' Miri does the Charleston in her bare feet. 'Hip-hip-hip-hooray!' She picks up a pair of shoes and throws them at the man's head. Russell, that is his name – Denise remembers now. He lives in Hexham and is allergic to peanuts. He grabs the shoes and his clothes and clatters downstairs for the door as fast as he can.

'Jesus, Miri, what the fuck?' Denise should be in the library writing up today. But if the last few minutes are anything to go by her hangover will probably win out instead.

'Let's have a picnic, a *déjeuner sur l'herbe*,' Miri says. 'Look at this weather! It's glorious.'

Denise rubs crumbs of sleep out of her eyes. She feels around for a glass of water that she dimly remembers getting in the night, but the man must have kicked it over on his way out and her hand lands in a soggy bit of carpet. 'Give me a few minutes to wake up,' she says. 'I'll grab a shower, then we can go to the shop. How about we walk down to the bridge over the Dene?'

'Fuck that,' Miri says and pulls a packet of sliced cheese and half a bottle of gin from the deep pockets of her dressing gown. 'You have to get dressed to do that. We have everything we need right here.'

There is something about her that is so self-confident. So like Darwin. And maybe that is why, after waking up in a strange room with a strange boy and being ordered around by Miri, Denise cannot tell her no. Will not. Being with Miri brings more fun into a single night of Denise's life than she has had in years.

Miri pulls at the wooden frame of the skylight. It lurches open with a rotten-sounding creak. She balances on the corner of the bed and starts to climb out of the window. 'Come on,' she says to Denise, a whip of coppery hair caught in her mouth, slicing her face in two. 'Last one on the roof has to pour the drinks.'

: 14 :

Brant Nazi Hooker: The New Profumo

Sources confirm that internal investigation in the Labour Party discovered Lionel Brant, the shamed party leader, was using his work emails to communicate with Miriam Goldstein, the prostitute known as 'Lamia' whose body was discovered in Cameron Bridge last month. The emails also confirmed that he shared potentially sensitive information with Goldstein. An individual close to the investigation commented that the ex-Prime Minister was expected to resign within the week.

Denise showered and dressed for work, avoiding the mirrors. She was working on getting out of the door without dislodging any black dust from bad thoughts into her head. Mornings were the worst. One unguarded moment, one stray glance in the looking glass, she could catch sight of a new bruise, and the downward spiral would start again.

Archie had come back from his work trip agitated and wouldn't say why. He arrived late, parked his car somewhere else, and roused her from bed to cook his dinner. She threw together a bowl of pasta and sauce. He ate greedily, looked through her, said nothing. She could tell as soon as she heard his keys in the door that he was on a shorter fuse than usual this time. They didn't talk about Miri. They hardly talked at all. He left early.

She traced her fingers along her collarbone, skimming the tender part where his fingers had dug hard into her. That was

88

a new spot. One he had not singled out before. The pain of it surprised her and he had broken through her rubber mask for a moment. The fingers were insistent, greedy. As if he was trying to break something. She changed her V-neck jumper for a high collared wool cardigan. Slightly too warm for the day, but no one would notice. She was always cold in the office anyway.

Whitehall sources suspect Brant and Goldstein used fake names to create webmail accounts and exchange messages without encryption. They are said to have shared an email account to make their illicit meetings, with one saving a message in the drafts folder for the other to read.

'The security of any information not logged through Parliament email servers cannot be ensured,' one source revealed. 'If they were sharing information about meeting times and locations of key committees – in order to facilitate the continuation of this sick, twisted affair – then it is fair to say that government confidentiality has been compromised. Any terrorist cell or rogue state could have intercepted this information, used it to blackmail Lionel Brant, or worse. We must have full access to all of his web and social media accounts immediately, to confirm how deep this goes.'

A representative for Brant did not respond to requests for comment.

Archie's laptop sat on the kitchen counter. Usually he would not have let it out of his sight, and often locked it in his car boot.

If she wanted to be at work on time she needed to leave now. Phone and tell him? He would tell her to stay put and she would have to wait another half hour for the next bus. It was her first day back since the collapse, and there was a meeting scheduled with the nurse who was helping collect patient data for her project. No, she couldn't miss that.

Denise nibbled at her thumbnail. A tightness crept up her neck, black threads reaching for her face with their cold fragile fingers.

She knew what Darwin would have done in the situation. 'If everything is forbidden, then everything is allowed.' It was one of his favourite sayings. Denise held her breath and pressed the touchpad. The screen flickered to life. Archie had set no password on his computer. For someone who was so cagey about what he did when he was away, it seemed entirely out of character. He had never added her as a friend on social media, citing 'security reasons' at work. Leaving a computer unguarded from random snooping seemed . . . odd. Was it a trap?

The internet browser was open and before she could stop to think what she was doing she opened its history to find a list of the sites he had visited.

The last two days' browsing included a large number of articles from news sites. She clicked through to see what he had been reading. He had found out about Miri's death – of course he had. From the looks of things he seemed to have visited every website that made any mention of it, from national news to local, BBC and a few forums. A few Denise had never heard of before.

She dropped her jacket and bag in the hall and carried the laptop through to the front room. Archie was not only visiting news sites and forums – he was commenting on them. She flicked between tabs. His browsing history showed that he was registered on a number of websites and appeared to be a frequent commenter.

Denise checked her watch. If she didn't leave now, she would be late for her meeting.

If everything is forbidden, everything is allowed. She slipped the laptop into her bag almost without thinking about it.

Denise stared at the passing streets as the bus trundled into the city centre. How did Archie spend his days away from Wallsend? Who did he talk to? What did they talk about? She had met his family over the years, but never felt close enough to them to confide in them, nor they in her. Even if she did ask they would have said whatever he wanted them to say – or worse, reported back to him that she was prying. If there was anything Archie hated, anything he warned her against again and again, it was prying.

'Josie never trusted me,' he lamented. Years after that relationship ended, he dwelled on the pain his ex had caused. 'A real bunny boiler,' he said. 'I can't believe we were together for seven years.' Denise learned never to ask for information he did not volunteer. Even benign questions could trigger him.

She found a photo once. Josie had been petite and blonde, with a nondescript oval face and neat figure. Denise studied the face for as long as she could, hoping to see something there, some flicker of the ruthless bitch Archie described. But whoever had taken the snap had been standing with the light at their back, and Josie's face, pinched against the sun, revealed none of her secrets.

She didn't want to be like Josie. Denise twirled her watch around her wrist. All she wanted was to see what he had said online about Miri. Then she would never look again. Then she would put the laptop back where she found it. Yes, that was all she would do. Anything else would be prying.

: 15 :

Nights at Lamia House are half-remembered dreams. The weather has turned mild and they take cabs everywhere, because when the party is going, why kill the vibe? It will be easy to buckle down once she finds permanent employment, she thinks. Soon she will be back in London and real life can resume.

Other people join them, in ones and twos, people Miri has approved, attracted to the house like moths to a light. Always more women than men. This is on purpose, Miri explains. It defuses the usual dynamic. The men stop feeling as if they have to compete, the women can relax. 'Plus the other entertainments on offer,' Miri says, which Denise takes to mean the drugs.

The usual rules are suspended here. Someone produces a wrap of coke. A few bottles of vodka appear from improbably small handbags. Lines of powder are chopped up on whatever surface is available: a table, a kitchen counter, a man's thigh.

She has tried it all by now. Denise discovers that she does not like marijuana: too slow to kick in, too slow to fade. Getting to the end of a sentence without remembering what she said at the beginning of it bothers her. She likes the intensity it gives to sensations, though, the way a hand carelessly brushing against a shoulder feels as erotic as being fondled by a lover. She likes the acute forcefulness she feels with cocaine, at first, though things too often devolve into self-centred bickering when everyone is on it. She likes ecstasy. The way it warms her, blunts her anxiety, makes her feel at one with everyone in the room whether she knows them or not. She doesn't enjoy the comedown. Alcohol is her entertainment of choice. And once things get going upstairs, the fucking.

Tonight Miri leads them into a formal sitting room that Denise isn't sure she has been in before. She would remember the William Morris wallpaper, the Liberty fabric curtains in peacock feather print. Most late nights at Lamia House are a blur of dark hallways, random drinks, and long, laughter-filled conversations she will forget by morning, true. But she is certain this is new.

Her skin feels tingly, electrified, the way it feels in winter when static has built up, just before touching metal to get a shock.

The natives in this land have a set of rules she is still learning. No one eats, not in public, a fact Denise finds a relief. Dresses are short and so are relationships. No one talks about work, families, or anything in the news. More often the topic – if there could be said to be a topic – is music or philosophy. Books, but not recent ones. The women throw their hair over their shoulders and flirt with the sort of men Denise would never have had the courage to talk to before. They can skip from Derrida to Byron to Melville in the space of a few sentences. She is getting there, but slowly.

It seems to come so easily to everyone else.

Sometimes they sleep in the same bed because of Miri's nightmares.

Miri falls asleep easily, her arms flung wide like a child's, her mouth open and whistling. She is as unselfconscious in sleep as she is awake. Denise finds sleep harder. Some nights she lies awake and still, letting the hours tick away until light brightens the room. The smallest movement might set Miri off and she does not want to trigger a nightmare. It has happened several times: Miri screams and sits up, her eyes wide and blank, speaking a language that sounds like nonsense. Denise understands it is dangerous to wake someone in this state. She does not want to make it worse.

Denise is afraid to ask what the nightmares are about. They might have something to do with a man. 'Promise me,' Miri says one morning, when they are trading sections of the previous week's newspaper over coffee. 'That if anything happens to me – if I go missing, or . . . well, anything – promise you'll do what you can to help me?'

It is so sudden, so unlike the Miri Denise thinks she knows. 'What sort of things? Who would want to do something bad to you?'

Miri shrugs. 'The usual,' she says. 'I got involved with some bad people once. The kind of people who make deals for stolen weapons, you know?' She sighs. 'I don't always have very good instincts when it comes to men.'

Denise frowns. She doesn't know what she could possibly do, or why Miri would ask her for help. 'I promise,' she says.

Miri throws her head back and laughs. 'Oh, you are always so serious!' she says. 'I was only joking.' But Denise, while thrown off by the remark, has a feeling that Miri is not joking. Not entirely.

One night they are together in bed when she hears Miri sobbing. Her eyes are closed but she feels the heat of Miri's body inches away from hers. 'I'm sorry, I'm so sorry.' Denise thinks, at first, it is another nightmare. *Stay still. Don't frighten her.* 'I can't go another day without saying anything. I was there, I saw him.'

Denise is in the same position they went to bed in. She slows her breathing. 'I was at Tonsai Beach, staying with friends. They came to the beach on a long-tail boat.'

Miri stops for a moment, and this is when Denise realises she is not talking in her sleep. She is awake, as awake as Denise. 'I remember them because he was an Asian man with a white woman; you don't see that often in Thailand, usually it's the other way round. I thought they must be American.'

Is she talking about Darwin? Her eyes stay shut. 'We were in a beach bar having morning cocktails. Everyone was talking about what they did, and I remember this guy saying he was a college athlete, and a swimmer, and that was when I noticed his accent, that he was English too.

'Everyone was having a good time. The water went out of the bay, about a mile. It was weird, no one knew what it was. Some people took pictures. I thought it must be because of the full moon. Then we saw it. It wasn't big, the wave, a few feet at most, but it kept coming and coming.'

Miri is whispering. Confessing. Denise can't open her eyes now; Miri would know she had heard it all. 'The water knocked the table over, knocked us off our feet. People were running, bits of smashed up boats were hitting us. I was knocked over. He grabbed my arm and we ran up the hill. When we got above the beach he panicked, his girlfriend wasn't there. He had saved me without checking where she was and couldn't find her now. He went back down.' A sob hiccups in her chest. Denise feels something warm on her cheek, a tear of Miri's. 'I'm so sorry. I should have stopped him. But he went to rescue her and I never saw him again. I'm so sorry.'

This rings true to Denise. The way she understood the event has not made sense before. The last time she spoke to Darwin he said that he and Shelley were going to be diving the next day. But most of the people who were diving survived; the wave passed through the deeper water like a rogue current. It was the weight of the surge hitting the shore that was truly catastrophic. People were stuck on beaches that formed under sheer cliffs with nowhere to run. Maybe they woke up that morning and decided to have a day off; it was Boxing Day after all. Yes, Denise believes what she is hearing. The divers in the water survived. It killed him because he was not diving that day.

She doesn't know what to do with this information. In that instant she knows her parents can never find out. They will not want this message from the past, dragging up their dead son from the depths. The treacherous sea makes sense to them in a way cocktails on the beach before lunch never would.

Denise struggles to control her breath. If she doesn't move,

Miri will stop, fall asleep again. In the morning she can pretend it did not happen.

She can imagine it. Darwin would have liked Miri. They are so alike.

Then a doubt creeps in, a finger of black thread tickling its way into her thoughts. What are the chances? It is too neat, too much like what Denise would want to hear. But if that's true, why would Miri try to manipulate her like this? *No*, Denise tells herself. She wouldn't. Miri is many things but surely she wouldn't lie about this.

Denise feels the mattress shift as Miri falls back to the other side of the bed. Within minutes she is snoring again.

: 16 :

Harriet Hitchin shrugged into a thin waterproof jacket and stepped out of the church hall onto Cameron Bridge high street. Her stomach was knotted, anxious. She had left ten minutes before the end of the meeting. It had been a mistake, going there today. All of it.

She glanced at a newspaper clutched in her sweaty paw. She'd bought it from the corner shop on her way into the meeting, in case she needed a distraction. Without a drink it seemed as if she had suddenly forgotten what to do with her hands.

The local paper was hardly worth reading any more. The news was almost entirely about that sex worker case now, syndicated content from the tabloids. Lionel Brant's resignation had not ended public interest in the story; far from it. Now the papers were baying for every last scrap of his private life to be held up for examination. Harriet shuddered. Her embarrassment in Leeds had been a trifle by comparison, but that hardly mattered to anyone who found themselves in the eye of a media storm. The hacks were relentless once they smelled blood.

Good old Britain, where nothing ever really changed. It was disappointing to see the small local paper, which usually reported on nothing more scandalous that planning permission conflicts, getting involved.

'Hey. Hey, wait up.' A voice behind her. Harriet didn't turn to look; it wouldn't be for her anyway. Nothing about this town was for her. When she first moved to Cameron Bridge, it had seemed like a good idea, the change she needed. She tried her best to embrace life here, the outdoors, the cold and damp.

Every day in Scotland was putting clear water between her and her past, she told herself. But now she was coming to see the grey sheets of perpetual rain for what they really were: walls keeping her from moving on.

A hand tapped her arm. 'Hey, you left the meeting in there, didn't you?' Harriet looked down to see a tiny young woman. She had black hair with bleached white ends, tanned skin, large green eyes. The face was somewhat familiar. 'I just came out too. I wanted to see if you were OK.'

'I'm fine. I walked into the wrong room I think.' Harriet brushed off the stranger's touch. 'I must have got a date wrong. I was at the wrong session.'

The young woman smiled and shook her head. 'If I had a pound for every time I'd said that when someone caught me coming out of an AA meeting, I'd have . . . well, enough to buy us both a coffee.'

Harriet looked away. She had been trying to muster the courage to go to an Alcoholics Anonymous meeting for weeks. She had not told Fiona, could not. There was no way her girlfriend would have understood. To Fiona, quitting was a simple question of mind over matter. Willpower was key, she imagined her saying, so why would Harriet need to go to a meeting, if she was truly ready to give up drinking?

The first few times she had sat in the car park opposite and watched people walking in and out. Then she moved on to hovering in the Tesco Metro over the road. Finally she had ventured as far as lingering outside the doors while the meeting was going on. This had been her first time inside, and it had not at all been what she expected.

'It's fine, you know,' the woman continued. 'It can be intimidating to even walk in there. Why don't I get us that coffee? You don't have to talk to me about anything you don't want to talk about. I hate to see someone feeling as if they don't belong at a meeting, that's all.'

Harriet decided she might as well. What was the worst that could happen? She stuffed the newspaper in a bin and they turned up the high street. Iain wasn't expecting her back at work this afternoon anyway.

'No, no, don't tell me,' the woman said. Her name was Lucy. Lucy was, like Harriet, another incomer to the area. From Yorkshire no less. Harriet was surprised, when she told Lucy she had moved up to Cameron Bridge from Leeds, to learn the person who had bought her a coffee and now shared a table with her was from Batley. They must have been practically neighbours. Harriet wondered if Lucy would have heard about the tribunal, would know about her shame.

Lucy's voice was silky and accentless. She had been a refugee, she told Harriet, came over from Kosovo with her parents in 1998. People in Batley ridiculed her family's broken English. So she did everything she could to blend in. Which meant removing any hint of history and geography from her voice, and following the customs of a Christian country, not her Muslim family. She changed her name from Lule to Lucy. Between Kosovo and Yorkshire she learned that fitting in determined your future, and that getting it wrong could lead to anything from ostracism to death. Harriet nodded, and felt terrible. The things this woman described had changed her life for ever, but Harriet could hardly even remember who had been on which side, and when.

The cafe door swung open and shut, letting in blasts of cool damp air. The windows were frosted with condensation; the sound of the till punctuated the air. 'You haven't said what you do yet. Let's see if I can guess.'

Harriet smiled, relieved to be off the topic of long-ago wars. 'Go ahead.'

'You're in office wear, so some sort of professional,' Lucy said. Harriet had selected a striped Oxford shirt and pair of grey trousers that morning from a selection of nearly identical outfits she now kept at Fiona's house. 'But no suit jacket, so you're also fairly senior.' Harriet nodded.

'You didn't know anyone in the meeting. That means you

don't work on the high street, so you are not an estate agent, banker, or solicitor.' Harriet nodded again and Lucy pressed on, counting off points on her fingers. She had two tattoos on her hands: a solid black ring around the middle of her right thumb and a tiny star on the heel of her left thumb. 'And you're English, unmarried I guess, with no family to keep you here. So you came for work. Which would mean your job is highly specialised, uncommon.'

'All true,' Harriet said. This was amusing her, but was surely also the kind of confidence trick anyone could pull off.

'I can stop here. The second A stands for Anonymous, after all.' Lucy drew a tobacco pouch from the inside pocket of her jacket and started rolling a smoke.

'No, it's OK,' Harriet said, and meant it. The forty min- utes she had spent in the meeting had been a small eternity of watching people greet each other like old friends. There were more women there than she had expected, more people who looked like parents. Curious eyes slipped over her but no one said hello. When other people spoke up during the meeting her throat went dry. If she told her story, what would she look like to them? An unrelatable posho whose problems had nothing to do with the normal rhythms of life in Cameron Bridge. Lucy's interest by contrast felt neutral, maybe even encouraging. 'I'm curious to find out what you come up with. Go on.'

'Your nails are short and unpolished, but you don't bite them; you use your hands in your work. A doctor? But you have a long lunch break – I haven't seen you look at your watch once. Which means you're not a GP and you're not at the hospital.' A look passed over Lucy's face as she made a calculation. 'I bet you're . . . ' Her eyes widened and she shuddered. 'No, that can't be it. Never mind.'

'What were you going to say?' Harriet said.

Lucy laughed and looked down at her own nails. They were painted black, matching her jumper and jeans, and were chipped. 'I was going to say you work in the morgue,' she said softly. 'Sorry.'

Harriet shook her head. 'No need to apologise about that,' she said. 'Because you are correct. I do work in the morgue. I'm a pathologist.'

'Wow,' Lucy said. 'That's, like . . . I have so many questions! As I said, the second A is for Anonymous. You don't have to go into it. Let's talk about something else.'

'You haven't upset me.' People usually recoiled when she told them what she did. 'Anyway, it's a job. Ask me anything you want.' She thought about the Goldstein case stories in the paper. 'Well – almost anything.'

'Well.' Lucy bit the corner of her lip. 'Do you ever see alcoholics in your work?'

'I do,' Harriet said. One of her first had been an alcoholic. His cirrhotic liver had been bloated, fatty and yellow, deeply marked from where it pressed against his ribs. He had been walking home from the pub one night and collapsed in the snow in his own back garden, where he died of hypothermia. He had been five metres from his own door. She remembered the smell of his stomach contents, the curdled vodka and chips. 'They don't usually die of alcoholism as such, but other things. After drinking.'

Harriet flushed. She had never been able to correctly gauge how far was too far when civilians asked her about work. She had probably gone too far now, and no doubt Lucy was thinking of the quickest way to end this conversation and never speak to her again.

Lucy touched her arm. 'You don't have to worry about offending me,' she said, as if she had read Harriet's mind. 'Death is a normal part of life. We don't talk about it enough in the modern world. That's why people are afraid of it.'

There were, she knew, such things as death-chasers: overly morbid people who supped on gruesome details of crime and killing, who could usually be found hovering around the edges of forensic science conferences, hoping to scoop up grisly morsels about notorious cases. But she didn't get that feeling from Lucy. 'So what do you do?' Harriet asked.

'I teach yoga classes at the community centre.' Her body was slender, and although she wasn't tall, she had long, lean muscles. Smoking habit notwithstanding, her skin was tanned and seemed to glow from inside. Maybe there was something to the yoga nonsense after all. 'But honestly? As little as possible,' she said. 'I moved up here for a fresh start.'

'Not the first place I'd imagine as a retreat for a yoga teacher,' Harriet said.

Lucy's shoulders shook as she laughed. 'No, I suppose not! I was studying to be a nurse until a few months ago, but that made the drinking worse, not better.'

'Oh?'

'Yeah.' Lucy looked ashamed. 'You know what you do? Bodies and stuff?' Harriet nodded. 'Imagine all that, but the patient is alive, and you have to have conversations with them as if nothing is happening,' she said. 'That was too much for me. Having to hold it together in the face of so much suffering. I couldn't handle it.'

'So you chose Cameron Bridge to recover.'

'New faces, new places, as they say.' She ran her tongue over her teeth, which were small like a little animal's. With the choppy edges of her layered black hair bleached nearly white, for a moment she looked older than Harriet had first assumed. 'I couldn't keep going back around my old haunts and expect that this disease was going to leave me alone. You know what they say the definition of insanity is. Doing the same thing over and over, and expecting a different result.'

'So I've heard,' Harriet said. From her old supervisor, in the last few weeks before the tribunal that saw her struck off from the list of Home Office pathologists. From Fiona, in whose mouth the line sounded like a motivational poster Blu-Tacked to the wall of a police interview room. When Lucy said it, it sounded different. Like hard-won wisdom. 'Where do you stay?'

Lucy laughed. 'You know, when you said that, you sounded just like a local.'

'Oh,' Harriet said. It was the same way Fiona would have

102

asked the question. 'I guess I picked it up from work,' she added and felt guilty. Why not say she got it from her girlfriend, if that was the truth? Why hide Fiona? She wasn't ashamed. Was she?

If Lucy noticed her discomfort she didn't show it. 'Past Inverlochy,' she said. 'Over the hill. It's small and boring. You wouldn't want to see it.'

'No, no, of course not.' Harriet laughed uncomfortably. Maybe Lucy had noticed.

The truth was that bit by bit, the cracks were showing with Fiona. Harriet found it harder to ignore the way she dismissed everything with a little nugget of cop wisdom. There was no news, no person and no situation that Fiona couldn't stick in a box. The police world was black and white in more ways than one.

She supposed that was why she hadn't told her about the meetings. The grey area between drunk and sober was unfamiliar ground. People assumed you stopped, and that was that. But it was hard. And she was scared. Scared she would be overtaken by a relapse at any time.

'How long have you been sober this time?' Harriet asked. They knew so much about each other already. It didn't seem unreasonable to ask.

'Let me think,' Lucy said. She reached forward, grabbed Harriet's wrist, and looked at her watch. Her face furrowed. 'About six hours. So you know, if you were thinking I could sponsor you . . . I am not that person.'

'Ah, I'm sorry.'

'You don't need to apologise to me,' Lucy said. 'Or for me. I've worked the programme so many times. I keep going in the hope some day I'll be ready for it to stick, you know?'

Harriet liked this woman. Something about her made her feel as if she had met a kindred spirit. Lucy wasn't put off by her work, or by her drinking, or by her brusque manner outside the church hall. Maybe Lucy was the kind of person she could talk to about what had happened in Leeds. Things she could never have said to journalists at the time, to her co-workers, or even now, to Fiona. Even if Lucy couldn't be her sponsor, perhaps she could be her friend.

'Hey, if you don't have to be anywhere, and it's not like I have appointments to keep, why don't we get another coffee?' Lucy said. 'It's been a while since I had someone to talk to.'

'Sounds lovely.' In spite of herself, Harriet smiled. She couldn't remember the last time someone had been so honest with her.

: **17** :

The night Denise meets Archie starts like so many others. Clubs, taxis, then back to Lamia House. In the multicoloured light of the Tiffany lamps, Miri is mesmerising. Her reddish hair contrasts with the dark green and grey of the winding vine wallpaper. She is wearing a gold bandage dress that shimmers like the skin of a reptile. Her feet are bare and the soles dirty. She lost her shoes in the club, walked to the taxi rank without them. It doesn't matter. Every head in the room turns when she speaks. She is talking about art, about Renaissance paintings of saints.

The faces around Miri are rapt. She tells them about Catherine of Siena's mystical marriage to Jesus after the teenage nun had visions of sucking blood from his wounds. 'Well she was sucking something,' Bodie, one of the newcomers to Lamia House, sniggers, and someone hushes him. Miri smiles. Catherine went back in the world to proselytise for her faith, wearing a ring of Jesus' foreskin as a wedding band.

'That can't be true.' Bodie turns to Denise. 'Is that true?' Denise shrugs. Her school was named for St Catherine, and she never heard about any of this.

'The Valentinianists knew,' Miri says. 'They wed their wise women to God in rooms with four mirrors. Those women's children would be born in the world to come.'

'Is that why you have mirrors all over your room?' Bodie asks. Miri says many odd things, and it is not always clear when she is joking. 'I assumed it was because you can't get enough of looking at yourself.'

'Catherine knew the old Gnostic ways.' Miri points at Bodie, grins. Her teeth angle in towards her tongue like fangs. 'She was born a twin, you know. Her twin died.' Denise shivers. 'She was the one who convinced the popes to move from Avignon back to Rome. Real power behind the throne. She never did get the recognition she deserved.' She pauses. 'She stopped eating. By the end she refused to ingest anything but the Eucharist. She starved to death.'

It is an uncommonly warm night, stifling. Miri signs her name on Bodie's bared back in ice water, dipping her finger in a cup after each letter, blowing on the skin so the droplets evaporate. She is left-handed. *Sinister*, she calls it. 'Some people think left-handers are the surviving twin when the right-handed one died in utero,' Denise tells her. Miri thinks this is hilarious.

'Can you imagine two of me? Never!' It is a strange thought, that you could be the mirror image of a person who never existed.

Denise accepts a swig from a bottle of tequila being passed around. The harsh alcohol hits the back of her throat and makes her eyes water.

How many men has she been with in the last few months? She can't remember. Mostly it is good, though the fumbling before sex is usually more exciting than the sex itself. There are no repercussions in this nighttime world, no judgments; people come to the parties to have a good time, to leave whatever is going on in their lives behind. The sex is as much a part of that as the drugs, as the conversation. She discovers that she enjoys being spanked. That she prefers older men to younger ones. And that it takes at least four, maybe five drinks before she feels unselfconscious enough to give a man named Roger a golden shower in the antique bathtub on the second floor.

It is nothing like the sex she imagined she would have and even further from the grudging sex education lessons at her Catholic school. Those had been delivered by a nun who looked about as comfortable answering students' questions as she might have done explaining the finer points of evolution.

Sex rituals and religious mysticism aside, there is something to it that is more than physical, she senses that. It is more than simply the coming together of genitals, but it is also less than the nuns insisted. They said God wants you to save it, but why would He create something that can be enjoyed with anyone, if you weren't meant to enjoy it with everyone?

And it isn't only men. There was the married couple, the wife holding her hair back as if it was a short lead while Denise went down on her husband. He smelled too sweet, like sugar, and was circumcised. When he was done, they switched places and she tasted the woman too. They stroked and stroked her afterwards and asked her if it was good for her. She said it was. She mainly recalls how dry her mouth felt, how her lips were numbed from the effort.

Denise passes the booze on to waiting hands. Already music is playing from elsewhere in the house. A tangle-haired woman is dancing alone in the corner, the top of her dress pulled down to show a satin bra. Her arms wave, defiantly out of time to any music, real or imagined.

The sound of a wolf whistle cuts through the room and brings everyone to silence. 'I say, I have an announcement to make.' A confident voice rises above the crowd. Denise turns to see a man standing on a chair next to the fireplace, one leg propped against the mantle. He is holding a champagne bottle. He swipes a lock of blond hair away from his eyes. 'Today is my thirtieth birthday,' he says. A smattering of applause ricochets around the room. Denise cannot remember having seen him before. 'Also, today I got a promotion. You are looking at the Revenue's Regional Investigation Agent!'

He grabs a short sword hanging on the wall. 'Ladies, the champers is on me!' With a swift single motion, he slices through the neck of the bottle. It rolls under the pouffe where Denise is sitting. A wild spray of bubbles bursts from the neck and a couple of women, laughing, run to catch the booze in their cups.

Denise picks up the cork from the floor. It was a clean slice through the neck, the cork still snug in the mouth of the bottle.

'Would you mind awfully? Only I'm looking for my cork.' Someone is barking in Denise's ear. She turns.

'Sure.' Denise hands it over. He smiles as his fingers close around hers, and she smiles back.

'I said, have you really never been to Scotland?' he says.

She doesn't remember talking to him before now, but maybe she did? 'No,' Denise says. 'Newcastle is as far north as I've been.'

A sharkish grin spreads across his face. 'What a ludicrous bunch of people Londoners are,' he says. 'Let me guess, you think the North means Watford. Silly, silly people.'

'Oh, leave off,' Miri calls from a tangle of bodies leaning over the cocaine-powdered table. 'Ignore him, Denise, he thinks negging works on women.'

Denise turns to Miri. 'Negging?'

'You know.' Miri detaches herself from the crowd and puts a possessive hand on Denise's shoulder. 'Negging is when a man thinks that being mean to you will make you fancy him more. It's a trick pick-up artists use.' The man blushes red to the roots of his floppy hair. Even his scalp, showing through the blond, is pink. 'They have websites and everything, where they share tactics on how to trick women into having sex with them.'

'I say . . .' the man stammers.

'It's so schoolyard. Might as well pull her pigtails while you're at it.' Miri flips her coppery hair over her shoulder. 'If you want to have a conversation with my friend, have a normal conversation with her.'

The man drops his voice, conspiratorial. 'Blimey, had I known you come with an attack dog I would have been more careful.' His smile is uneven. He peers up through his hair and she thinks he looks sweet. 'My name is Archie. You are, evidently, Denise. And Scotland is very beautiful, and I am deeply sorry for negging you.'

: 18 :

The light faded from the sky. Denise had not switched on the lights when she came home, had not put on the heating, had not even removed her coat. She sat, still and straight, and waited.

Ordinarily she would have stayed late at her desk and gone straight to running. Tuesdays were long runs, and tonight's would have been one of her favourites, along the course of the Blaydon race. Mark and the others in the club knew not to ring if she wasn't there on time. There were things she needed to take care of at home tonight, and they could not wait.

The house was cold. She tried to remain calm. The shadows of the furniture drew dim patterns on the walls, the plain white plasterboard Archie often mocked. He called the decorating style 'Landlord Chic'. In the near dark it all looked the same anyway.

She could tell from the sounds of the neighbourhood what time it was. The teenagers over the road came home from football practice: six, or possibly as late as ten past. The bus turning the corner on its way out to the Coast Road: quarter past seven. Judy's television switching on next door as she settled into her nightly routine: eight o'clock.

Archie had not let her know what time to expect him. She would simply wait. When he got home, she would be there.

She must have fallen asleep, because the sound of Archie's key turning in the lock woke her. 'Fucking cunt,' she heard him mutter. 'Where's that dozy bitch disappeared to now?' A shiver went through her. Until that moment she wasn't sure if she was brave enough to do what she knew she had to do.

He stepped into the front room and put the overhead light on. It took him a moment to spot her, but in that fraction of a second she watched his face rearrange from a scowl of irritation to fake concern.

'Kitty, what are you doing in here on your own with the lights out?' he cooed. 'Aren't you chilly? Here, take my coat . . .'

'Stop,' Denise said. To her surprise, he did. His arms were splayed wide as he bent forward. It was an odd posture, an ambiguous pose that reminded her of drunks in Renaissance paintings. He could have been coming to hug her or to strangle her. It really did not matter.

'Is everything OK, Kitty?' he said.

It was not the first time someone had asked her the question that day. She had been vomiting so hard at work that she left early. But she had her strength back now.

'Is everything OK in there?' Someone knocked at the door of the staff toilet while she heaved her guts into the bowl. 'Do you need me to call anybody?'

Denise had pulled the front of her cardigan tight against her shoulders but it did nothing to stop the shivering. She had been vomiting so furiously that even the bitter yellow froth was done, and her chest was tender from dry-heaving.

What she learned about Archie was worse that she expected. Worse than she feared. The pieces he had left comments on all had titles like 'How To Crush a Girl's Self Esteem' and 'Why Fat Girls Don't Deserve to be Loved'. One typical comment noted: 'a woman with excessive confidence is like a man with a vagina. It's an attribute that is at best superfluous and at worst prevents women from fulfilling their natural biological and social functions.' That was only the start of it.

The girls who attracted my interest were the ones who were the most insecure, the most emotionally vulnerable.

'I'm fine,' she'd croaked. There had been a brief silence on the other side of the door, then the sound of footsteps in the stairwell. She was not fine, but no one wanted to hear differently.

*

Denise took a deep breath. She could do this, she could. She took a piece of paper from an inside pocket, unfolded it. She considered the words printed there a moment, what saying them aloud would do. Whether she was ready for the consequences.

She was.

'What women don't understand is that they might be able to fake orgasms, but men can fake entire relationships,' she began. *'It is a scientifically proven fact that men are not wired to be monogamous so why try? Simply hook a fanciable filly, do the minimum to keep her onside for six to eight years, then dump her when you have identified a new, fresher target. My missus thinks things are going swimmingly. Little does she know we are in year seven and the hourglass is rapidly running out.'*

He said nothing. She continued.

'I have a couple of likely lasses on the horizon and am ready to throw off the shackles, it is simply now a matter of biding my time with this miserable sack of neuroses before I pack up and disappear. It goes without saying Her Indoors is so wrapped up in her selfishness that she is unaware any of this is coming. Fine with me. I like a quiet life.'

Denise looked at Archie. His face was a frozen clown's grimace. 'What's that?' he finally said. But his heart wasn't in it. Even he could not maintain the lie in the face of his own words.

'You tell me, TrueGeordieGent,' Denise said. 'That's the name you use on the Rome Must Burn forums. Also on the *Times* and *Guardian* comment sections. When you post to men's rights and pickup artist sites, you're TallArch69, or sometimes LongArchSilver.' She kept going. 'It's been interesting finding out what you think of me and of our relationship. If your internet history is anything to judge by, then the next girl is in for a hell of a time.'

Archie dropped his arms. 'Come on, Kitty,' he said. His face shuffled and reformed again. Flickers of expressions before one settled, as if he was choosing from a flip book. 'It's so silly. Last month I thought someone had hacked my email account. I would have told you but I didn't want to worry you . . .'

Denise looked away. His tone of voice was the same one he used when he was trying to think of a reason why his car wasn't parked at home again, or why his phone had been switched off when she tried to ring. The same tone whenever she asked where he was working this week. Pleading, but also a little bit belligerent, ready to flip if she dared question his story past whatever thin excuse he was offering. 'Don't,' she said. 'You sound ridiculous trying to lie about it now.'

'You don't understand,' Archie said. 'Those accounts . . . they aren't real. It's online culture. No one tells the truth on those forums, it's where people go to blow off steam . . . no one believes a word of it . . .' Already he had ditched the hacking explanation for a worse one, and expected her to believe it.

'Oh?' Denise said. 'Because I had some time to read through your posting history for the last two years. If you're blowing off steam, you certainly are very consistent.'

Archie's eyes flicked back and forth. His voice shifted further downward as he changed tack again. 'I can't believe you would snoop on me like this. It's your paranoia,' he said. 'That is the real problem in this relationship. I refuse to apologise for problems you caused. You should be apologising to me.'

Denise had seen it before. He was going through all of his acts, one after the other: wheedling, lying, changing the subject, trying to turn it around on her. And she supposed, to give him his due, it had always worked in the past. She had either let him believe that she believed him, or given up arguing to stop anything worse from happening.

That was the Denise of twelve hours ago. The Denise of this morning and earlier, who was so cowed that what he might think of her stopped her from finding out the truth.

This was a new Denise.

The old Denise would have fallen into line at the first sign of his anger. Would have cowered as if each word was a slap, then cried when the blows started to rain down. He shook his hands at her, his loosely curled fists at the level of her neck. A gesture she had seen so many times before. But New Denise refused to move.

To the new Denise he was ridiculous, a child throwing a half-hearted tantrum and being surprised when he didn't immediately get his way. 'You do not get to talk to me like that.'

'Pardon me?' Archie put one foot forward. His voice was creaking at the top of its register, but he had not started yelling, not yet. He was inches from her face. The hands, her neck. She did not flinch.

'You. Do not. Get. To talk to me like that,' Denise said.

Archie moved, but he was slow and sloppy, and she was ready. As he lunged for her she crossed her forearms in front of her face to take the brunt of the shock, then pushed back against them as hard as she could. She was half his size, but the surprise of her doing anything at all was enough to knock him off balance.

Archie stumbled to the other side of the room, half-crouched, panting. He moved again, though not for her this time. He picked up her work satchel from the ground and swung it, both of his arms straight, like an Olympic athlete preparing to throw a hammer. His body twisted as he let go of the handle, and the bag crashed against the wall feet from Denise's head. She heard the crunch and smiled. He had not yet realised that he had tried to destroy his own laptop.

'You do not. Get. To talk to me. Like. That!' she shouted.

Archie screamed, a strangled, awful sound. Instead of reaching for her this time, he attacked himself. He clutched at his face and raked his nails down the cheeks. The white pressure lines of his fingertips gouging the flesh turned bright red. Tiny pinpricks of blood mottled his skin.

Denise went to the front door. 'Get your coat, Archie,' she said. 'You can't stay here any more.'

His eyes looked like little black holes in his red face. She saw his legs tense up as if he was about to launch himself at her. She did not move, but braced herself, ready for the impact.

The doorbell rang.

Archie twitched and his face fell, distracted by the sound. Denise looked out of the small glass square in the door frame. Blue and red lights flashed outside. She saw the black-clad shoulders of two figures on the step. It was the police.

'You fucking cunt,' he hissed, but was already pulling himself together, smoothing a hand through his hair as he glided towards the door. His swagger had returned, though there were dark sweat stains spreading out from under his arms, the sharp tangy smell of violence on him.

Archie flung the door open. 'Good evening, officers, may I help you?' This was another of his voices, the hail-fellow-well-met act, the jaunty chap used to getting his way.

'Evening,' the smaller figure said. It was a woman. Denise stiffened: they usually sent a woman to investigate domestic violence calls, didn't they? Archie cut his eyes in her direction; he was probably thinking the same thing. 'My name is Officer Shalit, this is Officer Smith,' she said and indicated the man with her. 'We wish to speak to Archie Lyndon about a sensitive matter. May we come in?'

Archie grinned but did not step away from the door. 'May I ask what brings you to my home?'

The two officers exchanged a look. 'Ah, well, it's a bit of a tricky situation,' the man said. 'We had a phone call—'

'Oh, a phone call!' Archie chuckled heartily. 'Dear me, of course. I'm so sorry. This is all a misunderstanding. You see, my partner and I were simply watching an action film, and she tripped over, and happened to drop her bag. Now I appreciate that perhaps someone who passed by or overheard might think, well, they might think what they were hearing was an argument.' He looked at Denise, his eyes bright and unblinking. 'But as I'm sure my partner will be happy to confirm, it was nothing of the sort.'

Officer Shalit's nose only came up as far as the middle of Archie's chest, but she did not look up to him, rather addressed her words at his shirt buttons. 'We must insist on coming inside, Mr Lyndon,' she said. 'If you prefer, we can take you to the station. This is a matter of some urgency.'

'Mmm.' Archie looked back at her colleague, electing to address the man instead. 'Well, as I have said, I am certain you have the wrong end of the stick entirely.'

'Mr Lyndon,' Officer Shalit repeated. 'If you could please – this is a matter best addressed somewhere other than the doorstep of your home.'

'I'm sorry,' Denise said to the policewoman. 'I can't talk him into anything he doesn't want to do.'

'Well, there you have it,' Archie said. 'Now either say whatever it is you have to say, or come back with a warrant.'

The woman's colleague loosened a pair of handcuffs from his belt. 'Have it your way, Mr Lyndon,' she said. Her partner's massive hands closed the metal bracelets around Archie's wrist. 'You are under arrest in connection with the death of Miriam Rachel Goldstein. You do not have to say anything. Anything you do say may be given in evidence . . .'

: 19 :

Harriet set two places while Fiona put the finishing touches on a venison and black pudding stew. 'Smells amazing,' she said.

'Thank you.' Fiona pulled two wine glasses out of the cupboard and a bottle of red from the rack.

'Do you know what?' Harriet said. 'Just a sparkling water, for me, tonight.'

A flicker of a smile passed over Fiona's face, as brief as the twinkle of a star in the night sky. 'Good idea,' she said. Her hand brushed Harriet's wrist. They toasted. 'How did it go with Morag the Moaner today?'

Harriet perched on the edge of a stool as Fiona stirred the stew and put bowls in the oven to warm. 'Mixed. She obviously didn't remember me at first, but that isn't surprising.' Unfortunately, as soon as Harriet reminded the politician they had met before, Munro went frosty. Recalling a minor media outrage over an image leaked by a former police photographer seemed to have rubbed her up the wrong way.

Harriet had suspected that might happen but didn't know where else to turn. The year before, Morag had dropped in on some flimsy pretext, talking about disaster preparedness and how instrumental the mortuary was to the area plan. And while those plans seemed to have been shelved somewhere between Cameron Bridge and Westminster, Harriet still hoped there might be something in it that could save the facility.

Morag's smile had been static; Harriet outlining the trouble the mortuary was having with the council seemed to bounce off the MP like water off a hot pan. Then, much to Harriet's surprise, she brought up the matter of the Goldstein case. News had broken that day of an arrest down in Newcastle. Morag asked whether the pathologist thought that there was anything unusual about the circumstances, anything the police and public had overlooked. Harriet had to admit that, yes, she did think so.

'"The New Profumo", as I believe some of the tabloids are calling it,' Morag had said. 'Certainly given the woman – sex workers, as I suppose we must now call them – had such a complex social life, it does seem a bit too tidy, doesn't it? Ex-boyfriend, apparently?'

Harriet hesitated. Morag looked at her and smiled. 'Chatham House rule,' she said. 'I wouldn't dream of telling the press anything you might want to share with me about the case.'

Harriet emphasised that the autopsy itself had been ambiguous about the cause of death. The neck could have been broken after death, it was difficult to tell. Goldstein could have been murdered, or she could have killed herself. There wasn't enough evidence to say for certain either way. Morag seemed pleased to find out this titbit, and open to the idea of revisiting a mention for the Cameron Bridge mortuary in her consultations as a result. It wasn't a promise to help Harriet, as such, but it was better than nothing.

'The department might get something out of it. I don't know what else to do.' If the only option was buttering up Munro or losing her job, Harriet knew which she would choose. But something about the encounter with the MP had made her uncomfortable. Something she couldn't put her finger on, except for a persistent thought once she left the constituency office that it was she who was about to do a favour for Morag – not the other way round. 'Anyway, enough about me. How was your day?'

'Oh, there was good news. You know the mummy arrest? Forensics in Newcastle came back with sample matches from the boot of the suspect's car. Looks like we can close this out,' Fi said. 'If his solicitor has any sense he'll push to plead guilty and it will be over before the month is out.'

Harriet squeezed a wedge of lime into her glass of soda. 'You must be pleased,' she said cautiously. It flew in the face of her suspicions – and what she had told Morag only hours ago. 'Any idea why he did it?'

'Who even cares.' Fiona tasted her stew, considered, and ground more black pepper into the pot. 'He was probably an old boyfriend or client, I guess. Or maybe a pimp.'

'I guess.' It sounded so pat when she said it like that. In Harriet's experience, people's relationships to each other were rarely as simple as they seemed on the surface.

Harriet had already been concerned about the way things were likely to go, and her meeting with Morag only heightened her feeling of dread. Something about it still didn't scan. Of all the people connected to Goldstein in life, the police had interviewed no public figures about her death? That was odd. 'Will they be bringing him up here for a trial?'

'No.' Fiona shook her head. 'The prosecutors contacted the sheriff already. The suspect lives in Newcastle, so did the victim, and there is no evidence that the murder happened in Scotland. They could bring him here on other charges, I guess. But if he is convicted down south I doubt anyone would be bothered to do it.'

'And that's it?'

'That's it.'

'Wow. They don't want you to interview anyone here? At all? Maybe one of the local sex workers knew the victim . . .' Harriet was aware she was babbling. Fiona had not been impressed by her failure to turn up at the scene. It was clear what came first, in Fiona's mind.

'I doubt that,' Fiona said. 'The women we pick up for prostitution, they're the same women we also pick up for drugs, vagrancy. The ones who advertise online, they live outwith the Highlands. They don't mix with local prostitutes.' She snorted, a small laugh. 'They think having a website makes them "high class" or something.'

'Doesn't it trouble you that Newcastle takes the body and the paperwork out of here, and then that's it? If you're lucky, you get a phone call about what's going on?'

'I guess,' Fiona said. 'Alastair's pleased we can take it off our boards, and our budget. As long as it's solved it's a win for us.'

Fi turned back to the cooker and Harriet sipped her water. And it was fine, she was fine without the wine. Mostly.

But not everything was fine. The Goldstein case troubled her. It had been a long time since anything in Harriet's career had the power to haunt her outside of work hours, and she couldn't fathom why this one would. She glanced down at her phone. Would it be so terrible to text Lucy now?

Maybe it had finally happened. The thing other people always whispered about in morgues. They were all living on borrowed time until the big one came along. The one that changes you. The death that worms its way into your psyche, breaking down the barriers between professional and personal life.

For some people it was anything to do with children. When Harriet started working on shaken baby cases, there had been reluctance to assign them to her. She was a woman; the going wisdom in forensic science was that women were supposed to have too much empathy to handle these cases. It was a ridiculous assumption and a sexist one.

Dead sex workers were not a daily occurrence, but they were not uncommon either. There was the woman who had been killed and her body thrown into a stream in the Dales. Insects had eaten away all the soft tissue from the exposed upper half. The hands and lower body, perfectly preserved in the icy water, led to her arrest records for solicitation. There was the one who had been stabbed while loitering in an industrial estate near Holbeck. She survived just long enough after the attack to give police a description of a suspect. There were no credible leads; no one was ever arrested for the woman's murder. Harriet had shrugged off those cases and many more. It was not a problem. Women were not a problem.

Miri Goldstein should have been no different. Yet the thought of her still scratched away, demanding attention.

'Does it not seem a little convenient to you? That this is so cut and dried,' Harriet said.

Fiona ladled two servings of the stew, carried them over, and pulled up a stool. 'Not really,' she said. 'The majority of the time, once you have a victim ID, it's easy-peasy. Someone close to them. Which this was. Why?'

'I don't know,' Harriet admitted. 'Something about this doesn't scan for me. Why Cameron Bridge? If she was killed in Newcastle, why dump her here?'

'Some murderers want to be caught,' Fiona said. 'Not consciously, but they make simple errors that defy any other explanation. It happens all the time. Maybe they can't face up to the guilt, so they sabotage themselves.'

'Maybe,' Harriet said. 'Did you find his car on the CCTV?'

'No.' Fiona shook her head. 'Thanks to forensics in Newcastle, we don't have to bother. And thank fuck is all I can say to that. That would have been weeks down the drain.'

'What if it turns out he has an alibi? What if he was somewhere else?' Harriet could hear desperation in her own voice.

Fiona set her spoon down on the nubby linen napkin. 'It's not your problem what happens once the body leaves the morgue, and thanks to the arrest, now it isn't my problem either. It's just some hooker, killed by a guy she was probably fucking. It's no big deal.'

No big deal. Just some hooker. Harriet's food caught in her throat. Fiona surprised her with this attitude, this callousness. Harriet knew how other people saw her, what they assumed from the kind of job she did. That she was dead inside, that she had no soul. Or else was so numbed by drink she had no feelings left. Whereas police were meant to be the ones who did what they did out of a sense of purpose, of duty to members of the community. The thin blue line. Serve and protect. Fi was already talking about something else. Her hands waved animatedly over the table. Chatting about the new building, her work tea breaks, as if her curt dismissal of another human life was nothing at all.

But Fiona was also right in a sense. Sex workers were easy for people to write off. Maybe that was why they were at such risk, Harriet thought. Because people wrote them off. Not the other way around.

She knew she didn't have much goodwill left in the forensic science community and her reputation was mud. But she was sure of something: she was not going to mess up again. Whatever the truth was, she was going to find out.

: 20 :

The police station was a brick building in the centre of Wallsend. Not the one the police had taken Archie to. That was in town. Denise's hands shook: she had been up all night, unable to sleep, worried about what would happen in the interview. Imagining every possible scenario. What they would ask her. What she would say.

Every possible scenario, except for the one that had actually occurred.

They listened. They made notes. They told her something that shook her deeply, so deeply that she struggled to hold herself together, get up, and get out of the room without breaking down.

Denise pushed open the door to the waiting area and froze. Archie's mother was sitting on the other side, hands fussing at her figure-eight bun.

Christine Lyndon was the sort of mother who filled her pebble-dash bungalow in Morpeth with heavy furniture meant for a grander house. She laid the table with silver and candles for dinner even when serving ready meals and went ten miles out of her way to shop at a more expensive supermarket. She was the one who had saddled her son with his unwieldy name – Archimedes Finnbarr Lyndon. Family names, she claimed. Legacy was important to her.

Christine looked at Denise, then at the empty chair next to her. Denise sat down.

'It's an utter shambles is what it is,' Mrs Lyndon said. No greeting, nothing. 'How can they treat him like this? They won't let me talk to my own son.' She pursed her lips. 'For three days. Three days! First he was railroaded into an arrest, now they may refuse to release him on bail . . . A mother has rights.'

Denise took a breath. 'Are you here to give a statement?' she asked.

'Of course I am,' Mrs Lyndon said. 'What a silly question.'

Denise stood up. 'I have to go. I don't think they would want us to talk to each other first.'

As she tried to push her way past, Mrs Lyndon grabbed her wrist. Denise looked down; the older woman's hand was clawed and rough from a lifetime of gardening, and surprisingly strong. Its shape she recognised as Archie's. How many times had he grabbed her in almost the same way, as if he had a right?

'Don't go,' Christine said. 'Don't leave me here on my own.' There was real fear in her voice. Denise knew that sound. It was the same sound her own parents had in theirs when they first heard about the tsunami. 'I just need to know . . . Tell me you gave his alibi.'

Denise sucked in her lips. Did Mrs Lyndon know? Know what she had found out, from the police, only minutes ago?

The interview had started on time. Two uniformed officers, a man and a woman, sat with her in an interview room. One took notes while the other asked questions. Her name, her address. Her place of work. Her relationship to the suspect.

From there the questions turned towards the discovery of Miri's body. Had Denise known she was missing? Had she known she was dead? Had Archie mentioned Miri recently? Where had she been on the day the body was discovered? Where had Archie been?

Denise told them Archie had been at work the week that Miri's body was discovered. She said that she did not think he was involved.

The police officers exchanged glances and asked if she was certain. She had nodded. They asked her to give a verbal answer, for the recording. She said yes.

That was when they told her about Josie Shawcross's statement.

Archie's ex-girlfriend Josie. Bunny boiler Josie. Josie, who Archie had split up with before he ever met Denise.

Josie, who had contacted the police, saying she was his current partner. And that they were living together. The woman opened a folder and pushed across a signed statement from Josie. There was a look of pity on her face.

Denise read. Josie's statement said she and Archie left for a minibreak to Prague two days before the body was found. But they had an argument while there and he flew back early. She couldn't account for his whereabouts on the day the body was discovered. Denise didn't see him until he showed up unexpectedly at hers a day later.

The day Denise had collapsed at work. 'We figure there's a twenty-four hour window where he could have driven up to Cameron Bridge, dumped the body, then driven back to Newcastle,' the man said.

Denise was stunned. Given all she had found out in the last week, perhaps she should have seen it coming. It didn't change the fact that it still hurt. Hurt her to realise after all that time, as badly as he treated her – as much as she put up with – she was still not his first choice.

Mrs Lyndon lifted her chin and looked out of the window, at the daffodils raising their sleek heads from the dirt. 'I cannot even believe they are wasting police time on this,' she said. 'I mean for goodness' sake, the woman was a common prostitute. They should be rounding up the criminals in this city, not harassing people like him.'

'Miri was my best friend,' Denise said. 'Or at least she used to be.'

Mrs Lyndon kept talking. 'His solicitor said there had been a tip-off call . . . something about airport parking? That's why they took the car. The forensic tests . . . they get those wrong all the time, don't they? It will all come out in court, I suppose, in time. Still.' She looked at Denise. 'You were with him on the day the body was found, weren't you?'

'He was with Josephine Shawcross in the days before,' Denise said to Mrs Lyndon. 'Not me.'

She watched to see what the reaction would be when Archie's ex was mentioned. 'Yes, well,' Mrs Lyndon sniffed. 'You, or not you, whichever. I never can keep his women straight.' Christine Lyndon did not even flinch. 'But you can provide an alibi, can't you? Surely you wouldn't want him to go to jail. Over something that's a terrible mistake.'

So she had known all along, then. Known that Archie was still seeing Josie in Wylam, less than twenty miles away. Denise clenched her jaw and stood up. 'I told the police what I knew. If they need to talk to me again, I will tell them the truth.'

'At a time like this, a man needs to know who is loyal to him and who is not.' Mrs Lyndon pursed her thin lips, but her voice turned soft, conciliatory. The gentle wheedling that Denise knew all too well from her son. 'You could have been with him,' she offered. Mrs Lyndon did not say *you could lie*, but Denise knew what she implied.

Even if she had wanted to lie it was too late. Archie's name was all over the papers. The papers had been phoning her mobile since seven that morning. She locked herself inside the house, ignoring the occasional doorbell. Unplugging the phone was the only way to stop the landline from ringing.

Denise focused her eyes on the grey linoleum floor. It was almost too much to process: her best friend dead, her boyfriend arrested. Was he even her boyfriend? His mother, not only complicit in his cheating, but now asking her to commit perjury for the sake of . . . what? A misplaced sense of duty? To try to prove herself, to curry favour with a woman who had never thought of Denise as much more than her darling son's exotic piece on the side?

'Come now, dear,' Christine said. 'We are practically family, after all.'

Family. The word rankled. Mrs Lyndon's pain was not her concern. How long had she known about Josie and said nothing? Did she have any idea what else her son did, what he was really like? Denise went to the door. 'I told the truth,' she said. 'Which surely is enough.'

She walked quickly across the car park, shaking. Being New Denise was harder than it seemed. Getting sideswiped by the spectre of Josie had been bad enough. Lying was even worse.

Because Denise hadn't told the truth, not as such. She had answered the questions the police put to her truthfully. But was that the whole truth? Was it? Denise remembered Archie's early return, the day she collapsed at work. His strange mood. How he had started parking his car elsewhere. She should have said that to the police. She should have told them about it.

She should have told them about the bruises. About why, when the police first came to her door, Archie thought someone had phoned them in as a domestic disturbance.

That was not all. She remembered what had happened at a party at Lamia House one night years ago. The first time, perhaps, when she had realised what he was capable of. What he could do to her – to Miri. The first time she should have walked away.

That said, the party had been her idea. So maybe that made what happened almost her fault.

: **21** :

Denise passes her master's course by the skin of her teeth. Her supervisor looks at her sternly, there are corrections to the dissertation to be made, but she doesn't care. It is good news. She asks Miri if she can have a party at Lamia House. Not their usual weekend get-together – a real party.

She brings boxes of snacks and decorations, crates of wine to the house. Miri, amused, watches her from the kitchen table where she sits wrapped in her kimono and smoking. 'Anyone would think you were planning a wedding,' she smirks. But Denise has extracted a promise from her, that this will be a proper party. Shenanigans will be kept to a minimum. 'Shenanigans?' Miri scoffs. 'Is that the way you talk now?' And Archie will be there. 'Oh, him.' Miri scowls.

The invites specify fancy dress; attendees are to come as works of art. Early in the evening, Denise spots three Mondrian colour block dresses and two Screams. A few nonspecific velvety britches wander around. Lord of this, Duchess of that. A Madame Pompadour sits in the garden having an intense conversation on her mobile.

Denise adjusts the orange satin kaftan hanging over her shoulders. Miri made it from a set of old sheets, and the coral fabric drapes beautifully even if it does smell slightly of mothballs. The turban is less convincing: a white pillowcase wrapped around her hair and fastened with a costume jewellery brooch. 'Perfect,' Miri declares, after anointing Denise's lips with the same pink lipstick she was wearing the night they met. 'It's as if you stepped right out of the canvas.'

Hers is only half of the costume. The other half is Miri's, who has yet to make an appearance. Denise puts out snacks in bowls even though she knows no one will eat them. Opens bottles of wine. Everyone is fine, everything will be fine.

'Kitty, there you are.' Archie kisses the back of her neck. 'You look nice,' he says.

'Thanks.' Archie takes off his jacket. He is bare chested and wearing a woolen kilt. He throws a sheepskin over his shoulders. 'Remind me what you are again?'

He waves his hands in front of his bare chest. 'What do you think I am?' he says.

'Ah.' He had warned her that art was not his thing. 'Well, the bottom half says William Wallace, but the top half is a sort of . . . Biblical vibe, I guess? Esau maybe. Or Isaac,' she says. He says it is a party and he doesn't think anyone will mind. He pours two glasses of wine. Hers is only half as full as his. The wine is dark and tastes of iron. He toasts – to us.

'Tell me what you are then,' he says.

'It's from a Klimt painting,' Denise says. '*Die Freundinnen*. Miri is going to be the other person in it.'

He thinks. 'I don't know that painting,' he says.

'Me neither, Miri made the costume for me.'

Archie's distaste for Miri is evident whenever they are in the same room. He often comments how much time she seems to take away from Denise's studies. 'She's my best friend,' she reminds him. She tries to tell him about Miri's family, how they disowned her, but he is not interested in any of it.

Denise wants Miri to see how happy he makes her. He takes her to the cinema, he takes her out to eat. He always chooses where they go. He opens car and restaurant doors with a flourish, waiting for her smile of acknowledgement. Real dates. Not the erratic and casual hookups she has had recently, or the drawn-out and fruitless crushes from her teenage years. An old-fashioned gentleman, to use his phrase.

It gives him pleasure to see her happy. And she is happy, she is. How could she not be?

Archie is by anyone's yardstick out of her league. She has a good enough body but her face is less so. She remembers boys at the Catholic school calling her a 'butterface'. She asked Darwin what that meant later on, then wished she hadn't. But they were not wrong; her long face and thin lips were unappealing even to her eyes. Some women might know what to do with makeup to disguise their faults but Denise is not one of them. She has good hair, and good legs, but then so do horses. Another word the boys at school used when describing her. Someone like Archie would never have looked twice at her before. She is acutely aware that he is not only the best she's ever done, but the best she might ever do.

He says he has never before felt the way he feels with her. That she is destined to be his wife, the mother of his children. And they will have their own kids. He feels strongly about this; they will never adopt. The last thing he wants is a cuckoo in the nest. 'Our children will have the best of both worlds,' he says. 'Hybrid vigour.' As if she is a prized strain of cattle.

Denise refills her glass. 'Hey there,' Archie laughs, and puts his hand around her wrist. 'Pace yourself.'

The din of voices and music is suddenly dwarfed by a booming noise, a metallic wave that moves through the air. Everyone falls silent. Someone has rung the gong on the first floor. They all look up to the source of the sound.

Miri appears on the landing. She is completely naked.

The entire house holds its breath to watch her walk down the stairs, barefoot. She is not unadorned; jewelled cuffs go halfway up her forearms. Her hair is tied, a few tendrils caressing her flushed cheeks. A scarf is draped backwards, untied, across her neck; the ends hang between her shoulder blades. Her turquoise eyes are bright, the pupils vanishingly small, pinned.

Denise's breath stops in her chest. She has seen Miri so many times that the physical fact of her is something she takes for granted, like having a pet mermaid. Her slim white fingers stained yellow from smoking roll-ups, the shell pink nails crushing out a cigarette. Her round calves poking from under the bottom of her dressing gown, her shoulder when it slips down, like the shoulder of a classical statue. All these and more Denise could no longer see for the minor miracles they are. And now here Miri is, reminding them of her power. Reminding her.

There is no one in the room who hasn't seen Miri at least partly undressed. It does not matter. Her skin is glowing, white, as if bloodless. Her little breasts like pears sway with each step. The nipples, usually so pale, have been darkened with lipstick. Her thighs are wide and smooth and look carved from marble. In a room where everybody is dressed like someone from a painting, Miri is the real work of art.

She arrives at the foot of the stairs and loops her arm through Denise's, rests her head on Denise's shoulder. 'Here you are,' she exhales. Denise can smell her, vanilla, face powder, and sweat. 'The rest of my costume.'

Archie's mouth opens and closes. His face has gone blotchy, nearly purple. 'You mean she's wearing it?'

Miri laughs, a laugh that sounds like sex. 'No, silly,' she says, and pulls Denise closer. Possessive. 'She *is* it.'

Denise is on the toilet with the orange dress bunched under her arms when Miri bursts in and locks the door behind her. 'Jesus, Miri!' Denise instinctively puts her hands between her legs. 'You can knock next time.'

Miri leans towards the mirror and rubs a fingertip under her nose. It isn't even dark yet and already she has been at the coke. 'Don't worry, it's nothing I haven't seen before,' she slurs.

The bathroom is as large as a bedroom and tiled in the style of Newcastle's Victorian pubs, with a hammered copper bath in the middle of the room. The effect is more like a mausoleum than a spa. Apart from the toilet room in the attic it is the house's only working bathroom. The one on the ground floor has had its fittings torn out and never replaced.

Miri turns and crosses her arms over her chest. 'So, about Archie,' she says. 'How serious are you two now? He gives me the creeps.'

'Wow, that's . . .' Denise knows Miri can be blunt, especially when high. But it has never been directed at her before. Now that it is, it wounds her more than she imagined. 'I don't mean to sound judgy, but Rembrandt is dealing smack to Mona Lisa in the front room, you are literally walking around naked, and you're worried about who I'm dating?'

'That's the thing, though, isn't it?' Miri says. 'You never *mean* to sound judgy, you just . . . always do.'

Denise bites her lip. 'You should try to get to know him. He's really nice. We have loads in common.'

Miri turns back to the mirror, picks at a curl of hair stuck sweatily to her neck. 'Out of curiosity, does he offer any of these common interests without you prompting him, or does he wait until you say something, and then that happens to be exactly what he's into as well?'

Where has all this come from? 'Just because it isn't something you are interested in doesn't make it *de facto* uninteresting,' Denise says. She stops herself from saying there's more to life than parties and drugs, but it hardly matters – Miri has caught her eye in the mirror, and her nose crinkles as if reading Denise's thoughts.

'Listen, I didn't want to tell you this,' Miri blurts. 'But I remember the first night he came back here. I was talking to Bodie, you know, about plans for your birthday, and – God, it was meant to be a surprise! – I said I was going to take a group of us up to Cameron Bridge and hire a hostel and go hiking, because you've never been to Scotland before. Anyway, that guy Archie leans over and starts asking all these questions about where and when, and I guess me and Bodie thought he was someone from your course or whatever.'

'So he's keen,' Denise says. The thought of Archie targeting her in this way sounds odd, and makes her feel uncomfortable. She remembers the negging – a pickup artist trick, wasn't that what Miri called it at the time? But Miri has backed her into a corner. She has no choice but to defend him. To defend herself. 'Does it matter?'

'Does it occur to you that maybe he's using you?'

'What, for sex?' Denise says. 'Not that it's any of your business, but we haven't gone there yet.'

'What?' Miri is surprised. 'That's rather unlike you, isn't it?'

'Don't you mean, it's rather unlike *you*,' Denise says. 'Archie thinks we should get to know each other better first. And I happen to agree.'

'So you're bankrolling his lifestyle and he's not even giving you the D?' Miri laughs. 'You are more of a sap than I thought.'

More of a sap? Has Miri always thought of her this way? 'I'm not "bankrolling his lifestyle", as you charmingly put it,' she snaps.

Miri nods. 'You so are. I saw him parking up his car. Audi, is it? Bit out of his price range. If I had known you were throwing that kind of money around, I might have tried to seduce you myself.'

'I didn't buy it, I loaned him some money for the deposit,' Denise bristles. 'His Corsa was on its last legs. I thought, you know, he drives me around so much, then his exhaust went. He said it would be eight hundred pounds to replace. All those short journeys, you know, picking me up and city driving. That's more than his car was worth. He didn't even want me to help buy a new one, but . . .'

'But he let you anyway.' Miri nods. 'Isn't that convenient. Come on, Denise, isn't it obvious? He's after you for your money.'

Denise's face grows hot. That is not who Archie is. Not who she is. 'He doesn't even – we don't even talk about that.'

'No, of course you don't. I bet he makes a show of pretending not to care about it, doesn't he?' Miri plucks a pair of tweezers from a jar by the sink. She lowers her eyelids and looks down at her hands, cleans the grime from under her fingernails with the steel edge. 'Pretends to reach for the cheque until you get that bank card out. Because he's a gentleman, right? Someone who winces if he hears the work "fuck", but would fuck you over in half a second if the price was right.'

Miri pauses and looks up, drinking in the shock on Denise's face. 'But it isn't a one-way street, no. You get something out of it, too. You let him play that role, pretend to be a white knight. You're happy to do it in fact. Because you feel guilty for being alive when your brother is dead. For having the money at all. So here comes Archie, with his empty wallet and his expensive taste. Finally you have someone else in your life, someone who exudes entitlement. All he needs is the money to back it up. And you have a way to deflect your guilt.'

'Shut up,' Denise says. Her voice is shaking. 'You don't know me. You don't know us.'

Miri is not finished. 'I had him all wrong, you know.' She smiles. 'That first night he was here, and his silly performance with the champagne bottle? The negging? I thought he was trying to manipulate you into bed. But he has actually come up with something better. He's manipulating you into paying his way. And the cherry on top? He doesn't have to have sex with you at all!'

'Shut up, Miri, shut up.' Denise holds her hands over her ears.

'What are you scared of, Denise? What don't you want to hear?' Denise shakes her head. 'Too scared to hear the truth? Here it is. I've met men like him. They are all alike. Impressed by money and impressed by themselves. He loves you for your money, but he isn't faithful to it. Trust me – if he isn't getting sex at home, he's getting it somewhere else. Guaranteed.'

Hot tears weave a path down Denise's cheeks. She is trembling. Her mind is spinning. Where is this coming from? Why is Miri attacking her?

'Oh my God.' A thought dawns on Denise. It is a ridiculous thought, unimaginable. 'Are . . . are you jealous of me?' Denise says. It is a whisper. 'For being able to hold on to a man? Or.' Her voice is stronger now. 'No, it's not quite that. It's that Archie wants me and not you, and you can't stand not being the centre of attention.'

Miri exhales a puff of air. 'Don't be ridiculous,' she says.

Denise examines her face. Miri is high, her cheeks bright pink and her eyes glassy. She is impossible to read when she is like this. 'You don't want me to meet someone, do you?' Denise says. The words coming out of her mouth seem to belong to someone else. 'Because if I get a boyfriend – a real one – if that happens, I'm not your little Asian sidekick any more.'

'You think this is about pulling?' Miri's mouth drops open. 'God, Denise, go out there and pull anyone else. Go crazy! Start an orgy upstairs, whatever. I don't care.' Miri starts to pace, her tiny feet slapping the tiled floor. 'No – correction – I do care. I want that for you. I want you to loosen up and do stuff that has no consequences and no strings. Embrace all life has to offer, even the darkness, you know? Just don't get involved with that sub-Wodehouse creep set on dragging you down.'

Denise can't believe what Miri is saying. She laughs and the laugh doesn't sound like herself to her ears, either. 'Dragging me down? Do you know how ridiculous you sound?' she says. 'You have it exactly wrong.' Feeling brave now, she plants a finger on Miri's chest. 'You're the one who put me in danger of losing my real life. He is the one pulling me back to reality.'

'Reality, huh?' Miri swipes Denise's finger away. 'That pound shop David Niven is lying to you. A new exhaust should have cost him two hundred, tops. And, silly girl, you bought him a whole new car.' She licks her lips, pale in the middle now where the lipstick has been eaten away, and disappears in the direction of the top floor bedrooms.

Denise goes back to the kitchen, hands shaking. She takes a deep mouthful of wine, then another and another. She feels the warmth spread through her body, relaxing the knot of tension in her shoulders and the tornado of thoughts in her head. She pours another glass. Before she knows it, the bottle is nearly finished.

The lights in the kitchen flicker and die. A groan goes up from the room, then more as people elsewhere in the house real-ise the power has gone out.

'I'll handle it,' Denise shouts over the crowd. *Please don't let everyone leave.* She has never been in the cellar – Miri always says it is too damp to use. Someone hands her a lit candle. She pulls the door open, stiff and swollen in the jamb, and walks into the dark.

Downstairs it smells of dirt, and an earthier smell, like leather. It is surprisingly dry and warm. The circle of light from the candle is small and it takes a minute for Denise's eyes to adjust to the darkness. She reaches an arm out to feel along the wall, trying to locate where the fuse box might be.

There is an old bathroom suite in a far corner, a claw-footed bath and a sink, covered over with plastic sheeting. She lifts the corner of the sheeting; the bath is filled with sand for some reason. Piles of boxes are stacked next to old cases and trunks.

'Fuck you . . . you fucking bitch . . .' Denise stops. A familiar voice from the other side of the boxes. She peers around the corner.

A mop of blond hair, shaking up and down. It's Archie. She opens her mouth to say something, but then she sees he isn't alone. His kilt is thrown back, and someone is kneeling on the ground in front of him.

Miri.

His cock is in her mouth. He has one hand buried in her hair, pulling it viciously, while the other hand gropes for purchase around her neck. Even in the low light Denise can see the indentations his fingers make in her flesh as he forces his way down her throat. There is snot and sputtering from Miri's nose and lips every time he pulls back. Her body twists and struggles, the rough concrete floor scratching her bare knees. Denise's heart starts beating in her ears as she realises she is watching her boyfriend rape her best friend.

'Sh-sh,' he says, over and over. 'Shut up, bitch. I'm nearly there.'

His body finally tenses and he grunts as he releases his load into Miri's mouth. Finished, he pushes her off of him. Her body falls back against the damp wall.

Denise freezes in fear. If he realises she is there, he might attack her too. She should get upstairs, call the police, but she can hear other people at the cellar door now, threatening to come down, wondering what is taking her so long.

Archie faces away from her, doing up the buckles of his kilt. Denise inches forward quietly. If she can attract Miri's attention, maybe she can get past him, call for help.

Something snaps under Denise's knee. Miri's head whips around. 'Who is it?' Archie says.

Miri's eyes find Denise in the low light. She reaches to her mouth and wipes her lower lip with a sticky finger. 'It's no one,' Miri says to Archie, and shakes her head at Denise. 'No one at all.' She reaches her arm back behind her to the wall, where the open fuse box is, and flicks the main circuit breaker on. A weak lightbulb comes to life above them. She tugs at the corner of his kilt. 'You taste delicious. Let's do that again.'

Archie turns, his mouth open, hungry. He bends down and kisses her hard, pulling away with Miri's lip still in his teeth, drawing blood. She yelps, then looks out of the side of her eyes at Denise, and smiles.

Denise scrambles to her feet. Her heart is beating, hard. Her mind whirls. What has she just seen? Was Archie assaulting Miri? Or was that consensual? Or . . . something else? She reaches the top of the stairs as the power in the rest of the house comes on, slams the warped oak door behind her. A clutch of people applaud. 'Well done, thanks for sorting the lights.' Bodie smiles and pats her shoulder. 'Seen Miri anywhere?'

But Denise is lost for words and can only shake her head.

'Latest poll has you at three to five points ahead,' Arjun said as he swiped over his phone. A car whisked Morag Munro through central London for an appearance on *Newsnight*. Smeary lights moved across the rain-streaked windows. Morag preferred to read hardcopies to absorb the details, but she was an old hand at multitasking and had him reading the latest from social media while she sifted through a pile of printouts.

'Still well within error margins.' Morag frowned.

That bloody Vernon Coyle was making rapid progress. Her early favourability ratings were starting to plateau. If she was a hustings, he was a soundbite. She was an essay, he was a meme. While she had no problem getting endorsements from the trade unions, the one-member, one-vote system the party had adopted was new, untested. No doubt media presence would play a larger role than it ever had before.

'In a two-man race, sure,' Arjun said. Morag gave him a stern look over the top of her reading glasses. 'A two-person race, I mean. But you have to count on protest votes as the date gets nearer. Salinas is still holding on to a solid seven per cent. It might be enough to split the younger voters and give you the edge.'

'Salinas is holding because his "solid seven" would find the reanimated corpse of Karl Marx too right-wing for their tastes. I wouldn't have said he has mainstream appeal.'

'Don't throw the Marx out with the bathwater. It's all the rage on Tumblr these days.'

'Really? Well, goodness knows how I've got this far in politics without that crucial Tumblr vote,' Morag said. 'Bring me up to speed on the show tonight.'

'Usual stuff: government dragging its heels on Brexit, how have things changed, and so on.'

'Other panellists? What are they saying online?'

'Mackie will be there, of course. He's on so often I'm surprised when he isn't,' Arjun said. 'Tweeted out a few *New Politician* analysis pieces on the party earlier. Predictable, dependable.'

'As tedious as the rag he edits.' Morag nodded. 'And only about half as bright as he believes.' She deeply approved of Brian Mackie, tortoiseshell glasses and supercilious attitude notwithstanding. Old lefties like him loved to imagine they were playing hardball by throwing her the same five questions they had been recycling since 1996. 'Who else?'

'You won't like this,' Arjun said. 'It's that Woad person.'

Morag made a face. 'The Rome Must Burn one? Commodus, was it? Really?'

'I'm afraid so.' Arj turned his phone so Morag could see the screen, where Harold had been tweeting triumphantly about his invite to the show. Hashtag, a star is born. To her, his nickname said it all; who willingly named themselves after a corrupt, failed ruler? Maybe he thought it was louche and ironic. But to anyone over the age of twenty it smacked of student pretension. Her thin lips pressed in a line.

Her assistant noticed her displeasure. 'Probably best to prep some neutral talking points and let him and Mackie take chunks out of each other,' he suggested.

Arj was right – a war of words with Woad would not end well. Even if she bested him she knew what to expect from the online hate mob he headed up: abuse. Worse, online abuse had the habit of turning into newspaper thinkpieces about whether she deserved it, which tended to dissolve into accusations that she was a feminazi, an old harpy, or a battleaxe. She hated it, but that was the world they lived in now.

The car deposited them at Broadcasting House. Morag accepted her visitor pass at reception and was whisked over to the studio floor. Woad was in the makeup room already, tissues tucked around the collar of his fuschia shirt to keep the airbrush from staining his clothes. And what clothes they were: the lurid shirt, ripped jeans, Dr Martens, and a tweed hacking jacket a size too small. Brian Mackie was in the chair next to him.

'Oh, Morag,' Brian called when he heard her heels clicking past. 'Do you have a moment?'

'Brian,' she said, rolling the 'r' around in her mouth. 'A pleasure to see you as always.' Woad eyed the two of them in the mirror's reflection.

'Harold Woad,' he said and stuck out his hand.

'I know,' Morag said.

Woad's lacquered face betrayed only a hint of annoyance. He swivelled towards Mackie, his hand still out. 'Harold Woad.'

'Brian Mackie,' the professorish man mumbled but did not offer his hand. 'How do you do.'

'Harold Woad,' Harold repeated. His hand was still hanging in mid air.

'Yes, you said,' Mackie said. 'Commodus, is that what they call you.' A statement, not a question. 'You are the one with that website, aren't you.' Another statement. 'Fascinating stuff,' Mackie continued even though Harold had said nothing. 'Well, it was nice to have met you.'

Arjun waved urgently at Morag in the mirror. His eyes were wide and his face ashen. Harold strode over with his extended hand.

'Harold Woad,' he said. Arjun waved him away. 'No need to be rude,' Harold mumbled.

'Soz.' Arjun caught Morag's eyes again and pointed at the mobile. 'Everything's going haywire right now. Have you seen? Brant's topped himself.'

'What?' Harold and Morag said at the same time.

Arjun rolled his eyes. 'Get this one, the social media guru,' he said. 'The story broke five minutes ago. Have a look at your phone.'

Morag switched on the television and Arj gave her the précis.

Pills, apparently. His wife found the body at home. Brant was already the top trend worldwide. She gritted her teeth. 'Not fucking again,' she said. 'After that nonsense with the Major last year. Well, I won't do it.' She switched off the television. 'Text the producer, get her up here. We're going home.'

Harold sank back into the makeup chair. 'Fuck. Fuck.'

'What's the matter?' Arjun sneered. 'I would have thought you would be as happy as a pig in mud. After all, you did break the Nazi hooker story.'

'Yes,' Harold said. 'I mean no. For one, everyone's asking why I haven't put a piece up on the website yet. For another, what use is a dead man? The story ends. There's no content everyone else won't already have. And there's no chance we'll scoop the morgue photos before TMZ does. If I can't come up with something juicy on air tonight, I am screwed.'

Arjun wrinkled his brow. 'So you're upset that someone else might publish the corpse while you're on national television. Not that a man is dead. An interesting angle.'

'Yeah, well,' Harold said. 'What's your angle? Pretending to be upset that he's dead, or happily pushing your boss into his position? Or a bit of both?'

Morag opened her mouth to answer, but stopped herself. Give him nothing, give him nothing. Arjun pressed a finger to his chin. 'It's funny,' he said to Harold. 'Because you act like someone who thinks he has principles, but that can't possibly be the case. Given how cheerfully you ruin people's lives.'

'Real journalism is printing what people don't want you to print,' Harold snapped. 'Everything else is publicity.'

Arjun stepped forward until his chest was inches from the shorter man's. 'I don't usually tell people like you what I think of them, *Commodus*.' He enunciated each syllable with care. 'But in your case I don't mind making an exception. In a profession that is not lacking for unlikeable blaggers, you are by a long way the least credible fuckwit to trawl the gutter in a very, very long time.'

Woad was scrambling for a reply when an efficient-looking

woman in a grey pencil skirt walked in. Arjun backed away, but his eyes were still looking daggers at Woad.

'You're pulling out then? Are you certain?' the woman said to Morag.

Morag nodded. 'Afraid so.'

'OK, I understand,' the woman said. She turned to Harold. 'Hi, I'm Beth Chambers, the assistant producer. We spoke on the phone.'

Harold turned on his smile. 'A pleasure.'

Beth nodded briskly. 'I'm so sorry, Mr Woad, but I'm afraid we are going to have to bump you from the show tonight.'

'Bump me?' Woad's face went ashen under his makeup. 'But why?'

'I'm afraid Ms Munro won't be joining us this evening, so in lieu of having a panel of guests we'll be rerunning Brant's appearance after the European referendum,' Beth said. 'All looks a bit in bad taste now, doesn't it? Morag won't do a death. And Brian won't do it with only y . . . I mean, he won't do it without Morag. They're old friends.'

'She won't do a death,' Harold fumed. He looked back and forth between Beth, Arjun, and Morag. 'What the hell does that mean?'

'We were caught out on live television when Major Gaspar died last year,' Arj said. 'There's no point.'

'Are you joking?' Harold said. 'This is live news, you can't just bugger off. If I don't go on tonight, and I have nothing for the site, I'm fucked.'

'It's her choice.' Beth pouted sweetly. 'We have to respect that.'

'Well, whatever,' Harold said. 'But you can still have me.'

'You're right, and we'd love to, really we would.' Beth pulled her face into a concerned frown, the kind that clearly indicated she didn't mean a word of it. 'But we've not had you on the show before. Without some sort of . . . balancing guest, it would be too much of a risk.'

'Are you saying I'm too much for your viewers?'

'I'm saying that without knowing how you perform on air, we wouldn't have you solo,' Beth said. She started backing away from Harold. 'Please understand, it's not you, it's us. We've been caught out by loose cannons in the past. If it was a normal night, maybe. But not when a nation is in mourning.'

'In mourning?' Woad sneered. 'A man loses a general election, shags a Nazi hooker, and this is about mourning?'

Beth raised her palms. 'I don't make the rules,' she said. 'But it is exactly comments like that we can't chance going out live.'

'Fine, have it your way,' he said. 'But I'm billing you for the taxi home.'

'Of course,' Beth said. 'We cover the travel expenses both ways for all of our invited guests.' Harold frothed wordlessly, then spun on his heel and made for the elevators.

'Oh, Harold?' Arjun called after him.

Woad paused, then turned. 'Yes?'

'Nice outfit.' Arjun smiled. 'That is *so* what I would have been wearing two years ago.' Harold turned round again and disappeared into the stairwell. A peal of laughter erupted from the group as the door slammed shut.

: **23** :

Denise's boss phoned her desk when she got to work. Co-workers parted like the Red Sea as she made her way from there to his office. The looks on the secretaries' faces told her all she needed: they knew about Archie's arrest.

The boss was a bald Irishman. Overgrown tufts of hair over each of his ears stuck out, giving him the slightly surprised look of a baby owl. A reporter had been to the department while she was on leave, inquiring about her, about Archie. She cringed. He asked her to take unpaid leave. She knew it wasn't a question. This is a children's hospital, he reminded her. It did not matter that she was not clinical staff, that the only patients she had access to were on paper.

The media had also turned up when police came back to her house, this time with a dog. A corpse-sniffing dog, they said. Some kind of hound that walked through the house wagging its tail. She opened the loft hatch above her bed and pulled down the ladder. Apart from old cardboard boxes she had shoved up there, there was nothing. Nothing to see, nothing to smell.

Denise stood outside while they finished their work. The neighbours had gathered. They came out of their houses, in ones and twos, stood in their gardens and watched the police, watched her, standing on the pavement in her work trousers and cardigan. Not one of them said a word to her, though a few did whisper to the reporters. She could guess what they were saying. She had always kept herself to herself. She had never fitted in here.

Only Judy gave her anything like a human look, watching

from over the fence that divided their gardens. The press hung about until it became clear she would not be giving a statement. She hoped that would be the extent of it.

She arrived on time to visit Archie. Early, even. 'Phone, keys, and handbag,' the woman at the security check recited. She did not lift her eyes from the desk.

Denise had not brought a bag. She emptied her pockets into a small plastic basket and peered at the woman's nametag. Just an initial, 'L', and the last name, 'Bailey'. L Bailey extended her hand for the book Denise had brought. Denise passed it over and Bailey flipped through the pages. 'Do I need to sign anything?' Denise asked.

Bailey slid the basket onto a shelf behind her. 'I'll remember you,' she said. Denise stopped herself from asking how, given the woman had hardly looked at her or her ID. She knew how.

The large open room could have been anywhere. A cafe. A hospital lunchroom.

'The fuck . . . that wasn't ninety minutes! That was nowhere near ninety minutes!' A pair of policemen rushed into the room and took away a man dressed in a dull grey uniform. A woman and baby sat at the table he was being dragged away from.

There were officers stationed at the doors of the room, cameras, reinforced glass barriers between sections. Sitting there felt like being at school, when someone had done something wrong and the teacher lectured the entire class. Even if you hadn't done it you couldn't help but feel guilty, ashamed.

Archie walked out in his own clothes. His mother must have brought them. A stiffly starched office shirt and a pair of jeans. The laces of his shoes had been removed.

'You got my letter,' he said. His bulk was too much for the moulded plastic chair and he shifted uncomfortably.

'I did,' Denise said. Five pages of A4, closely handwritten on both sides. It was a struggle to read. His writing was unpractised and his sentences ran on and on. 'Well, this is an odd situation.'

Archie looked away and scowled. 'I'm not the one who should be here. If anyone should, it's you.'

Denise inhaled sharply. 'Oh?'

'This is entirely your fault. It was you who brought – that woman – into my life,' he said. 'My life was fine until you entered it.' His eyes narrowed, though he was looking at the wall, not at her. 'Now the train has gone off the rails and everyone on it is dead.'

'You asked me here to blame me for you killing someone,' Denise said. She supposed she should have been upset, but that was the old Denise. The new Denise was not about to take his abuse any more. She had come to get the answers to questions, and if he was going to try and pull his usual tricks, there was nothing in it for her. She pushed back from the table. The legs of the chair screeched against the lino. 'If that's how you are going to act, I'm going home.'

'Wait!' Archie looked up. There was a glaze of confusion in his eyes. Usually it would have been him policing her reactions, and now the shoe was on the other foot. He seemed to struggle to come up with something appropriate to say. 'Please,' he said. 'I just . . . I haven't been able to sleep. It's so noisy here, and they never turn off the lights, and my mind keeps going and going and . . . I didn't mean that. I didn't. Please, Kitty. Please don't go. You can't just leave me here.'

Denise lowered herself back into the chair. Even now, in a prison and accused of murder, he did not seem to appreciate how much the ground beneath him had shifted. She was not his Kitty any more. 'You're scared, that's why you're lashing out at me. Fine,' she said. 'Do it again, and I walk out of here and you will never hear from me again. Do you understand?' Archie nodded. 'I brought you something,' she said, and slid the book across the table.

Archie glanced at the paperback. 'Thanks,' he said. 'There's plenty to read here.'

'Flip through it,' she said. 'Look at page fifty.'

Archie did as he was told. She watched his eyes go over the

sentence faintly pencilled in the margins. *Do they know about the guns?*

He opened his mouth – old Archie again – then thought better of it. He shook his head. 'How did you know?' he said.

'Does it matter?'

'No,' he said. 'I guess it doesn't.'

The bad thing. She had been snooping. Was it her fault? He had been acting so strange in the weeks before his last trip away. Yes, it was wrong of her, she knew that. Bad Denise. Bad, bad Denise. Right now she did not care.

She had found the ring receipt, and she had found something else in the boot of his car: a zippered sports bag filled with smaller nylon bags. Curious, she had opened one and almost dropped the pistol inside, she was so shocked. They must have come from a car boot somewhere. Maybe he had been selling them to buy the ring, she told herself. She spun a story in her imagination, no matter how unlikely, anything to believe that there was a reasonable explanation that made it all make sense. She also supposed – at the time, anyway – that asking him about it would have done her no good at all.

That was then. Now she needed to know what kind of danger she was in. Even if writing the message in the book had been a potential risk. She needed him to start telling her the truth.

But Archie said nothing. She decided to put all her cards on the table. 'There's more.' She folded her hands. 'I know about you and Josie,' she said. His face went pale. 'The police told me. Cheers for that. The papers haven't mentioned her yet, but you can imagine how that is going to look for you, when they decide to print it. Guns, two girlfriends, a double life – when the press find out about all of this, you are not going to be a very sympathetic figure, are you?'

Archie shook his head again but still said nothing.

Denise felt a prickly heat flooding her cheeks. This was infuriating. Why wasn't he talking? 'What did you tell her about me, all this time? What cover story did you spin? Was it anything like the one I got? That you were being stalked by some girl named Denise, who was a real bunny boiler?'

His head dropped. Not a word came from his lips.

'Do you call her "Kitty" too? Is that what you do? So you don't have to worry about getting our names mixed up?' Now it was all pouring out, and she did not know if she would be able to stop. 'I saw your mother. Do you know what she told me?' Archie shook his head. 'She told me to invent an alibi for you – to lie to the police – because Josie refused to give one.'

It had been so seamless, how Mrs Lyndon had gone from acknowledging her son was a cheat, to asking Denise to lie to protect him. There had been no apology in any of it. No shame.

'Seven years with her, seven more years while you were with me . . . Tell me, did I mean anything to you?' Denise asked. 'Anything at all?'

Still he said nothing. Denise snorted. 'Don't imagine I'm here because I support you. I just need to know what hell is in store for me next. When the police are going to knock on my door again. Did you know the press have been camping outside my house?' He shook his head. 'They tried to break into my office, too. They had to be escorted off the premises by the police.'

Now that she had read his online posts she was able to piece together how he had lied for so long. He had rehashed his successes to an appreciative audience of men with monikers like SeductionKing and MingeMagnet.

It was, he told his pickup artist friends, not enough to maintain two lives and try to juggle them. His preference in paying for things in cash, instead of by card, was now explained. He carried his phone with him everywhere, but used it as little as possible with either her or Josie, preferring instead to turn up unexpectedly. Two phones would have looked suspicious. His job was genuine, but also a decent cover for unexplained periods of time away. He never gave real gifts, no jewellery, no showy cards, putting the emphasis, instead, on 'gestures' of romance. An impromptu night away. Recreating scenes from romantic films. Reciting poetry, which had the same effect as writing a love letter but without the pesky evidence. Assembling the ingredients for her favourite meal. (She could cook them for him, later.) Also, as he pointed out, gestures were cheap compared to real gifts. The only women who deserved to have money spent on them were the ones who were Wife Material. Win-win.

Every detail of their relationship – from his view, the one he had kept hidden – was right there online. She wondered how long it would be before the press found all that, too. When people had examined Archie's lies and found them wanting in the past, he bullied them with his charm or with his fists. Neither option would work now.

Archie leaned forward. He opened his mouth and only a whisper came out. 'Please,' he said. 'You have to believe me, Kitty. I didn't kill anyone. I need you to know that.'

Denise sighed. How long had she waited to hear that he needed her? That he cared what she thought of him, that her support meant more than what strangers thought? Now that he was saying the words, they meant nothing. 'I don't know what to believe,' she said.

Archie put his forehead on the table. A horrible sucking sound came from his nose and she realised that he was crying. 'It's not Miri,' he sobbed. 'It can't be. They've made a mistake.'

Denise was flabbergasted. He was still living in la-la land. Believing that if he insisted something often enough, that it would be true.

'They matched her fingerprints, Archie,' she said. 'They took genetic samples from her family and from the body. It's her.'

He looked up. His eyes were as swollen as if he had been punched. 'What do scientists know?' he said. 'They get it wrong all the time. Maybe there was a mix up in the lab, some kind of contamination—'

'They didn't get it wrong, Archie. Talk to your solicitor. This is real. This is really happening.'

The forensic evidence pointed to him, he had no alibi, he had the opportunity, and if Denise revealed what she knew about his personality he was as good as done. The knowledge sat on the edge of her tongue, sharp like a lemon pastille. She could crush him. No, much more than that. She could bury him.

And yet.

Denise had always been able to tell, in the past, when he was lying. He would stammer and bluster, as transparent as a toddler. She had not always known what he was lying about but it hardly mattered.

This was not the same. Yes, he was selfish. Yes, he was still ignoring her needs. But her gut feeling told her he was not lying this time. It was a small voice, one she wanted to ignore, but she could not let the thought go. He had lied to her so often that the truth, as little as she wanted to believe him, was recognisably different.

She closed her eyes. Behind her lids, fish lined up row after row, their stares blank and milky. She had not saved Darwin. She had made a promise to Miri, all those years ago. Denise couldn't save her, but maybe she could help bring whoever did it to justice. If she told the police how Archie had treated her, it would build the case for him being a murderer. Not for being an abuser. He would go down for something he hadn't done instead of something he had.

Miri would not have justice.

She swallowed the bitter pill resting on her tongue. 'I'll help you,' she said.

Archie blinked. 'What did you say?'

'I said I'll help you. But I won't do it by lying. You need to tell me the truth, Archie. Let's start with what I found in your car.' The guns. She nodded at the book. 'Do they know about those?'

'I did not kill anyone,' Archie said. His voice was barely a whisper. 'But yes, there were . . . you know. I . . . I was trying to sell them for someone else.'

'Who was it, Archie? You have to tell me,' she said. He did not reply, only stared at his hands. The nails were bitten down to the quick, the skin of the cuticles torn and pink. 'Archie, are you in trouble?' His eyes met hers. There was a look of fear in his face. Real fear, something she had never seen in him before. 'Is someone going to come after you here?' She gulped. 'Jesus Christ, Archie, speak up. Is someone going to come after *me*?'

: **24** :

Harold Woad clicked between browser windows with his right hand and tapped cigarette ash into a jar lid with his left. On one tab, he watched the stats for Rome Must Burn. Where visitors were clicking from, how long they stayed on the site, and where they clicked to. On another tab, he monitored submitted comments as they came in.

Dead tree media called him a troll. He didn't consider himself a troll, not in the strictest sense of the word. More of a devil's advocate. A classical liberal in the de Tocqueville tradition, he liked to say.

The week's stats were not encouraging. Hits for the site were way down. The *Newsnight* fiasco had hurt badly, and he was struggling to catch up after being caught on the back foot by Brant's suicide. Instead of hits coming from social media as they normally did, he was picking up traffic from Google searches – and the punters weren't staying. Not even the registered ones.

He could see all of his errors now in glaring technicolour. RMB's content had been ripe for stealing. He should have watermarked the escort photos, right across the woman's face. Technically the copyright was not his, true. It belonged to whoever took the original picture. But was that person ever likely to come forward? Other media outlets had ripped off the stories he broke. Some even went so far as to lift entire blog entries, nearly word-for-word, and post them on their websites without so much as a byline credit or a linkback. Woad was a dyed-in-the-wool supporter of freedom of speech and all that, but surely that was taking the piss?

Even the tried-and-true free speech route post-*Newsnight* had not attracted as much attention as he hoped. He had photoshopped two pieces of tape over the mouth of one of his headshots and penned a screed on how the BBC producers silenced him. But the piece was pulling in his lowest numbers for weeks. A surprising proportion of commenters urged him to 'have some respect' for Brant, saying that 'the body isn't even cold yet'.

He needed a new angle. Fast.

Harold tapped his teeth with a fingernail. The problem was, in the days since Brant's suicide, the now very former leader's reputation was undergoing rapid revision. Everyone rushed to eulogise him. Columnists urged their readers to look past the peccadilloes of the Nazi sex scandal, and remember instead the selfless public servant who had given decades to his party. Vernon Coyle came out strongly with warm recollections of his 'close personal associate' Lionel Brant. The papers ran photos from party conferences in the 80s and 90s, when the sharply coiffed Brant was a fresh young face shaking up politics, tipped for bigger things. And they had new ones of his widow, looking pale and drawn as she followed the funeral cortege into church.

It was as if, in the past week, the entire country had been hit with a bout of collective amnesia. What happened to the Lionel Brant of the last few years, the leader whose handle on his own party's policy was so weak, the Shadow Cabinet often had to pull U-turns simply to explain his gaffes? Or Brant, who failed to make any public statement about the Nazi hooker, not even to deny the stories? It was as if none of it had ever happened.

Even his own commenters were banging the drum for 'decency' and 'respect'. Ridiculous. Getting caught with a dead prostitute was simply the final straw in Brant's overlong and shambolic career, and he deserved to be remembered that way, not retrospectively canonised.

The mobile on Harold's desk vibrated. Number withheld. He swiped it to voicemail, but it started ringing again. 'Hello,' he barked.

'Harold Woad,' a voice said.

'Obviously,' Harold snapped. 'What do you want?'

'I think the question is, Harold, what do you want?' The voice was familiar but Woad could not immediately place it.

'Well, you could start with who you are and what this is about.'

'Have a think, Mr Woad. I believe you know who I am. We met recently and I admired your suit.'

His suit, his suit. Oh, right. Woad rolled his eyes. Now he recognised the voice. 'You're that bloody assistant of Morag Munro's. To what do I owe the pleasure?'

'In a word? Your reputation for having no journalistic ethics whatsoever,' Arjun said. 'Or to put it another way, I am calling to apprise you of a situation where your services may prove helpful.'

'Go on.' No doubt the call was being made from an unlisted mobile by Morag's assistant because he was about to be asked to do something important. While he had no interest in helping Morag Munro – no more than he would have helped anyone who was not himself – he was interested to see what kind of information was being offered. Not to mention the colour of her money.

'As you may know, Lionel Brant's demise has brought your media moment to an abrupt end,' Arjun said.

'Not to mention your boss's lead in the polls. Coyle is the man of the hour, wouldn't you say?'

Arjun ignored his remark. 'It is unfortunate to see such a . . . unique new voice extinguished so soon. I am sure you agree, and I wonder if we couldn't do something to help revive your flagging career.'

'That is generous of you,' Harold sneered. Trying to make your mark feel like they owe you something when you want something from them: the oldest trick in the book. He wasn't falling for it. 'But I'm sure it's you who needs the favour from me, not the other way around. I'm not the one angling for the leadership.'

'Call it enlightened self-interest,' Arjun snapped. 'You need a story. And Vernon Coyle needs bringing down a notch or two. I happen to have leads which could do that.'

'I see.' So Munro was going to go directly for discrediting Coyle? Coyle was younger than she was, he was smart enough, he was good-looking, he had a wife and two young children the cameras loved. He even produced a tear the moment the coffin was brought in at Brant's funeral – a tear that was broadcast on every news update for the following two days. Morag could not compete with that, no matter how expensive her suit or well-styled her bobbed hair. Her public statements in the wake of the death sounded exactly like what they were: rote, mechanical. People wanted aspirational leaders. No one aspired to be Morag Munro.

'If you need me to publicise something, why not send it in an email?'

'Don't make me spell it out for you,' Arjun said. 'I'm sure you're smart enough to figure out this contact is not happening at all. I have a list of names I'm going to read out, if you are interested. That is the end of our phone call. Do you have a pen?'

'Do you have money?'

Arjun snorted. 'You must be joking. The exposure you would get from this is worth far more than a paltry payoff. And we can't be having a paper trail now, can we?'

'Are you saying you've never met a journalist in a public place and handed over a bag of cash for publicity?' Given some of the stories that had been attached to Morag Munro in the past – whispers of an affair with a radio producer in return for positive coverage, rumours that refused to lay down and die – he found this unlikely.

'I'm saying that if you think that's how this goes down, you're barking up the wrong tree. Journalists pay for information, not the other way around. And I'm about to give you something for free, or would do, if you could stop interrupting me.'

'One question first – why me?'

'You want me to stroke your ego. Well.' Arjun sighed.

'Because you have the ear of the reactionary underbelly of the internet,' he said. 'The people who make and break trends, the ones who shift the Overton window. Because this story needs confirmations that don't yet exist. Because it has to come from someone who would never be connected to my boss in a million years, and she despises you. Will that do?'

It was not exactly what he wanted to hear, but Harold enjoyed the affirmation anyway. 'OK, hit me,' he said. He scribbled the six names Arjun read out on a notepad next to the phone. Four of them were people he recognised. Two newspaper columnists, a television pundit, and one of Coyle's former parliamentary secretaries. The other two, he didn't. 'These are all women,' Woad said.

'You're observant. There'll be a reason for that, and when you put it together, there is your story.'

'Sexual harassment?' Coyle was a blue-eyed public school-boy with the requisite cheekbones, charm and a head of close-cropped hair that had gone prematurely silver. He did not come off as someone unpopular with the ladies. Much the opposite. Still, appearances could be deceiving. And if his real kink was power, then it made sense that consent would not be required.

'Got it in one,' Arjun said.

'No way,' Harold said. 'I don't touch any of that social justice warrior nonsense. If these women had legitimate complaints about Coyle they should have gone to the police.'

'That's a bold statement, considering the power differential between, say, an MP and an intern. But I understand. As you wish,' Arjun said. 'I'm off to talk to the *Telegraph* women's editor next . . .'

Harold gulped. It had been days since he had anything fresh for the site. Sexual harassment might not engage his readership base, but it would attract attention from the wider media. Was he making a mistake?

'Wait,' Harold said. 'Don't go to the papers. They wouldn't do a story like this the way it deserves to be done. You said that

the confirmations don't exist. Not to mention, sexual misconduct accusations are serious claims. A story like this would be
legalled out of existence before a paper even touched it.'

'No, we're good, you said social justice is not your jam. I
heard you. Thank you for your time, any—'

'I'll do it,' Harold blurted. He needed the content, needed it
badly. He could figure out the spin later. 'But I want something
in return.'

'Unlikely, but you're welcome to ask.'

'When the libel suit hits my doorstep, I will need a solicitor,'
Woad said.

'I should have thought you would already have someone re-
tained. Didn't I read a quote that your website spends twice on
legal what it does on editorial?'

'Two times nothing is still nothing,' Harold said. There was
no point not being honest. 'That was to discourage the more
cheeky threats. The only lawyer in my contacts is a conveyan-
cing solicitor.'

He thought he heard Arjun stifle a laugh on the other end of
the line. 'Understood,' he said. 'I need to know that you will
pull no punches before I make any kind of introductions.'

'You have my word,' Harold said. 'I'll do my worst.' While
it was unlikely poking around in Coyle's past would reveal anything as shocking as the Nazi pics, if he could get anyone on
tape saying the word rape – even if they refused to be named
– he would draw crowds. Guaranteed.

'I can make some calls. If it's a free speech issue, a few of the
bigger legal firms might be willing to take it on no-win no-fee.
But as I said – no direct connections.'

'Then we're on.' Woad grinned. If he did publish and Coyle
hit him with a libel suit, then all the better. Free speech über
alles.

: **25** :

With no work to go to Denise poured her effort into finding out who really killed Miri. She approached the problem the same way she would any scientific investigation: with what information she had, however imperfect. It was a starting point, a frame for data. Her first instinct might not always be the right one, but she had to pick a direction to guide her research before she would find out where the real answer lay. Just like her professors used to say: there has to be a theory before a theory can be disproved.

Archie had been frustratingly vague after the gun revelation, and refused to give her names. There was not much she could do with his side of the equation: Josie didn't know anything about it, he said, and all he would tell her about the other people involved – the people who could have been his alibis – was that she did not want to know.

Walking away was an option. *I can leave this behind and never come back, and then he really is fucked*, she thought. *It would be no less than he deserves.* But she would never be able to square it with her conscience. She remembered the promise she had made to Miri: that if something ever happened to her, Denise would protect her.

She also couldn't shake the feeling that whoever was involved – both with the guns, and with Miri's death – would, at some point, come looking for her.

Archie's RMB account details were her starting point. They allowed access to the original articles about Miri, which had now moved behind a paywall, and all of the forums, even the unmoderated ones closed to unregistered users. Denise started by categorising posts as 'of interest' and 'not of interest'. The ones that were of interest, she scoured for links, unique data, and big summaries. Most of the RMB forums were onto the next scandal – sexual harassment allegations about Vernon Coyle, who was running against Morag Munro to replace Brant. She scanned a few of the pieces but there was little to interest her. Unnamed sources, vague suggestions of more to come. What was the saying about newspapers? Tomorrow's chip paper? It was interesting to see how true this was on the internet as well.

One name kept turning up in the comments of the RMB articles she accessed: HighlandLad88. It wasn't one of Archie's accounts. The user was a prolific and early commenter on the Brant stories, and had contributed to some of the Coyle reports, but not much in between. She checked their profile, but apart from a birth year – 1988 – it was empty. In spite of commenting over 200 times in the space of two weeks, the user had not uploaded a photo.

While a lot of commenters seemed to come and go, the specificity of HighlandLad88's interest seemed unusual. Was this someone who had met Miri? A client perhaps? Denise noted the name, then moved on to the next part of her plan: trying to find out who Miri had spent time with, and when.

She went to the escort message boards. Unsurprisingly, putting in Archie's email address and RMB password showed he had accounts on those too. A quick search for HighlandLad88, by comparison, turned up nothing – but whoever it was could have had a different handle for different places if he was a punter.

The escort sites were split into forums, adverts, and reviews. The amount of data on the sites looked huge but most of it was just noise. She decided to focus on the adverts and reviews. First she searched service providers in the Northeast and their availability and date ranges. Who else was based in Newcastle? Who toured there? If she could reach some of these people, they might know something.

As far as she could see the escort business in Newcastle was small compared to, say, London. The number of sex workers who provided domination services in the Northeast was smaller still. Reading through old forum posts and following links, a picture started to emerge. That picture suggested a story that had not, as yet, appeared to interest the police. The story not of who Miri had worked for – who her clients were – but who she worked *with*. Her friends, her colleagues.

Denise kept landing on the profile of one person in particular: a dominatrix in Newcastle named Sandra Jones.

Sandra had attracted her fair share of press over the years. A trial for evading taxes in the early 2000s revealed she had gone from streetwalking on the Bigg Market to running one of the largest escort agencies in the Northeast – all black girls, catering to sports stars and anyone else with loads of cash. Her little black book was made public, and more than a few of those footballers endured taunts about 'brown sugar' from the terraces for years. Sandra retired after the trial but only for a few years. Now she seemed to run a much smaller business out of a flat in central Newcastle.

The woman in the photos was striking. Sandra Jones favoured sharply tailored power suits, perhaps vintage pieces left over from her previous success? Even in middle age she looked ageless, timeless. Denise wondered if it was the same woman she had seen in town with Miri, all that time ago.

The more Denise probed, the more it looked like Sandra's emergence from retirement coincided with Miri's earliest escort adverts online. Adverts that started not long after Denise drifted out of her life.

Something bothered her about this. She told herself there was no reason to, but she couldn't help but wonder. Had Miri really gone from zero to full dominatrix in so short a time? What had those parties really been at Lamia House? Were they, in fact, events where Miri vetted clientele? Or even looked for new women to work with? Was she being *groomed*? The dark rooms, the people in them – a swirl of bodies and faces. Were any of them famous? Were any of them paying?

No, she told herself firmly. They were friends, end of story. Those were house parties and that's all they were. Still the questions bubbled up. If Sandra had ever been at one of those parties, Denise would have remembered her. Wouldn't she?

Miri and Sandra's adverts did not specify the addresses where either of them accepted clientele. But the description of the facilities for incalls – when the punter visits the escort, as opposed to outcalls where she goes to him – matched almost word for word. Both mentioned a central location, well-equipped dungeon, elegant bedroom suite, and minibar. She compared these against the other people offering domination services in Newcastle, and then in the UK generally.

When new adverts appeared for one of them, there had usually been a fresh ad for the other within days. On one of Sandra's photos she spotted what looked like a corner of a leopard-print bedspread. It was possible, of course, that it was something else, or that it wasn't the same one. But the clues were coming together.

Denise created a new spreadsheet on her laptop to enter data. In the first sheet she noted dates and locations of tours and reviews. In the second she took down repeated and similar phrases on the websites, with the dates they appeared. On a third sheet she recorded what details were known about Miri and when they first appeared in the media, and where.

Tour reviews from the south of England and Scotland showed, for at least 75 per cent of the instances she found, overlapping dates for both women. Bristol and the Southwest in 2011. West Midlands from 2012 onwards. Not exact date matches in all cases, but then they possibly did not travel together. Maybe they shared hotel suites only after they arrived.

On the page of Sandra's site detailing how to book her services, Denise found:

Embrace all that life has to offer, all of its beauty and its darkness. When life is dragging you down, show it you can take the hits and come back for more. Surrender your flesh to the reptilian mistress of the night. Explore the joy of pleasure and pain in the manner of the great artists and poets. Everything is up for grabs and your pleasure is non-negotiable. This sweet thing is a guilt-free, after-eight treat for adults only. Delectable debauchery awaits.

Her heart skipped a beat. Denise could all but hear Miri's breathy voice in her ear as she read it. The art historian with an eye for the dramatic? Of course she would have helped a friend write the copy for her site.

She didn't have everything she needed, nowhere near enough to go to the police, to show them Archie was not the person they were looking for. But here was someone who must have known Miri, who might have been aware if any of her clients had seemed threatening, or if Miri had done something to provoke someone. This Sandra Jones couldn't have come so close to Miri without knowing something. It was a truism of Denise's profession: correlation is not causation. But it was also true that there was no causation without a correlation. It would be remiss of her not to follow the leads and see where they went. As her supervisor often said, sometimes the strongest weapon in the epidemiologist's arsenal is their intuition. It might not please the scientific method fetishists, but in the history of discovery it was often a coincidence, a chance encounter, or a hunch that led to a breakthrough.

What would be ideal would be to get inside Sandra's flat, see if Miri's photos matched up. To try to massage some information out of her, about who Miri knew, who she saw. But how? If she just turned up at her door and told her she used to know Miri, Sandra would be unlikely to share her story. Someone like Sandra wouldn't just open the door to any stranger. Denise needed a story, a reason to visit.

How on earth could Denise get in? She could not plausibly claim to be a repairman, or someone from the council. Denise sipped a diet Coke while she thought. The answer hit her with shocking clarity. A call girl would have no trouble getting inside. Of course. Sandra had recently put a message out on the boards, looking for someone to tour with. But Denise wasn't a sex worker and wouldn't even know where to begin—

Unless she really had been in that world all along and never knew it. Unless those parties at Lamia House were more than just friends getting together for a good time.

An escort could do more than just compare the premises to the online description. An escort could conceivably get access to the client list and figure out who was where when Miri went missing. The idea frightened her. But once she had the thought Denise found it impossible to set aside.

Why not? She could fake it long enough to get the information she needed. And if she needed to go further, she asked herself, could she cross that line? Was being an escort really so far away from what her life had been like when she was a student? Getting with random men, throwing herself into the moment, going out with nothing more on her mind that having a good time.

It wasn't that different, really. On paper. But the reality was another matter.

What was the worst that could happen? Her mind ran through the scenarios almost without trying, processing data, assessing risks. She could be strangled by a client. Shot by one. Raped. Sandra could find out she was spying and attack her. She could be arrested. Worse – she could be arrested, and the police might think she was involved with Miri's death.

What would you do to save the person you loved most in the world?

There was a noise outside her window. It sounded like someone walking up the drive. Denise froze. Neighbourhood kids had taken to coming up to her door, ringing the bell, then running away. But these were heavier steps.

She waited. The doorbell did not ring. The footsteps seemed to get further away – a car door slammed. She waited a moment, went to the window, and peeked out of the crack between curtains. The street was dark but for pools of light slipping out through other people's windows.

A car was outside her house, parked across the driveway. One she didn't recognise. She tried to make out the registration plate or the model but neither was visible.

It's just someone parking there while they visit a neighbour, she thought. She tucked herself behind the curtain and waited. When she peered out again, she saw a brief flare of light, like a match being struck. There were two people in the car. A reporter and a photographer? Or something else? The black threads seized her chest again, and she crumpled to the floor.

: **26** :

'So, A-levels.' The woman waited for Denise's answer.

Denise's hands were clammy. She hated interviews, always had. She felt like she was skirting the edge of a panic attack. 'All As. Chemistry, biology, further maths . . .'

'Oh, baby, not those A-levels.' The woman across from her laughed. 'I mean anal. Do you do anal?' Denise's eyes widened and she nodded. The woman in the power suit adjusted her gold-framed glasses. 'How old did you say you were again?'

The cafe was centrally located. Anonymous. Denise felt conspicuous in a red silk dress and heels, but after the circuitous route she'd taken, she was sure the press weren't following her. And she knew what she was doing wasn't illegal. So why did she feel as if she was breaking every rule by sitting down to have a coffee with this woman? This . . . dominatrix?

'Twenty-nine,' Denise said. It was more or less true.

Sandra Jones looked at her a long time. 'We'll say you're twenty-two on the website.'

Sandra looked very much like her photos. She'd clearly had work done. No one's skin looked so taut and flawless into their sixties. Not even a black woman's. But the overall effect was of someone who took care of herself out of pride, not desperation. Her high cheekbones were flawlessly contoured, the tiniest crinkle of laugh lines had been allowed to remain at the corners of her deep-set eyes. The tricks of a clever doctor, and a well paid one.

Sandra let Denise observe her for a moment. She seemed to know what the younger woman was thinking. 'Looking good is my business,' she said. 'And business is good. If hydration and genetics have got you to thirty looking like you do now, great. But nothing lasts forever.'

'It's not just about looking good, though, is it?' Denise said. When Sandra told her the meeting place, she had said to choose a seat near the window. Denise supposed it was so she could change her mind, in case Denise turned out to be a stalker or a cop. She wondered if anyone else was watching. A pimp, from the high windows of the office block over the road? A bodyguard?

'That it is not. Do you want to see my flat? Have a look at what we'll be taking on the road. Decide if it's for you.'

Denise had hoped to see the flat but was not prepared for everything to move so quickly. What would Miri do? Miri would brazen it out. 'I'd love that,' she said, more confidently than she felt.

Denise had sent her an email from a throwaway encrypted account, attached a couple of old photos. A blurry one of her in a black strappy top at one of Miri's house parties, a later one from a schoolfriend's wedding with Archie cropped out. If Sandra recognised the setting of the first snap she didn't say. But she did say that she had no problems taking a newbie on the road. 'Aptitude matters more than experience,' she said. 'Clients love the idea of someone who's fresh to the business. They'll fall over themselves to be the one who posts your first review.' *First review*, Denise thought. *Go back and check who was Miri's first review.*

'How many men have you been with?' Sandra asked in the taxi.

'Two,' Denise said. It was a lie, but she was playing a part, right?

'Are you joking?' Sandra laughed. She looked at Denise, expecting a punchline, but did not get one. 'Oh, honey. I guess you really need the money, huh?'

'My last relationship was . . . abusive,' she said. It felt strange saying it out loud. But it was the truth. 'I don't really care about sex any more.' Also true. One lie, two truths. Good enough.

Sandra instructed the driver to stop at a plain door between a shop and a chippy and paid him with a crisp fifty-pound note. 'Keep the change, baby,' she said. The keys jangled in her hand.

They walked up the narrow staircase. 'Well if I've heard a story like yours once I've heard it a thousand times,' Sandra said. She opened the second door, the one to the flat. The place was larger than Denise had expected and more understated. 'Make no mistake, getting paid is nothing like real dating. It's a transaction. They pay, you perform. But if all you ever had was men who treated you like dirt, then it's not so bad, either.'

Denise looked around. The reception area looked like a dentist's waiting room. This was nothing like what she was expecting to see, nothing like Miri's photos or descriptions of the incall. She wondered if she hadn't made a huge mistake.

'Do you want a drink? Coffee, something stronger? You won't mind if I have a glass of wine.' Sandra walked through the open-plan room to the kitchen area. Under the stainless steel refrigerator was a cooling drawer stacked with bottles of pinot grigio. She poured herself a generous glass.

'I'm good, thanks,' Denise said. 'How about a tour?'

'Sure, honey.' Sandra walked her around the rest of the flat. The large bathroom was stocked high with disposable toiletries, fresh white towels, and towelling dressing gowns. Another generic-looking room, Denise was disappointed to note.

She had all but lost hope of any leads when Sandra opened the final door with a flourish. The back room was papered in black flock, with mirrors covering the ceiling. This was more like Denise had imagined from the website descriptions. What she had at first glance taken to be a collection of candles on a silver tray was in fact several dildoes. In the centre, a bed on a raised platform was spread with a leopard-print cover. Denise's heart fluttered – it was exactly like Miri's photos. *Don't get too carried away*, she told herself. *Maybe every escort has leopard sheets*. But intuition told her this was the one.

A painting hung on the far wall, uplit as if in a gallery. It showed a nude woman in shades of black and grey, yellow and orange. Her body was turned to face the viewer, her head in profile.

'Mata Hari,' Sandra said. 'That was a gift from a client, years ago. An art dealer.'

Art dealer? Now that would surely be the kind of client who would have met Miri, or wanted to. Denise turned to Sandra and smiled. 'She's beautiful.' There was something in the pose, the frank presentation of the body, that was arresting. Classic, like a statue. But with only half a face, and that partly in shadow, what she might be thinking was a mystery. 'Do you like Klimt?' she blurted.

'Some of his works,' Sandra said. 'Though all his women look a little . . . like they're not quite there. Pretty-pretty but not very deep, if you know what I mean.'

Denise nodded. 'I think so.' Had the print she saw on the wall when she went back to Lamia House always been there? The two women, one naked, leaning on the shoulder of the other one in her turban and orange gown. *Die Freundinnen*. She couldn't remember. She turned to her host. 'Maybe we should talk about particulars.'

Sandra's eyes crinkled. 'You don't hang around, do you?' she said. 'So, my next tour is up to Scotland. Cameron Bridge, Inverness, Aberdeen. That's a good way to start – you're less likely to run into anyone you know.'

Denise gulped and nodded. Scotland? Maybe this could lead her to HighlandLad88, if indeed he was a punter.

'My standard for a Highlands tour is one-fifty per hour, incall. That's when they come to you. Two hundred for out, anywhere in a ten-mile radius. Any further than that, it's a two-hour minimum booking plus transportation. Add a flat fifty for couples.'

'How much of that do you keep and how much do I get?' Denise said.

'A third of the fee comes to me, but if you get any tips you can keep those. As this is your first tour, you should stick to incall. We'll book suites. I'll be on the other side of a door if you need anything. Until you find your feet. What kind of services would you offer?'

'I think I can handle GFE,' Denise said. She had done her research, trawled the review sites and tried to pick up the lingo. GFE meant girlfriend experience. 'I know I can do submissive.'

'Good, good.' Sandra smiled. 'One of each. Old and young, domme and sub. Customers like variety and I like to give it to them. We can put doubles on the table, someone books us both, then it's two fifty per hour. Put on a little show, they'll be gagging for more. You still keep the hundred.'

'Do you always work with someone else?' she asked.

'Most of the time,' Sandra said. 'Not so much lately. I had someone rip me off a little while back.' She shook her head and sighed. 'You'd think as long as I've been in this industry I would have seen it coming. I thought old clients were going cool because they couldn't afford it any more, double dip recession, you know how it is.' Denise nodded. 'Too late I find out she was nicking them out from under me. She was going through my emails, finding who responded, then contacting them on the sly, undercutting the agreed price, then telling them to cancel with me.'

'I'm sorry.' Was Sandra talking about Miri? 'Any idea why she would do a thing like that?'

Sandra threw up her hands and sighed. 'Same old story. Girl was up to her neck in drug debts,' she said. 'Not my concern, and anyway, it's why some people start working. Pretty girl, you wouldn't have known it for the most part. Only at some point she started shooting up. That's how I found out the rest. One of my regulars on the last tour saw the marks on her feet. She turns up at his hotel high as a kite, trying to jerk off his soft cock into a condom, mouth covered in sores, you name it. Some guys wouldn't notice but at one-fifty for the half hour you bet they will.'

Denise drew in her breath. Miri had never seemed to regard

drugs as more than entertainment, but then, it had been years. Things change. People change. Could it have been her? 'Wow.'

'He walked out of there, didn't even pop once. Came straight to my hotel and told me the state she was in. I cut ties and took the adverts down before anyone else noticed. I gave him a refund if he agreed not to leave her a review – something like that is pure poison on the boards, and as she usually toured with me, well, you can imagine. It would have cost me more in business than giving the guy his money back.'

'And that was it?' Whoever that one was, it didn't sound like he would have killed Miri. The killer surely wouldn't be stupid enough to go straight to Sandra afterwards.

'More or less.' Sandra paused to sip her wine. 'She went loopy when I chucked her out, accused me of – well, you name it. Crazy isn't even the word. Came out with some paranoid rant about people trying to sell her out to MI5 or whatever, accusing me of being in on it. Gun dealers and all sorts. Nuttier than squirrel shit. At first I thought it was a joke, but she wouldn't stop. I wasn't about to keep her around and find out.'

'You never had political clients?' Denise was surprised.

'Oh, I have. Everyone has. But I don't get involved in any of it beyond doing my job. In my line of business, I don't ask questions about my clients and they only tell me what they need me to know. I learned that lesson the hard way a long time ago.' Sandra smiled again. 'Anyway. I found out she took my tour stash out of the door with her too. Water under the bridge now, water under the bridge.'

'That's terrible,' Denise said. Surely she was talking about Miri. It had to be. 'It's good of you to keep it in perspective.'

'Perspective, hell.' Sandra held Denise's gaze. 'Who needs perspective when the bitch is dead?'

Denise choked down a cough. Sandra raised her wine glass. 'Don't worry, you wouldn't do a thing like that, would you? You probably haven't even smoked a spliff in your life,' she said.

Denise nodded mutely. Sandra. Of course, Sandra. In all

her research Denise had imagined Sandra was the link between Miri and her killer. That it had been a bad client, someone they both knew, a HighlandLad88 or someone similar. She hadn't considered that it could have been Sandra herself, and sat on her sofa, the thought now was terrifying. If this was a woman who would kill someone over a few thousand pounds, what would she do if she found out why Denise was really there?

If Sandra noticed Denise's sudden turn she didn't say. 'We have to get you some real photos, something that plays up your assets. That hair. And the punters are going to go crazy for those legs. The dress you have on now is good, pretty but not too revealing. Keep the mystery for your first time out. Girlish, ladylike.' She sipped the wine. Her dark purple nails looked like raptor talons against the glass. 'You know, I had a good feeling about you as soon as I saw you in that window,' she said. 'I always trust my instincts. We're going to get along fine.'

'Photos, yeah.' Denise did not want photos. She did not want to be in the flat a minute longer. Her heart was thumping, and if she didn't leave soon, she would probably collapse. She blinked the black threads away. 'Can we do it another time?'

'You have to go?' Sandra said.

'Sorry. I was going to go for a run today, then . . .' Denise trailed off, unwilling to furnish the lie with more details than were necessary.

Sandra waved her hand. 'Don't worry about it. Get your run. You take care of those legs, I'll take care of the rest. We'll do it tomorrow or whenever. Use the time until then to get a manicure, yeah? Now get outta here.'

Denise ran down the stairs and out of the front door. She left so fast, she never even noticed the car that mounted the pavement twenty metres behind her as she did. Or the man in black crocodile boots who caught the door in his hand a second before it shut.

: 27 :

Seminole Billy paused at the top of the stairs, nodded at Buster, and stood aside to let him make their customary entrance.

The big man shouldered the door open. Billy was in behind him. Billy's leather-soled boots tapped the floor as he made his way across the room. He was faster than he looked, and stronger, too – within moments he had twisted one arm behind the woman's back and pushed her up against the wall. His other arm barred the back of her neck and kept her from moving. 'All right,' Billy said. 'Where the hell are you hiding her?'

'Hiding who?' Sandra twisted to get a look at the two men. The short white one with his all-black clothes, the tall black one with his ginger dreads. 'I take it this isn't a social call.'

'You know who,' Billy said. 'We're looking for the French girl. Augustine.'

Sandra struggled against Billy's grip but it was no use. 'You got the wrong flat,' she said. 'I don't know any French girls.'

'Like hell you don't,' Billy said. He jerked his head at Buster, and the big man sidled off, gun drawn, to check the other rooms. 'We saw her come in here last night.'

'Nonsense,' Sandra said. 'No one was here last night. What does she look like?'

Billy sighed. 'Don't play stupid with me, woman. You know who she is. Brown hair, short. Like Louise Brooks with a tan.'

'Louise Brooks, huh?' Sandra raised an eyebrow at the mention of the silent film star. Her lipstick smeared the wall where her face was pressed. 'You've got rareified taste for a pimp.'

'I ain't a pimp,' Billy said and ground his arm deeper into her neck. Sandra's breath laboured against the force of it.

'Boyfriend, pimp, burglar, whatever,' she croaked.

Buster returned from his brief tour and shook his head. 'No sign of her,' he said. Billy asked if he'd checked the windows. 'Two storey drop, no fire escapes. She's acrobatic but that'd be stretching her chances.'

Billy sighed. 'You must have nodded off, then,' he said. 'I knew we should have both been staking it out.'

Billy stepped back from the wall, releasing Sandra. She wobbled on her heels as she turned to face them. The makeup on one half of her face was smudged, the skin under her cheekbone scraped raw and already starting to swell, but she shook her head and threw her hair back over her shoulders as if they had been having a normal conversation all along. 'I told you, there's no one here but us, chickens,' she said. 'Wine, gents?'

Billy frowned. 'Water for me,' he said. 'And for Buster.'

Sandra walked to the kitchen in the corner of the room. 'So he's Buster. But I guess you're the brains of this operation. What's your name?'

'Seminole Billy,' he said.

'Billy, hmm,' Sandra said. She handed each man a glass of tap water. 'I thought I detected a bit of a Yank accent there.'

Billy bristled. 'Not that it matters to you, but Yanks are the people who live up north. I'm from Florida.'

'If you say so.' A hint of a smile flitted across Sandra's lips. She turned to Buster. 'How about you? Bristol, is it?' Buster nodded. 'Florida and Bristol. Well, now we're all introduced, why don't you sit down.' She indicated the club chairs opposite the sofa.

Buster remained standing. Billy scooched his thin backside into the seat. He smoothed the crisp denim of his jeans over his thighs and crossed one foot over his knee. His polished black alligator boots were finished with silver tips. He observed Sandra noticing this, then watched her notice the slight bulge under Buster's jacket at about hip level where the butt of the Glock 34 distorted the line of the fabric. 'You're pretty chill for someone who claims not to know who we're looking for,' he said.

Sandra shrugged. 'You're a man. Not a cop. Not one of my clients. So you either have the wrong place or you are here to rob me. Either way, not my first time.'

'How did you know we're not clients?' Buster said.

'Apart from the sidearm and the fact I don't take walkups?' she said. 'You two aren't the kind of men who pay for it. Pay for it directly, I mean. No, I think you are straight up criminals. Maybe you really are looking for this Augustine, whoever she is. Or maybe it's a story you made up to bust in here.'

'A fine thing, getting judged as criminals by a prostitute,' Billy said. Sandra shrugged but offered no excuse or apology. Billy uncrossed his legs and reached into the pocket of his corduroy bomber, pulled out a pouch of tobacco and a packet of skins. 'There's an Augustine all right. But I care less about her than I do about the money.' Seminole Billy rolled a cigarette and stuck it in the corner of his mouth. 'Mind if I smoke?'

'I don't imagine I could stop you.' Sandra pushed a crystal ashtray across the table.

'Thanks.' Billy lit his roll-up, took a drag, exhaled. He stuffed the tobacco pouch back in his pocket. 'I gotta tell you, I don't like Newcastle. Last time we were here, I had to almost kick a man to death on the Bigg Market before we even got to where we were going. And if—'

Sandra held up one hand. 'Spare me the details,' she said. 'I know what you do, or at least I have a pretty good idea. Tell me what you want.'

'We're here for the rest of the money,' he said. His pale eyes shone like glass marbles in his weather-beaten face. 'Or the guns. Preferably both.'

Sandra puffed air from her cheeks. 'I don't keep more than a thousand pounds on the premises,' she said. 'And I don't know about any guns.' She gripped the stem of her glass. 'But if you want whatever money I do have here, it's yours.'

'Augustine said twenty thousand, cash, small notes,' Billy said. 'You seem reasonable. Understand I'm a reasonable man, so I'm gonna ignore the fact that she was supposed to deliver two weeks ago. But Buster here.' Billy jerked his head over his shoulder in the direction of his friend. 'Buster gets real upset whenever someone violates a verbal contract. Don't you, Buster?'

Buster cracked the knuckles of one large hand in the other. 'I'm a stickler for protocol,' he said.

Sandra lifted her wine to her lips and took a sip to disguise the gulp in her throat.

'So we'd like that money right now,' Billy said. 'Cash, obviously.'

'I've never heard of either of you before, certainly never promised you twenty grand and I've never seen these guns you're getting so worked up about,' Sandra said. Her words were firm but the tone of her voice less so. 'Never heard of the woman you're so convinced that I know. As I said, I don't keep a load of cash here. Everything gets banked daily.'

Billy snorted. 'Bitch, please. This ain't my first time at the rodeo,' he said. 'Let's have the money.'

Sandra grabbed her handbag, opened it and showed the men the jumble of makeup and receipts inside. 'Look,' she said. 'There's no money.'

Billy unfolded the leg across his knee and stood up, walked a few paces towards the door, stopped, and tapped the toe of his boot on the floor. There was a slightly hollow sound. 'There's a space under this floorboard,' he said. 'You either got the guns or the money down there, maybe both, so play ball and we can all be out of here before teatime.'

'That's hours from now, man,' Buster said. 'We gotta be somewhere else by then.'

'Shit, what?' Billy's face wrinkled up as he examined his watch. 'I thought y'all took tea at two, maybe three in the afternoon,' he said.

'Nah, man, you're thinking 'bout high tea. That's some middle-class London bollocks. We're in the North here. Tea is dinner and dinner is on the table before six.'

'You're confusing me now,' Billy said. 'I thought dinner was lunch.'

'It is, except when it's not,' Buster said. 'But tea is definitely early evening.'

'Well that makes no fucking sense,' Billy said. 'That's too early to eat. What happens if you get hungry again before bed?'

'I think that's supper,' he said. 'But to be honest I'm not so sure myself.'

'Damn,' Billy said. 'Y'all have an extra meal and I didn't even hear about it before now? Is this a new thing?'

'Buggered if I know,' Buster said. 'I just know they do things differently up here. Maybe it's because of the coal mines or something.'

Billy considered the point. A decades-long career of crime with spells in and out of the joint had not done much to introduce him to the subtler points of British class and regional markers. On the one hand, his background was a plus. With few loyalties and fewer ties he had no boundaries, next to no compunction about carrying out a job. So long as he was getting paid. On the other hand, he could now recall at least three instances of getting a meeting time wrong that in retrospect had been his fault. Up to and including the job that led to his last spell in Belmarsh.

On the other other hand, it was also where he had met his partner, Buster. Apart from the Thatcher job fuckup that meant Buster had to travel in the car boot, their partnership was a good thing. Silver linings and all that.

'Um, guys?' Sandra tapped a nail against her glass. 'I'm still over here, and you still haven't told me what this is about.'

Billy held up his hand. 'Hold on, I gotta get this straight in my head first. Teatime is when?' He pointed at her. 'When is it to you?'

'Your friend is right, it was half five in our house every night,' Sandra said. 'Soon as Dad came home. How long have you lived here?'

'Like, fifteen or sixteen years,' Billy said. 'It never makes any more sense.'

'You could always go home,' she offered. 'I hear Florida is nice this time of year.'

'Yeah, and you could mind your own damn business. Besides which your girl kinda ran off with my retirement fund so, y'know, I might have a problem procuring the one-way ticket off this rainy fascist island that I so was looking forward to.'

'If that's the case' – Sandra's pursed lips clearly demonstrating she did not think that was the case – 'then you are going to have to tell me what this is about. Assume I know nothing, because I do.'

Billy rolled his eyes. 'We made a deal with Augustine last year. We, uh, came into possession of a number of collectible firearms and needed someone to sell them on. She wired the deposit and instructions for the dead drop. We dropped the stash at the airport. Went back a week later, and the drop was gone. Not empty – gone. Tried to get in touch other ways, and then . . . well, the wild goose chase that led us to your door. Which brings you more or less up to date.'

'Damn.' Sandra couldn't help but smile. 'Maybe you should have vetted your associate a little more carefully.'

'We knew her for a couple of years,' Buster said. 'No reason to think she wouldn't come through this time. Sometimes you gotta believe in honour amongst thieves.'

Sandra nodded; he had a point. 'Still. That's gotta hurt.'

'It'll hurt less in about five minutes. For me, anyway.' Billy nodded at his feet. 'Buster, break up the floor.' Buster withdrew the gun from the holster and aimed it at the floorboards. He straightened out his long arms and slipped his finger down onto the trigger.

'OK, fine! Stop it! Put that thing down.' Sandra slid a long nail under the corner of one piece of flooring and gently lifted it, then a second and a third. There was indeed a small safe, as Billy had predicted. Sandra looked up at the two men. 'Do you mind looking away so I can enter the code?'

Billy sighed. 'You gotta be kidding me, lady,' he said. 'We're taking whatever's in there. It doesn't fucking matter if we see you enter the combination or not.' Buster slipped his gun back into his holster and put a hand over his eyes.

Sandra entered a six-number code on the keypad and the door popped open. Inside were bundles of money. Twenties and fifties rolled up and secured with an elastic band. Billy scooped up the lot – about two grand, if he was right, and he usually was. He juggled the cash in one hand before slipping it into an inside jacket pocket. 'This really all you keep in here?' he said. 'No offense, but that's barely enough to get a girl out of town in case of emergency.'

'About all I can float without raising eyebrows,' Sandra said. 'I learned my lesson the hard way when HMRC came knocking.'

'And you really have no idea about Augustine. Or the guns.'

Sandra stood up and crossed her arms. 'Until you two busted in here, I hadn't seen a firearm in ten years at least,' she said. 'As I said, once you've had the taxman wiggle his nose around your affairs . . . nothing puts the fear of God into you the same way. Not even the police. And definitely not some Tesco Value hitmen.' She sashayed back to the sofa and retrieved her drink. 'You going to tell me why you thought someone was in here, or nah? Because if you have nothing else to say, we're done, and I'd appreciate if you two could run along. I have to get ready for my five o'clock.'

Billy massaged his deeply lined forehead with one hand. 'She came in here. Yesterday. We were watching out from over the road. It was definitely your door.'

'Bull and shit,' Sandra said. 'I was at an outcall last night. No one lives here but me.'

'She rang us from a landline one time,' he said. 'Burners after that. We traced the landline number back to this building. That's how we knew where to find her.'

'Yeah well,' Sandra said. A flicker of worry passed over her face. 'You must have been mistaken. No one else has worked here in over a year. My business slowed right down, I can't be carrying some newbie. I don't even have a cleaner any more.'

'What about johns?' Buster asked. 'Any of them have a key?'

Sandra shook her head. 'No way,' she said. 'I don't leave them in here alone. Things can get messy if I don't keep an eye on the boys. I specialise in CBT, you see.'

'CBT?'

Sandra smirked. She probably shouldn't enjoy conversations like this one as much as she was about to, but she was a born dominatrix through and through. 'Cock and ball torture. Needles. Hooks. Electrical shocks, that sort of thing.' She watched both men's faces go ashen. 'My playmates generally can't be left on their own with good reason. Though if anything does go wrong – and that is a possibility, especially with the popularity of testicle crushing lately – the hospital is less than ten minutes away.'

Billy had broken into a cold sweat as she talked. He extracted a handkerchief from his jeans pocket and swiped the back of his neck. Both he and Buster looked keen to go.

'So when was this landline call supposedly made?' she said. Her voice was bright and artificially helpful, as if all she had been describing was car insurance or the weather, instead of genital torture.

'January 16th,' Billy said. 'Afternoon.'

Sandra shook her head. 'Must be crossed wires,' she said. 'I was on tour that week. First paycheque after New Year's is always Scotland, they're gagging for it. Check my online diary if you don't believe me.'

'And there's no way someone else could have gotten in here?' Billy asked. 'You're sure no one has the key?'

'Trust that I take my security more seriously than you can possibly imagine. No one was here.'

'Previous owners?'

'I've owned this flat for fifteen years,' Sandra said.

'Any chance you still have the CCTV from January?'

Sandra shook her head.

'Shit, this is going nowhere.' Buster pushed Billy's shoulder.

'I told you it was too easy.' He withered under the smaller man's glare. 'Sorry, mate,' Buster mumbled.

Billy did not move. 'You said you were in Scotland that week – where?'

'All over,' Sandra said. 'Edinburgh, Inverness, then down the West Coast. Cameron Bridge, Oban, and Glasgow. I would have to check my diary to say exactly where.'

'Check it.'

Sandra threw her hands up. 'Fine.' She took a few moments tapping at her smartphone. 'Here we go. Old online tour diary – Cameron Bridge.' She turned the screen towards the men so they could confirm she was telling the truth.

Billy's pale eyebrows rose. 'Huh.' He leaned to whisper something in Buster's ear, and the big man nodded. 'Could you tell us who you saw when you were there?'

Sandra laughed. 'What part of "client privacy" was unclear? They pay me to do evil things to them, yes. But they are also paying for discretion.'

'You don't pay a call girl to turn up, you pay her to go away,' Billy said. 'Dashiell Hammett, wasn't that?'

'Errol Flynn, actually,' Sandra said. 'As reported by a Holly-wood gossip columnist. So apply the appropriate grain of salt. Either way the sentiment is, mainly, correct.'

'It can't be that hard to find out, anyway,' Buster said. 'After all that Nazi hooker stuff all over the papers, everybody knows where the reviews are. All we have to do is find a tame computer person, maybe that Erykah lady you met last year . . .'

'Actually, it might be harder than you think,' Sandra inter-rupted. 'My clients are not the sort of people who hang around on punter forums comparing breast size and bareback blowjobs.' She sniffed. 'Not that they are better than that or anything, but they have good reason to be paranoid about their proclivities becoming public knowledge. And for what it's worth don't call her a hooker. It makes you sound like trash, not her.'

'Geez, lady, I was just saying.' Buster raised his hands in surrender. 'You don't have to go all Sunday school on me.'

'It's a simple matter of respect,' Sandra said. 'Remember that.'

'Thing is, we were in Scotland then too. So what I'm thinking is, you were in Cameron Bridge, so were we, and someone just happens to call us from your house? Too much of a coincidence for my comfort,' Billy said. Sandra shrugged. 'Are you going back to Scotland soon?'

'As it happens I was interviewing someone this afternoon for a duo tour,' she said. 'The Chinese girl. You probably saw her going out on your way in.'

'You seeing the same clients you saw the last time?'

Sandra snorted. 'Do I look like a mind reader?' She drew a purple varnished nail across her forehead. 'Does it say "Madame Brown: Tarot and Fortunes" up here?'

Seminole Billy nodded. 'Well make arrangements for two more on the road trip,' he said. 'It looks like you ladies just scored yourself a bodyguard and a driver.'

: **28** :

The library is where Denise belongs. After the disastrous party she hits the books with a vengeance. The corrections to her dissertation must be in before the end of the month. She runs dozens of computer simulations of genetic epidemiology over again, checks and rechecks the references in the literature review chapter. During her lunch breaks, she walks out into the library courtyard and unwinds with books on anything to clear her mind. Ancient civilisations one day, Greek mythology the next. It is in the last pages of a dusty hardback she spots a familiar word. Lamia.

Lamia was the queen of Libya and mistress of Zeus. Zeus's long-suffering wife Hera, enraged by the human's desirability to all who saw her, killed Lamia's children. She changed the queen into a demon that fed on souls and killed babies as they slept. Hera tore off Lamia's eyelids so she could never venture into direct light. The unblinking reptilian creature clung to the edges of shadows, ready to devour families, trying to feed the deep hunger inside of her that nothing could fill.

Denise chews an apple slowly as she reads. She recognises now that every painting, every piece of art in the house in Jesmond had some connection to the myth. Dozens of gilt-framed prints and paintings told and retold the myth. Women whose eyes were wide open, never to close. Women encircling men with snake-like limbs, leading children into caves and the underworld, beckoning to the viewer from velvet-draped chaise longues to come closer, closer.

Lamia is the half-snake, half-woman who was too beautiful

to be allowed to live. Denise spends her days finishing her dissertation research and her lunch breaks chasing the story from mythology through art history and poetry. She has been borrowed and revived across many cultures and times but her faces are always similar. She is a temptress, a succubus, a reptile and a vampire. Draper and Waterhouse painted her as a beautiful, milk-skinned woman whose languor was openly sexual. Elizabeth Barrett Browning immortalised her 'moonlighted pallor'. Banished to the shadows forever, Lamia still glows.

Unlike most of the feared women in mythology, Lamia was not a crone or a hag. She was a nightmare in spite of being so desirable. Because she was so desirable. Harlots and courtesans of old adopted her name as a popular tribute, Denise reads.

Denise's favourite version of Lamia is the one in Keats. Lamia, the serpent, takes the form of a human woman. She stands on a road where she knows the beautiful youth Lycius will pass on his way to Corinth. Lycius sees her and falls violently in love. She spins him a tale of her past, of her family obliterated by disease and disaster. Together they walk to where she says she lives. She shows him an abandoned mansion, far grander than any he has ever seen before, though it is in ruin. There they indulge in sweet sin and eschew the company of others. He is obsessed by her, this bewitching woman with the murky past who seems only to exist for his pleasure. She is everything he ever wanted, and many things he did not know he wanted.

Lycius decides they should marry on the eve of the feast of the virgins. It is an enchanted day, when those who are unmarried perform rites that reveal the true name of their beloved. Lamia tells him there is no point in a public celebration of their love, and anyway, she has no one to invite. Isn't love alone enough to sustain them? But Lycius feels the pain of being apart from his family and the only world he has ever known. So she agrees – on the condition that Lycius will not invite his oldest friend, the philosopher Apollonius, to the feast.

Lamia summons daemon servants to decorate the banquet hall and furnish it with rich foods of every kind. They hang tapestries on the walls, arrange vases of peacock feathers and fresh flowers. They lay silver platters of roasted meats and candied fruits, olives and capers. Mead and hibiscus sherbet are poured from amphorae the size of men. When Lycius' guests arrive they marvel at the scene. None of them knew there was such a magnificent palace in Corinth. Hiding at the back of the crowd is Apollonius. He has come uninvited.

At the height of the wedding feast, Apollonius makes his way to the head table. Being much older than his friend Lycius and partly blind, he has not yet seen the bride. He begins to stare at Lamia, to examine this seemingly perfect woman. Lamia starts to turn, literally, green. Lycius asks what is wrong; she says nothing. The feasting and the music stop in the awkward atmosphere. Turning to Apollonius, Lycius commands him to stop staring at Lamia.

Apollonius lashes out. He has saved young Lycius from every danger to cross his path in his short life, only to watch him become the prey of an enchanted serpent? He shouts at Lamia: 'A serpent!' At the words, she takes back her true shape and slithers through a crack in the stone wall. At that moment Lycius falls to the floor dead.

Denise closes the book. Her mind is troubled by questions. She realises she doesn't know anything about Miri from any source other than Miri herself. She is such a blank canvas, so free of attachments, even though she appears to be living in the same city where she was born and raised. Growing up in a stifling ultra-Orthodox family explains some things but not all. In spite of surrounding herself with people, none of her friends or acquaintances knew Miri before the year she and Denise met. That can't be possible, surely. Nobody leaves no footprint.

Miri told Denise that her family had mourned her as if she had died. But the dead don't simply disappear, Denise knows this first-hand. Years after the tsunami, Darwin is still present in her family's life. A photograph, a news story. A forgotten note in his scrawled, pointy handwriting falling out of the back of a book. Every bank statement Denise receives, every bill she pays. In phone calls and cards from her grandmother in Macau. The empty place at the Christmas dinner table. No one is traceless. Especially not the dead.

Denise is disturbed by the sudden intrusion of a thought she can't shake. What if the story had been told to her the wrong way around? What if it wasn't Miri who was dead to her family, but they who were dead to her?

She goes for a run. It has been weeks since she last talked to Archie. She doesn't know what to tell him. I saw you getting a blowjob from my best friend at the party? It seems such a banal thing to say, the kind of betrayal that might happen in a soap opera, not the quasi-violent scene she witnessed. And then what?

She decides to take a path through the Dene that day. At the halfway point she slows and stops to tighten a bandana tied around her forehead. She draws her chin in, sets her eyes on the ground in front of her, and takes off. As she begins to speed up, she runs straight into someone.

'Why don't you look where you're—'

'Hey! Get out of the—'

'Sorry!' She is looking right at Miri. Denise jumps back, surprised. 'What are you doing here?'

'What are you doing here?' Miri says at the same time. To her surprise Miri is smiling. It seems genuine. 'It's good to see you,' she says.

'Thanks,' Denise says. She doesn't know what else to say.

'If you're almost done running maybe we could . . .' Miri nods in the direction of Lamia House. 'I mean you could drop by for a cup of coffee after you're done. If you want.'

Denise bites her lip. Miri looks luminous. Innocent almost. Fruit-ripe, the skin of her cheeks glowing pink from the sunshine. Even in that moment, remembering everything that happened, Denise cannot bring herself to turn and walk away. Not without saying something. She owes her that much, right? 'I'm pretty much done,' she lies.

Miri waits as Denise moves through her stretches. The walk to Lamia House is silent. Denise keeps to the edge of the pavement, leaving almost a body's width between them. She tries to think of what she will say and how she will say it. *I know you know I saw you. I want you to know I'm making a commitment to Archie and I don't care what you think.* She is anxious. What if Miri laughs at her? What if she picks all of Denise's carefully composed words apart, challenges her to defend them?

Miri stops suddenly on the path, stoops, the bright circle of her plaited hair a crown on her head. 'Come look at this,' she says. Denise leans down, and sees her pluck a mushroom from the dirt. It is velvety and purple with deeply ridged gills. 'Amethyst deceiver,' Miri says. 'The warlock mushroom.'

It is delicate and deadly looking. Miri's fingers tear into its flesh. The mushroom is as purple inside as it is out, a bright, dangerous little thing. She pops it into her mouth and smiles.

'No!' Denise lunges forward, but Miri dodges her and laughs.

'Silly. It's edible. Warlock is an old Norse word, the caller of spirits.' Like the forbidden nightjar, the passion of Catherine of Siena, Denise is amazed at how she knows these things. Where would a normal person learn any of it? Where would Miri, her access to the world once carefully controlled by her family, have done so? 'Mushrooms are very important,' Miri explains. 'Knowing the good ones from the bad ones kept my people alive in the forests, the many times we had to flee killers in Europe.' Denise supposes she means Jews, but she never heard of Jews living in the woods, and is afraid of seeming stupid if she asks.

Inside the house the kitchen is bright, the windows of the conservatory angled to catch the spring sun. It could be any morning of the dozens Denise has woken up here. Miri pulls mugs out of the cupboard and sets a coffee percolator to brewing. If Miri notices her awkwardness at being here again, she doesn't mention it.

'Milk?' Denise shakes her head. 'Oh right, I remember now. Black like your soul.' Miri laughs her deep laugh. She pours the coffee. Denise's eyes crawl over Miri's face, taking in every faint line, every pore. Somewhere between the top of the mug and the bottom, Denise's anxiety begins to shift. What she feels isn't nervousness, now. It is something else.

Is this really the same woman she had obsessed over for months? Miri's world is so flat, so one-dimensional. She goes out. She parties. She makes new friends as quickly and easily as she loses old ones. Has it always been this way, and she never noticed? Has Denise's life been so stagnant that this woman was the most exciting thing to have happened to her in years?

'You OK?' Miri smiles. Her little pearly teeth, rounded and separate. The way her pointed chin draws up when she waits for an answer, exposing her neck. 'You seem quiet.'

'No, I just . . . it's nice to see you.'

From the first time she met Miri, when they changed clothes, everything about their friendship had felt fated, electric. Irresistible. Simply being around Miri made her bristle with interest and envy and lust. The woman's very existence was like an allergen landing in a sterile room.

Miri swirls the liquid in her mug and looks up through her pale reddish lashes.

Denise suddenly feels a sharp pain, like something cracking inside her. A growing rage flooding her insides.

She realises that she hates Miri. And she realises that feeling has been building for a long time. The strong emotion coming over her in waves, it is feral, it is vicious. She had been letting her life spin out of control, in thrall to someone who had no idea what that was worth. Denise realises she hates Miri for the things she has done, but also for all the things Denise hasn't done. She hates herself for taking so long to see it. It is her fault as much as it is Miri's. Not only for being tricked, but for allowing herself to be tricked. And none of the things she can say, that she plans to say, can change anything that happened.

She realises she will not feel better until she hurts this woman.

'I'm sorry, I . . . I shouldn't be here,' Denise says. She puts her mug on the kitchen counter, too hard. 'I have to go.'

Miri sets her mug on the counter next to Denise's. 'Yeah,

I guess so,' she says. She turns and crosses her arms under her breasts. 'If that's what you want. I mean . . . I hoped we could straighten things out between you and me. After what happened.'

'You want to talk?' Denise's heartbeat hammers in her neck.

Miri shakes her head. She reaches over and loosens the bandana around Denise's hair. Her fingertips brush the skin by her ears and Denise shivers. Miri's mouth is parted slightly, her breath smells of coffee. 'You should have a hot bath before your muscles get cold,' she says, and starts to rub the base of Denise's neck. 'I need a bath too.'

Denise feels her body responding in spite of herself. The touch of Miri's fingers sends shockwaves down her, hardens her nipples, makes her breath shallow and quick. She closes her eyes and moans. Now Miri's lips are close to hers, firm and silky. Denise wants to bite through them as if they are meat, as if they are fruit.

With much effort Denise lifts her hands and removes Miri's from her neck. 'No,' she says, and steps towards the kitchen door. Miri moves forward to stop her from leaving. She presses her body against Denise, who feels the warmth of her flesh through their clothes where their legs, their stomachs, their chests touch.

'It was always you I wanted.' Miri's breath is hot in her ear. Her hands slip around Denise's waist, under her fleece top, and travel up the crevice of her spine. Her fingertips rub the damp skin under the band of the sports bra. Her hands inch around Denise's sides, brushing the crease beneath her breasts.

Everything feels slow, as if she is underwater, as if in a dream. When she was a teenager Denise had her first wet dreams, flashes of scenes that always ended with her waking up, sweating and twisted in the bedclothes, before reaching orgasm. She would cry in the dark at the pain and frustration. This feels to her like those did. As if a spell of sleep has been cast. As if she will wake up any moment and be alone, clutching the sheets, and Miri will be gone.

'Not like this,' Denise says. She feels a throb inside her pants, an aching pulse of needing to be needed. The walls of Lamia House draw in like lungs. And this is not a dream, this is real. She knows whatever else may happen she will be haunted by this woman.

'You miss me, don't you?' Miri asks. She presses her body more firmly against Denise's. 'I miss you too.' Her voice drops to a sinuous whisper and she rocks her thigh side to side against Denise's crotch. She is rubbing her arms up and down Denise's sides. 'Let me lather you. Let me scrub you.'

'No!' Denise says, the hate raging in her throat. 'Not like that.' She grabs Miri's hands, pulling them out from under her top. 'Like this.' She reaches up and roughly grabs the knot of hair at the back of Miri's head, pulls her surprised face to hers.

Miri gasps. Denise leans back, pulls Miri's top off over her head. She rubs her face in the scent of her sun-ripe skin, the dried sweat, the sour and sharp smell under her arms. She runs her tongue down the salty line of fine hairs on Miri's stomach. She rolls the tights away from her waist, and buries her nose in the wet scrap of fabric covering her lover's rich oyster pussy.

: 29 :

There was no reason to feel that she was being disloyal, Harriet told herself. She placed the coffees on a tray and selected a table for two nearest the window, with a view of the high street. This was not a date.

She was going to AA meetings regularly. Harriet had still not told Fiona and wavered about whether she should. They had not had a conversation defining their relationship. Were they exclusive, or not? Not that it mattered; in a small town like Cameron Bridge. It wasn't as if Harriet was overwhelmed with dating options. In any case she had nothing to feel ashamed about. She was taking control of her own recovery by going to meetings. And she was only seeing someone for coffee. Someone from her meetings, no less. This was good. She needed friends outside of work and outside of romantic relationships. If Fiona had known, she surely would have agreed.

So why did she feel so guilty when Lucy walked in the door? Harriet jumped up and waved, almost spilling her latte.

'Sorry about that, giant queue at the bank.' Lucy shook the rain off her jacket. She had dyed her hair again recently. The bleached tips of her black bob were now a jewel-bright royal blue.

'I got you a cappuccino,' Harriet said. 'Extra large.' Harriet worried for her; Lucy always looked slightly cold, being so thin. Even wrapped in heavy jumpers and jeans her elbows and knees showed through as sharp as her cheekbones. 'Thought I might as well get an order in before they get bogged down with the lunch crowd. Hope the coffee hasn't gone too cold.'

'Thank you.' Lucy raised the wide, steaming cup to her lips and took a sip. The foam left a little moustache that she licked off. 'No, it's perfect. God, it feels so good to get out of there,' she said and leaned back in the chair. 'I swear I thought Hughena was never going to finish talking.'

'Right?' Harriet smiled. Deconstructing what went on in the church hall after a meeting was one of her favourite parts of seeing Lucy. Harriet had gained in confidence, speaking up once or twice during the meetings, but was more content to listen. It was a relief to be in a room with people who knew what she was going through, and hearing their stories and the readings from the AA literature was helping her. She was sure of it. But at the same time people were people, and some of those people didn't know when to give up the floor. They enjoyed the attention the way Harriet enjoyed staying in the background. 'If I have to hear one more story about her son's move to Inverness . . .'

'Shh, shh.' Lucy leaned forward and laid her hand on Harriet's arm. 'Guess who just walked in.' She sat back, and her voice returned to normal volume. 'Anyway, how's work?'

'Fine,' Harriet said. Lucy raised an eyebrow. 'Rubbish actually. The council is trying to push the mortuary assistant out of his job. They put out the advert this week.'

'I saw that,' Lucy said. 'I subscribed to a job search website when I moved here, and it turned up in my email. The experience they're asking for is almost zero.' She chuckled. 'Even I'd qualify.'

'Iain is refusing to reapply for his own job, obviously, but he is going to have to interview whoever takes his place. Which is horrible. And they've started proceedings to have the building condemned, and . . .' Harriet sighed. 'I don't even know what to do any more. What I can do? I don't like it here, I can't lie about that. But for it to end like this? It isn't right. Not for Iain, not for the facility, not for Cameron Bridge.'

'Is there nothing that will change their minds?'

Harriet shrugged. 'I can't say we didn't see it coming. When they started cutting the library budgets, the writing was on the wall, wasn't it? The dead don't matter as much as the living. But it is still a travesty. Privatising the service might be a slow-moving disaster, but it's still a disaster. And one fuck-up is all it takes for people to lose faith in the system.'

Harriet had come clean with Lucy about what happened in Leeds. There were all sorts of excuses she could have made, but the truth did not change. Her standards at work had fallen. This was as much to do with her drinking as with the number of cases she was expected to handle as a junior pathologist. It didn't matter as much in the early stages of her career; senior pathologists were around to pick up on any errors. The problems came when she was promoted and did not change her working style. The laziness had become ingrained. As had the drinking.

She got away with it for several years. She collaborated in research, published a few academic papers, and gave evidence that was highly regarded on important inquests. She keynoted at a forensic science symposium in Las Vegas one year and shared a table at the conference dinner with the pathologist who performed Marilyn Monroe's post-mortem. She met her previous partner and they bought a house together. Producers from the BBC contacted her, hoping to shadow her at work for several weeks as the basis for a new crime drama. In public, things were going swimmingly. In private she felt like a fraud who was about to be discovered at any moment. Her drinking got worse. But her career continued to move from strength to strength.

Until it hit a brick wall. Her life in Leeds had not simply fallen apart, it imploded. An appeal against a shaken baby murder conviction uncovered the fact that her reports were written days, and sometimes weeks, after the initial post-mortems. She had no notes from the PMs, had made no voice recordings of the autopsies the way most pathologists did. The conviction in question was overturned and an appeal begun.

Harriet refused to defend herself. There would have been no

point. She had been told by police that the case was as good as in the bag and her contribution was simply a formality, but that had clearly been an exaggeration. It was no excuse for the gaping holes in her reports. Her lack of organisation spoke for itself. A fitness to practice panel convened by the GMC issued only a reprimand, but cautioned that 'professional misconduct at this lower end of the spectrum nevertheless warrants close attention going forward'. A dozen more people appealed their convictions as a result of her errors. She resigned her post in Leeds simply to save them the effort of firing her.

She was not sure what to expect when she told Lucy – not sure, in fact, whether Lucy didn't already know. The scandal had been all over the papers at the time. But Lucy listened, and did not judge. Afterwards Harriet wondered what she had been so worried about. Admitting it to someone else, or to herself? It felt good to say it, in fact. To get it off her chest.

'What about the high-profile cases?' Lucy asked. 'Surely after that recent murder the council won't be able to justify shutting the morgue. Not when you have the police depending on your work.'

'If only.' Harriet sighed. 'The Newcastle police have claimed it as their own. Police Scotland hardly got a look in. And they're convinced they got their man down south. Cameron Bridge was just a dumping point in this story.'

Lucy looked sceptical. 'You think they arrested the wrong person?'

'Maybe, maybe not. I think there is more to this than meets the eye,' Harriet said. 'They found DNA evidence in his car – fine. But from what I understand, the car was also left unattended for several days.'

'You think someone could have planted it there,' Lucy said. 'He was framed?'

'It's not impossible, is it? The fact that a sex worker who had ties to politicians turns up dead seems like more than a convenient coincidence to me. Not to mention the way the information was released to the press. Someone was holding all the trump cards in their hand and just choosing the right time to lay them down.'

Lucy's face turned serious. 'I'm not saying you can't be right,' she said. 'I don't want you to think that I don't hear you. But I was born around the time Tito died. To me, a conspiracy has a different feel. What motivation would anybody have to do something like this, anyway?'

'I know how it sounds. Believe me, I do. But the more I look at the story – and I know this is crackpot territory – the more I think something is wrong.'

'Such as?'

'Such as, the police seem to have been spectacularly uninterested in any other theory. Isn't it a tiny bit possible they are missing someone more obvious?' The more she spoke, the more Harriet was aware of how insubstantial it all sounded, but she couldn't stop herself. 'Of course, now that Brant's dead, well.'

'And what does your girlfriend think of this?' Lucy interrupted.

The way Lucy had said *your girlfriend* was pointed, and Harriet winced. 'Fiona thinks I'm wasting my time,' she admitted. 'It's not her job any more and it isn't mine. There are other things I could be focusing on. The future of the morgue, my personal life, recovery . . . and you know, she isn't wrong.'

'You might be obsessing over this for no other reason than it takes your mind off everything else.' Lucy swirled the last of her coffee in the cup. 'You have no control over your job, the people around you, or your addiction, but this is something you feel like you can contribute to.'

Harriet gulped. What she said rang true. Very true. 'Maybe it is, yes.'

'And you don't feel you are getting support from the people closest to you. Your girlfriend, for example.' Harriet nodded. 'There is a reason that they recommend not starting a relationship in your first year of recovery. Everything is so intense at the start, when you're trying to get dry. It has a way of making other things in your life feel more . . .' Lucy waved her hand, searching for the word. 'Important than they really are.'

'I guess.' Part of what had attracted Harriet to Fiona was how sane, how stable she was. Surely it was better to have someone like that in your life than not to? But she had to accept that Lucy had been doing this far longer than she had. It was still early days for Harriet. Both in the recovery and the relationship. 'What do you think?'

Lucy took a deep breath before she answered. 'I don't know,' she finally said. 'It sounds to me as if maybe Fiona's right.' Harriet's face, verging on hangdog, dropped even more. 'Don't take this the wrong way. It is not a reflection on you! Or on your intelligence. At all. You're obsessing. We've all been there. You can't let this case go, and it is nothing to do with the police or the murder itself. You've made this personal because everything else in your life is too much to deal with. As far as the relationship goes – it isn't my place to say.' She looked up at Harriet, her eyes sad. 'If I were in your shoes, a new girlfriend would be too much for me.'

The truth hurt. Harriet gulped. She wasn't ready, yet, to give up on either the case or the relationship. 'What shall I do?'

'There is no one-stop solution. I would start with self-care,' Lucy said and winked. 'Stop punishing yourself for things you have no control over, take time out to look after yourself. Put Harriet first for once. Spend more time doing the things that make you happy. Forget about all this conspiracy stuff.'

What made her happy? Her work didn't, had not done for years. She did not like where she lived. She had spent so long focussed on her career that any hobbies and activities she used to pursue were now long in the past, and as nice as it was being – whatever she was – to Fiona, she was wary of putting too much into a relationship without some idea of where things might be going. The only thing she had enjoyed since moving to Cameron Bridge was drinking. And that was now off the table. 'What do you suggest?'

Lucy chuckled. 'It isn't about what I want, you have to think of what you want. What makes you happy?'

A question to which Harriet had no answer at all.

: 30 :

Morag Munro gloried in those few precious hours on the sleeper train when the route swerved beyond the mountains before turning south into Cameron Bridge. Where the most important issue of the day was whether breakfast to her first class berth was on time, or not. Whether there was enough coffee for her to get in her customary four cups before the train slowed to a juddering halt at the tiny Highlands station.

She finished breakfast and reluctantly switched her mobile back on. After almost a minute spent finding the network – Cameron Bridge was civilisation, but only just – the phone started buzzing with incoming messages. Twelve missed calls from Delphine Barnett.

Morag rolled her eyes. If Delphine was calling, it meant that someone else had suddenly dropped dead, or that Morag was about to. Metaphorically speaking. Morag enjoyed a well-deserved downfall as much as the next person, but rarely had she met anyone who twisted knives with such glee as Delphine.

She took a deep breath and hit dial. The phone rang and rang; so much for the keen caller, then. She was about to hang up when Delphine finally answered, breathless. 'Morag, thank you! But I've just got off the line with your Arjun and he assured me there's nothing in it,' she gushed.

'Ah, perfect,' Morag said. She exited the station and darted into the tunnel towards the Cameron Bridge high street.

Morag had no idea what Delphine was referring to or what Arj would have said, but no doubt he had deployed one of the usual responses to media storms. Still, better not to reveal she was still outside the loop on what was happening. 'I've been on personal time this morning; has anything more happened overnight?'

'Not a lot,' Delphine said. 'Popular opinion seems to be that Woad bit off more than he can chew, and blaming you for the steer is about as credible as an eyewitness report of the Second Coming. Arjun explained how you cold-shouldered him at the BBC on the night Brant died. I can believe he'd be upset about that, but to stoop so low . . .'

Oh, that. 'Yes, Mr Woad is not noted for keeping the tone elevated, is he?' Morag said. 'But what would you expect from a new media cowboy? He has never had to toe the line that real writers such as yourself at the papers must do.' Not that Morag had high regard for journalists of any stripe, much less Delphine Barnett, who swanned into a cushy column job for a broadsheet. But there was no harm in buttering her up.

'Right?' Delphine chirped. She paused. It was a pause Morag knew well from Delphine's days as one of Brant's advisors. It was the pause that meant, *I am about to ask a question with which I hope to trap you.* Morag smiled; it was good to know some people never changed, even if their jobs did. 'I assume, in any case, there were no emails between you and him, and nothing more to say there.'

'No, obviously not,' Morag said. 'There may have been a group email sent from the producers of *Newsnight* to all of the guests beforehand on the night of Lionel's . . . unfortunate passing, but apart from that? I've hardly spoken to the man. He very much gave the impression of being someone to whom the less is said, the better.'

'OK if I quote that?'

'Please do,' Morag said, knowing full well she would whatever the response was.

'Brilliant,' Delphine purred. 'Well, I'll leave you to get on with your day. Ta-ra!'

Arj was waiting at the office with a pile of local papers and a cafetiere of strong coffee. He did not even raise his head when she came in. 'Libel suit,' he said simply.

'Coyle? On Woad?'

'Served yesterday.' Arj peeked out of the door to make certain no one was in earshot. 'Lengthy piece up on RMB. Luckily, a few people managed to grab the text in screenshots before the site itself went down.'

'Oh my.' Morag couldn't help but smile. 'Site down already? I had no idea the wheels turned so quickly.' She had been on the receiving end of the odd threatening letter from m'learned friends over the years, though a strongly worded letter remind-ing the senders about Parliamentary privilege was usually enough to scatter the bottom-feeders. And where that didn't do it, a reference to *Arkell v Pressdram* usually did.

'Coyle's not stupid. He laid it on the internet service provider, not Woad himself. I think even he might have been surprised at the speed they reacted.'

'Well, it couldn't happen to a nicer bloke. Which reminds me, I just hung up with Delphine . . .'

'Woad was saying you were the source of his intel,' Arj said. He paused. 'Obviously, you were in no way involved, and I'm sure whoever did it – if indeed this isn't some fevered invention straight from the mind of Woad himself – would not be so silly as to leave a paper trail.'

'Indeed, anyone who did that would be in for it,' she said. 'Is it making a splash?'

Arj snorted. 'Not even. He started a hashtag, JeSuisCommo-dus, and it didn't even trend in London. No, this is going to be sinking to the bottom of the pile rather quickly, I expect,' Arjun said. 'A couple of thinkpieces at most. Without his forums on tap, no one can be bothered any more.'

'Any movement in the leadership polls?'

'You lead is widening,' Arjun said. Morag's advantage had narrowed precipitously in the days following Brant's suicide. The Coyle rumours about sexual harassment seemed to bring that to a halt, and start to reverse the trend. 'All we need is to hold on to this, and you're in the clear.'

'Well that's a relief,' she said. 'Anything else I need to know?'

Arjun sniffed. 'Rather lengthy addendum on the Woad post, speculating that you were involved with that Media Mouse story last year,' he said. 'Obvious bunk. Sub-David Icke stuff. Down already of course, but repeated in a few places.'

'Incredible,' Morag said. For the most part people had forgotten her name was ever linked to a story about a female politician having an affair with a radio producer. It was true, of course. But she knew that her public image precluded anyone actually believing it. No one could imagine her having sex full stop, much less cheating on her husband. Anyway the story had been the inspiration she needed to jettison that dead weight of a boyfriend, so all was well that ended well.

'You won't want to see his tweets,' Arjun said. 'At last count it was twelve in a row swearing revenge on you. Ugly stuff. But suffice it to say, the longer he goes on, the more unhinged he looks.'

'Is he getting abusive? Perhaps contact Twitter and have him banned?' Morag was vaguely aware she possessed a social media account, but she had never used it directly.

'Best not,' Arjun advised. 'It might give some credence to his nonsense about being silenced. The social justice crowd will report him; no need for you to be involved.'

'Thank you for bringing me up to date,' she said. 'You're a star.'

Arjun handed her a folder of briefing notes. Under the day's agenda were prinouts of the latest polls and projections. The morning's news was yet to be processed, of course, but her lead looked safe for now. Once the membership's ballots were tallied it was surely only a formality before she was confirmed as new leader. Morag nodded, satisfied.

Arjun fussed with pamphlets by the door, studiously avoiding unlocking the front and letting constituents in until exactly one minute past ten. 'So, I've been thinking about my candidacy,' Morag said.

'Oh?' Arjun looked at her and smiled, his face a perfect, friendly blank.

'This has all come on rather quickly, hasn't it? Only a month ago it would have taken nothing short of a crowbar and dynamite to force Brant out of office. And now this. I can't say I'm not pleased. But it certainly is a surprise, the way things have happened.'

'Is that so?' He bustled over to a filing cabinet and flipped through a bunch of folders.

'Given that no formal plan was ever discussed. Everything seems simply to have . . . dropped from the heavens into my lap, I suppose. When all is said and done, no one will be able to say anyone was responsible for Brant's downfall more than Brant himself.'

'A good thing, if you ask me,' Arjun said. 'Time to dig up that absentee husband of yours. The press will be wanting photocalls soon.'

'Well quite.' Morag closed the folder. Her fingers drummed the desk. 'One thing still piques my curiosity, you understand.'

'What's that?'

Morag thought about how best to phrase her next sentence. 'Just how a small-town murder managed to be connected to one of the most high-profile politicians in the country,' she said. 'You would think, wouldn't you, that when a prostitute turns up dead the police and press would have no interest in digging any deeper. And – how shall we put it? – as exciting as call girls are, the press hardly have the manpower, much less the wherewithal, to assemble a story like this so neatly. Not without a leak. Especially not for a site as underresourced as RMB. Someone put in a lot of time doing that. For not entirely obvious motives.'

Arjun turned and crossed his arms over his chest. 'Yes, it certainly is a mystery. But, as my dear departed mother used to say, don't go looking a gift horse in the mouth.'

Morag nodded. She had not expected him to confirm it directly, and he did not disappoint. But she still had questions. 'Answer me this, Arj – how on earth did you ever pull this off?'

Arjun stepped towards her desk decisively and Morag felt, suddenly, in some kind of danger. He jerked his arm out and she flinched, but he was picking up the folded newspaper on her desk. 'Do you remember the first time I came to Cameron Bridge? One of the lessons I learned,' he said as he unfurled the local paper. 'If you want to find out what really goes on in a small town you have to keep up with the news. Maybe, in some ways, I became a true Highland lad after all.'

Morag nodded. 'I see,' she said. 'And the Nazi business?' The fact that photographs existed surprised her considerably less than that they had come to light at such an opportune time. She was not inclined to believe, she could be so lucky without some karmic balance in store for her eventually.

Arjun simply raised an eyebrow. 'I'm more than a pretty face,' he said with a practised certainty that sent a chill up her spine. 'I am also a very observant set of eyes. And a very sensitive pair of ears. Don't ever forget that, Madam Leader. Everyone has skeletons. Even you.'

: 31 :

'Hey,' Sandra said. She was fully made-up, in contrast to her casual clothes. She pointed at Denise's small overnight bag. 'Is that all you're bringing?' Denise nodded. 'Damn. I wish I could pack that light. Oh!' She snapped her fingers. 'That reminds me. I know the answer is probably no, but do you have any tapes?'

'Cassette . . . tapes?'

'You know, music,' she said. 'I mean someone your age, you probably don't even know what a cassette even is . . .'

'I have a few. Hang on.'

Denise ran upstairs and dragged a cardboard box out of the back of her wardrobe. A car horn sounded outside, tap tap. Sandra shouted that they had to go. She didn't have time to check what any of it was, just grabbed what was closest to hand of Darwin's old tapes.

Denise locked up and walk out to the kerb. She was surprised to see a weathered old Mercedes idling there, a real banger. It was not what she imagined Sandra would drive. There was someone else in the driver's seat. Sandra hadn't mentioned anyone else coming on tour. Maybe it was another girl. Fine, but that would make it harder to try to prise information about Miri out of her.

'Howdy.' The man in the front seat nodded at Denise as she opened the car door. He was a craggy-looking, skinny guy on the wrong end of middle age. He wore all black, like a preacher from a spaghetti Western. 'Better get in fast. Looks like you got some real curtain twitchers in your neighbourhood,' he drawled.

Denise hesitated and clutched her bag to her chest. She could run back into the house, lock the door, this could all be over. *No*, she scolded herself. *Do it for Miri.*

Denise slid onto the seat and closed the door. He did not bother to introduce himself and Sandra didn't offer his name, either. She supposed this must be Sandra's pimp.

The radio was on. Some news phone-in show. A syrup-voiced woman took calls from bored housewives and cabbies caught in traffic with their takes on the stories of the day. 'I brought tapes,' she offered, and laid the handful of cassettes on the seat next to her.

'Great. Put on some music.' The driver punched the accelerator with one crocodile boot and zoomed out of the Wallsend housing estate onto the A19. Within minutes they were on the A1 heading north and one of Darwin's mixtapes was on. Blues, mainly, heavy on anyone with 'Blind' in their names. At least he's driving in the right direction, Denise thought.

It was not, in short, how she expected to start the weekend.

Denise had opened the bookmarked pages she was working with on Thursday morning, expecting to get cracking on her spreadsheet. But to her surprise the pages were gone – all of them. Link after link came back with an Unable To Connect error. The Rome Must Burn website had been taken offline. Panicking, she clicked through and tried her other bookmarks. Miri's escort profiles were also gone.

She tried to find them on the Internet Archive, but like most adult sites, the profiles had code to prevent them from being indexed by search engines. The forums, because they had been behind a paywall, were impossible to get at all. Denise searched frantically, her heart sinking. It felt like a bad dream.

According to the news, Rome Must Burn's web host had been hit with the threat of a libel suit after the Vernon Coyle stories. Rather than get on the wrong side of a politician, the ISP had taken everything down. Miri's profiles, she supposed, had been removed as a matter of course by the review site's owners.

Denise squeezed her hands so hard the nails started to cut into her palms. She had screwed this up big time. She should have taken screenshots of the pages while they were still live and archived them herself. She couldn't believe she had been so careless, especially with something that was a daily part of her job. What was the first rule of data curation? Have three backups. One local, one at another site, and one in the cloud. It was an integral part of any research project; if this had been a work issue, she would have been in real trouble. As it was she felt even worse.

Apart from the news stories that lifted the escort photos and a handful of other pictures, none of the content was reproduced, only linked to. Denise gritted her teeth – so the news organisations were no better when it came to how they handled their sources – but in the end, blaming them went only so far. She had fucked up.

The tour to Cameron Bridge was all she had left. She needed more than ever to make this work.

The driver was careful to stay at ten miles above the speed limit, she noticed, neither too fast nor too slow. The car might have looked a wreck but he handled it as if he was taking his mum's treasured wheels out for a spin. Clearly he was someone used to flying under the radar.

The country and blues mixtape she had put on was the only sound in the car for ages. As each crackling song came on, four-string banjos plucking away, the man snorted. He tapped his thumbs on the steering wheel to 'Shuckin' Sugar Blues'. He looked at her. 'Where the hell did you get these?'

'They're my brother's,' she said.

'Your brother's.' He shook his head as if she had told him a very old joke. 'You or your brother ever shucked sugar?'

'No.'

'My stepdad worked the sugar plantations,' the man said. 'Hand cut it. Seasonal labour, down in Pahokee for Domino. Hard work. Jamaicans did it for years, too. Doesn't pay shit.

They got machines to do it now. He used to make shin guards out of oil cans so the scythes didn't cut his legs. We would get the cane tops as a snack, chew them till there was nothing left but the fibre. That was good. If you had molasses to dip 'em in, even better.'

'Cool,' Denise said. He was lost in whatever memory the song had shaken loose. She slipped her phone out of her bag and surreptitiously texted Sandra in the back. *Who's the creepy guy? I didn't think you had a pimp* and pressed send.

A buzz came from inside the driver's leather jacket. He withdrew a sleek, rose gold iPhone and glanced down at the screen. It was Sandra's phone. Denise's heart caught in her throat. Fuck.

The driver put on an indicator and pulled into a lay-by. She felt a cold sweat break out on her body. Now what? Maybe he was going to beat her up, or worse. Denise crept her right hand under her left arm and rested it on the door handle. When the car slowed down enough, she could make a jump for it. And then what? She looked at her shoes, the walking boots she had bought with Miri and never worn since. They were stiff, the leather unbroken. They would be difficult to run in. But she was fit and fast and would have a chance. The car rolled to a stop and the driver killed the engine.

To her surprise, the man chuckled. The sound was low and dry, almost reptilian. He held the phone screen over his shoulder so Sandra could read the text Denise had sent on it.

Sandra broke into a laugh. 'Oh, honey,' she said. 'I'm so sorry. I didn't introduce you to Billy and Buster. My bad.'

'Billy . . . and?' Denise looked over her shoulder, but as far as she could see there were only three people in the car, including herself.

'He's in the boot,' Billy said. 'It's a long story.'

Denise did not like the sound of a body in the boot. 'It's a long way to Cameron Bridge. I have time for a story.'

Billy glanced at Sandra, who shrugged. 'Well, go on,' she said. 'It's not as if you told me why he rides in the back either.'

Billy turned the ignition and pulled the Merc back onto the

road. 'He almost got done for a bomb job down in Archway a few years back, so he keeps it incognito.' Billy's pale eyes flicked sideways, and Denise gulped. 'He's not what you'd call easy to miss in a crowd.'

'So you're not her pimp then,' Denise said.

'Hell no he's not my pimp,' Sandra said. 'I only met these two last week. Same day I met you, in fact. No, they came to me about a little . . . side job in Cameron Bridge. Seeing as we were all headed up the same way, it seemed silly not to grab a lift.'

Denise tried to keep calm as the miles rolled by but it was difficult. Something about Sandra's manner seemed off. If she said this Billy person wasn't a pimp, then he wasn't. But Denise had a feeling she wasn't telling the whole truth either.

She is fifteen. A two-day school trip: one day walking around listening to a geologist bore on about igneous and metamorphic whatever. The second day they go a few more miles up the road to Alton Towers. Excitement is high; everyone is talking about what they are going to do, how much junk food they are going to eat.

Inside the park she hovers at the edge of Darwin and his friends at first while people suggest which rollercoasters they should go on. 'Runaway Mine Train,' she says, loudly, almost shouting. His friends look at her, silent at first, that's a baby ride, is she joking? Then they laugh and run off to join the queue for Nemesis.

Deserted, she buys a bag of doughnuts. Hot and sugared and six in a bag. She munches through the first three and starts to feel a bit sick. She tries to throw the rest away but the bins are surrounded by clouds of wasps, so she is stuck with the greasy bag.

'Gis a doughnut,' a voice says. A boy. He looks older than her, his hair cut so it falls across his eyes. She senses immediately that this stranger is exactly the sort of person who would beat up smaller kids for dinner money, so she hands the bag over. To her surprise he sits down next to her.

His name is Geoff. He's from Stafford. His school is here, too, but he took off on his own. Denise nods. He does not seem, yet, to have realised her status in the pecking order, how many levels of coolness someone like him is above someone like her, so she says nothing. He looks at her from time to time and watches her reactions. She lets him talk and talk. She is afraid to say the wrong thing so she says nothing,

The only boys she knows – apart from her own brother, obviously – are his friends. Denise is tolerated because of Darwin. Her brother tries to explain that the key to fitting in is not trying too hard. 'But you always work hard,' she says.

'Trying hard and working hard aren't the same thing,' he says, which she doesn't understand.

Geoff licks doughnut sugar off his short, wide fingers. 'Wanna snog?' he says, and because Denise doesn't know what to say, she nods. He takes her hand and they wait in the queue for the Haunted House. Standing next to each other, she realises they are the same height and she feels ashamed, sure now is when he will realise what she really is, but he puts his arm over her shoulder and strokes her neck anyway. Once inside and in the dark he reaches for her. His mouth is sugary, his tongue probes the edges of her gums and the roof of her mouth. She doesn't know what to do, is this it? In between snogging his hot breath in her ear says he likes her, she is 'cool' and 'doesn't talk too much'. Her knee brushes his, he grabs her hand and puts it on his crotch. He is hard. She pulls away but he shrugs and strokes the back of her neck for the rest of the ride.

Outside she sees Darwin's back in the doughnut queue. 'I have to go,' she says.

Geoff nods and shrugs again. 'That was cool,' he says. She wonders for a moment if she should give him her phone number, but what would be the point? London is miles from Stafford. He would only have to ring once, hear her mother's thick accent on the line, and realise she isn't the girl he thinks she is, she isn't cool. So she runs away.

On the way home, Darwin keeps looking at her. He senses

something is different, and asks where she disappeared to. He was looking for her for over an hour. He even missed Nemesis. 'Nothing,' she says, and stares out of the window of the minibus. 'Nothing happened.' It is the first time she ever keeps a secret from him.

'Have you been to Scotland before?' she asked Billy.

'Couple of times,' he said. 'Jobs here and there.' A long pause. She waited for him to expand on that, but he didn't. What did he mean by jobs? Robbing people? Dealing drugs? Or worse? 'How about you?'

'First time,' she said. 'I always wanted to go, but I never did.' It was meant to be Miri who took her. In a strange sort of way she was going now because of Miri. She gulped.

'First time for a lot of things for you this weekend, huh?' Sandra said.

'Uh, yeah,' Denise said. Was it better for Billy to think she was clueless, or not?

As the miles rolled by the scenery changed from the flat, scrubby coast and wide beaches of Northumberland that Denise knew well into a vista of heather-dotted hills. After a snarl of motorway junctions at Edinburgh the traffic grew less and less, with cars peeling off to their Central Belt destinations. The A-road turned inland and Denise felt her ears pop as they crossed a high moor. The distance between towns was longer now, and the towns themselves smaller, the houses blocky, small-windowed and short, built from grey granite.

'Come on, I need the loo.' Sandra pouted at Billy. 'Isn't it time we hit a service station? Don't you want a break?'

'I could use a stop too,' Denise said.

There was a service station ahead. Billy grunted and put the indicator on. He guided the Merc into the corner of the car park furthest from the entrance and switched it off. 'Well,' he said. 'I guess if you gotta go, we all gotta go.' He got out and opened the boot. A tall man with dark skin and red dreadlocks emerged. He went round to Denise's side of the car and opened the door.

When he bent over his jacket gaped and she could see a holster peeking from underneath.

Denise tried to hide her surprise. 'So you're Buster,' she said.

'My reputation precedes me,' he said in a lilting, Southwest accent. He turned to Billy. 'Hey, what the fuck was up with the music? That country shit was bad. Come back talk radio, all is forgiven.'

'And as we've established, you have terrible taste. Tape wasn't mine anyway.' Billy shook his head and jerked a thumb at Denise. 'Blame the girlie.'

'Thank you for stopping,' Sandra said and flashed a smile at Billy that Denise already recognised as professional, conciliatory. 'We'll be back in five minutes.'

'Not so fast,' Billy said, and grabbed Sandra's arm. She flinched, but did not dare pull away. 'No way you are going in there by yourselves. No offence, ladies, but I have a feeling if me and Buster stay out here waiting for you, we'll be waiting a long damn time. So let's pretend to be one big happy family if we want to get in and out without being remembered. Which, in case it wasn't clear, is exactly what we want.'

Denise looked at Buster's proffered elbow, then back at Sandra and Billy. She hesitated. 'We'll be fine. It's only a few minutes,' she said.

'I promised you a chaperone and that's what you're gonna get.' Billy looked at Denise for a few moments. His eyes were unnaturally light against his suntanned skin and she fidgeted under his gaze. 'You look familiar,' he said. 'Real familiar. Have we met before?'

Denise gulped. One or two of the papers had run a picture of her after Archie was arrested, but it was an older photo, one from school. 'I don't think so.'

Even thinking of it now made her feel ashamed. The police in her house while the neighbours dissected her with their eyes. The people at work and their barely disguised glee at being adjacent to scandal. It should not have happened; none of this should be happening.

Buster guided Sandra in the direction of the service station door. Billy's hand clamped around Denise's elbow like a vice. 'Wait a second, sugar. I want a word.' She looked down, noted the faded tattoo on the web of his hand, the letter 'B'. It looked like a prison tattoo. Suddenly she felt nauseated, light-headed the same way she had just before she collapsed at work. Her hindbrain knew. Fight or flight. This wasn't a game; men like him were dangerous.

'What's wrong?' she said as neutrally as she could manage.

'I don't know what you're up to yet,' he hissed, his voice low. Billy leaned close to her, so close she could smell the tobacco on his breath and the deeply embedded scent of smoke in his clothes. 'But I know you're up to something.' He nodded at Buster and Sandra's backs. 'This little act of yours might have her fooled, but I ain't no patsy.' His hand was tight now, cutting off her circulation, and her hand and fingers were starting to tingle. 'I'm keeping my eye on you.'

: 32 :

Denise grabbed Sandra as they walked into the toilets. She was shaking and angry. 'What is going on out there?' she said. 'I thought we were going to Scotland to work. You never said anything about being escorted by a couple of gangsters.'

Sandra shrugged off her hand and pasted the professional smile on her face as a shocked-looking family exited the loos. 'Calm the fuck down,' she said. 'They're not going to hurt us. Not if they get what they want.'

'Can you tell me, exactly, what it is they are doing here? Because as far as I can see, you have more or less enlisted me in . . . well, I don't know what. But I know it isn't what I thought I signed up for.'

'Settle down, woman,' Sandra said, and paused to examine her makeup in the mirror. She was not wearing a suit today, but a dark indigo, well-cut pair of jeans and a soft cashmere jumper. Her makeup, toned down from when Denise had met her, was still flawlessly precise. Overall the effect of her 'dressing down' seemed more formal, not less.

'Settle down? Are you having a laugh? We're being kidnapped. Those men are killers.' *Killers who might recognise me if I spend much more time in that car*, she stopped herself from adding. Denise took a deep breath. 'We walk out of here, and we go to security,' she said. 'We tell them to call the police, and arrest those men.'

'Girl, are you kidding me? Never call the police for any reason whatsoever. Especially not considering what you and me are going up to Cameron Bridge to do. What sort of being a hooker was unclear?'

'But – why wouldn't you call the police? I thought sex work was legal?'

Sandra blew air out through pursed lips. 'Yeah, it's legal. But sharing a room, like we're gonna be doing? Guess what, we're running a brothel. Soliciting, like I do when I put our adverts online? Forget about it. Call the police and they'll pick you up for pimping me. Then they'll turn around and arrest me for pimping you. Then because we both got here in a car? We'll get done for trafficking ourselves.' Her eyes narrowed. 'Like I said – never call the police for any reason whatsoever.'

'What if those two men attack us, or try to kill us?'

'Never call the police—'

'Isn't it worse to be hurt or dead than to get arrested? What's the worst—'

'—for any reason whatsoever. If someone is of a mind to kill me, I'll be dead long before the polis even bothers to turn up. If not, I'd rather not be arrested, and I'm sure you don't want to be arrested either, OK?'

'They might not arrest you.'

Sandra arched an eyebrow. 'In my experience, the only time the police don't arrest you is when they rape you. Sometimes they do both.'

Sandra's answer shocked Denise into silence. She should not be here. What had she been thinking? She reminded herself that it had gone too far now for her to bail out. Running was not an option. What would Miri do? She would dig deep and try to stay on top of the situation.

Sandra turned her back to the mirror, leaned against the sink, and crossed her arms over her chest. 'So this happened. Those men turned up in my flat last week. Someone has been using my address, my details, to scam them,' she said. 'They passed on a load of firearms to be sold and whoever it was ran off with both the stash and the cash, and is leading them on a wild goose chase to you'll never guess where.'

'Cameron Bridge,' Denise said. 'But why does he have your phone?'

'He's waiting on a text from whoever it is,' she said. 'I guess he still doesn't believe it isn't me. And he asked nicely.'

Sandra glanced down and Denise noticed thickly applied concealer high on her cheeks. Exactly the way you would put makeup on to camouflage a mark. It was a technique she knew all too well. Was Sandra hiding a black eye? Had they beaten her?

Sandra caught Denise's glance. 'Would you say no to a man like that?' Denise shook her head. 'Right. Now you know. It's not about kidnapping you and it's not about trafficking or pimping or whatever foolish idea your imagination has whipped up that ends with you chained to a radiator getting raped by fifty men a day.' Sandra's face transformed instantly into a butter-wouldn't-melt smile as a shell-shocked grandmother emerged from the last stall and scuttled out of the toilets without even stopping to wash her hands. 'All you have to do is mind your own business for the rest of this trip and we'll be fine.'

Denise opened her mouth and Sandra put up her hand. 'Don't even. Whatever you're about to ask, I already thought of every angle on how this could have happened, and the answer is, I have no fucking idea. But if they get their money or whatever up there, then it's over. OK?'

'OK,' Denise said. They were expecting to find someone in Cameron Bridge, someone who had set up a gun deal. Just like Archie had. What were the chances of that? She didn't know much about illegal firearms, but there couldn't be too many people moving loads of firearms around Scotland at the same time. Her head was spinning. It was possible – just possible – that whoever they were looking for was the missing link she needed to find the person responsible for Miri's murder.

If that was the case, that also meant they were certain to figure out who she was. Billy had almost recognised her. It was only a matter of time before he remembered from where. But she also had to keep Sandra from suspecting she had any ulterior motive besides work. 'I don't like it,' she said, and looked at the floor and tried to sound stubborn, doubtful. 'Those men are bad news. Didn't he say Buster was wanted for a crime? If the police pull us over, they could do us for . . . What do they call it, when it's a minor thing but they're trying to get the ringleaders?'

'Joint enterprise.'

'Exactly,' Denise said. 'You know how it is. The company you keep and all that.'

'Oh, I know *all* about that,' Sandra said, and touched the makeup at the top of her cheek. 'If they gave PhDs from the School of Life, the company we keep would be my specialist subject.'

They stayed at the service station for lunch. Sandra insisted. 'I get cranky when my blood sugar drops,' she said, and Buster mumbled something about feeling hungry too. Denise put on her best face, smiled and treated the men as if there was nothing odd about this at all. Just two couples enjoying an afternoon out.

'Last time anyone caught me queuing up to hold a dinner tray was in Broadmoor,' Buster grumbled, poking at a sausage roll that looked older than he was. Then he smiled, and Denise saw it was a joke. His lilting accent was difficult for her to parse. It made it sound either as if everything he was saying was a punchline, or else he was being sarcastic. She decided that if she assumed he was trying to be nice then that was fine.

Billy had a piece of fried chicken on a roll that looked tired from hours of sitting under the warming lights. From the expression on his face when he bit into it, it was clear it didn't taste much better than it looked. He picked off slimy slices of tomato and flicked them over the edge of his plate.

'Man, look at you throwing perfectly good food away.' Buster clicked his tongue. 'Picky attitude like that, people be tempted to think you never spent any time in solitary on the gruel diet.'

'You'll note we are not currently in prison,' Billy said. 'No reason for me to put up with the crap y'all try to pass off as tomatoes in this country any more than I have to. Only two things that money can't buy, and that's true love and homegrown tomatoes. Ask your gran in Trinidad. She'll tell you it's true.'

'Whatever,' Buster said and demolished half his sausage roll in a single bite.

'If the food here's so bad, why stay?' Denise asked. She only remembered eating one thing the short time she was in Florida, and it wasn't a meal.

One corner of Billy's mouth turned down. 'It was what you might call a shrewd career move,' he said. 'If you never move around, never – what would you call it? – diversify your CV, then no one will believe you're any good.'

'He's right,' Buster agreed. 'Showing your ability in different areas is key. If you want something you never had, you have to do something you've never done before.'

'Like stab a man, maybe steal his boat,' Billy added.

'Ah,' Denise said. She took a long drink of her diet Coke and hoped they changed the subject.

Sandra smiled at Denise. 'So I guess I need to give you some ground rules about working, seeing as it's your first time.'

Denise flushed to the roots of her hair. 'Here? Now?'

Sandra waved her hand. 'No time like the present,' she said. 'It's not as if anyone is listening.'

Denise was pretty sure that everyone in a small radius around them was quieter than usual, straining to overhear what this odd foursome was talking about, but Sandra either did not notice or did not care. 'Go on, I'm all ears,' Billy said to Sandra, and propped his head on his hands like a schoolboy waiting for a history lesson.

'First thing, the money,' Sandra said. 'Get it up front, always. Count it if you want to, or not, whatever. But if you come up short, my cut comes out of whatever's left. Understand?' Denise nodded. 'You're on incall, so I won't be far. Lobby or next room. Once you get the money, text me. Your time starts from then. And text or call again when they leave so I know when to come back up.'

'Cool, OK,' Denise said.

'Now, condoms. Up to you if you want to use one for oral but I guess I don't have to tell you there's no bareback intercourse. Don't even think about it. Some guy asks you for that and won't take no for an answer, walk. If he tries to slip it off during? Walk. If he says he can't wear one because of allergies – well, I brought polyurethane ones, there's no excuse. If he's circumcised, make sure you pinch the tip when it goes on, and if he isn't, pinch a little extra—'

'I know how to put on a condom,' Denise interrupted.

Sandra threw her hands up. 'OK, little miss two lovers. I'm only trying to help.'

Billy snorted. 'If she's only had two men in her life, I'm the next president of the United States,' he said, and looked at Denise. 'No offense, honey.'

Denise opened and closed her mouth, ready to protest, but he didn't expand on his observation and Sandra continued as if she hadn't heard him say it. 'Oh, and if they leave a good review online, leave a nice comment back. Helps keeps them sweet. Anything else . . . well, I'm sure more will come up as we go. If you think of something, just shout.'

Denise nodded. She slyly looked over at Billy when he was wasn't watching her. The other three kept talking about nothing in particular. Her ears pricked up when the subject of Lionel Brant's suicide came up, but they said nothing that had not been done to death in the news already.

Sandra caught her eye a couple of times and smiled. Denise was doing her best to fit in. They would be in Cameron Bridge soon enough. Make the others feel like you're the real deal, even if it's only for a few hours. Ordinarily that might have been a work tip. Now Denise knew she had to smile or die trying.

: 33 :

She dreams of Miri, frequently. Denise wakes in the night, twisted in the sheets, her heart pumping. The dreams are never explicitly sexual. More often they are about twilight forests full of birdcalls. About standing in an empty conservatory drinking cups of black honey. But a presence weaves its way through her nights, a presence that has a rich, deep voice and smells of sweat and vanilla.

Miri never gets in contact after the last time she left Lamia House. She never did before – Denise is not even sure if she has a mobile phone, she never saw one – but keeps hoping she might reach out somehow.

To say what? Miri isn't going to be her girlfriend. That is not how she operates. She careers through other people's lives, causing destruction, then flitting on to the next person, place or thing. But Denise can't help feeling that she wants there to be something more. It wasn't just sex. Was it?

If Miri knocked on the door one day and said she wanted to be with Denise then it would be easy. In the absence of any contact, though, she doesn't know what to do. Choose the friend who betrayed her. Or the man who did.

She could choose something else. She could pick neither. But that would be another unknown, and she isn't certain she is ready to start her life over again. She is too old.

She is twenty-four.

Against her better judgment she stops resisting Archie. It is not long before the relationship between them starts to settle into what it will become.

'You should not have put all your eggs in such a fragile basket,' Archie says one evening, standing over Denise's shoulder watching her cook. No names but they both know who he means. Being with him is not easy in many ways, but it makes it easy to start to see Miri's part in her life as a rapidly retreating past. An interlude between who she was before and who she is becoming now. A stage of grief, the last throes of mourning her brother. It doesn't feel like exactly the right narrative but it does have something going for it. A beginning, a middle, and an end. Otherwise, what was she doing? All those meaningless nights.

And who is she becoming? She doesn't know. The plan to move back to London after finishing her master's seems less urgent. When she talks to her parents, what was 'soon' becomes 'someday'.

Bit by bit she inches closer to Archie. His hand rubbing her shoulder as they curl up on the sofa at night has started to become less ruminative, more insistent. Yet something inside of her feels that giving in to him would be crossing a Rubicon in a way that she cannot yet define. She does not want her actions to have uncertain outcomes any more. Especially when it is a decision she can not take back.

It happens at his place. Archie took a room in a student house after Josie dumped him. His housemates are all younger than he is. It is there where she gives in.

She tells herself, no, he is not perfect but he makes her feel like someone worth possessing. Someone who is more than a face in the crowd. She spent half a lifetime losing to Darwin, the last year losing to Miri. If this is a competition then she wants to win. The thought appalls her, but there it is.

The others are out for the night. He has taken the house television up to his room. 'In case they come back and are being loud,' he explains, though she knows that in his room the only place to sit is the bed. He bought Scotch pancakes with sultanas and put them under the grill, smothered with butter. She finds them cloying and greasy and eats one out of politeness.

They watch a gentle drama about the contrived adventures of a young laird in the Highlands. It is set somewhere north of Cameron Bridge. Sunday night entertainment, aimed at the grannies. Denise finds the show fascinating. The well-worn plots are so familiar, the last line is inevitable as soon as the characters walk in the door. The scenery is lovely, almost comically so, with hazy heather-sprigged hills and distant, glittering lochs. It is how she imagined Cameron Bridge. The way Miri described it to her.

The laird argues with the maid, and because they are both young and blandly attractive, she knows this means they will get together by the end of the series. Most things are obvious. She knows tonight is the night, whether she wants sex with Archie or not. The last line was inevitable as soon as she walked through the door.

It starts with the caresses in the first advert break. She stays inert. Soon his body is on top of hers, heavy, and he is shuffling off his jeans between them, the buckle of his belt scraping a trail on her thigh. When she makes a noise he shoves his hand in her mouth, deep and painfully. It feels as if he is trying to dislocate her jaw. His eyes are closed; he is in his own ecstasy.

The view when she is pinned down, over his shoulder, is of a spherical paper light shade. With every moment he is inside her, every thrust, she is being pushed further and further into the future.

Afterwards he murmurs in her ear, 'You gave me a look as old as time.' His pillow talk is cobbled together from scraps of old bodice-rippers. Dimpled flesh, split peaches, butterfly wings. Euphemistic, flowery. None of it bears any resemblance to her or to what just happened. It is not an apology but it is apologetic.

Perhaps he knows that he went too far, but is unable to call it what it was. By not choosing, the choice is made for her. Isn't this how it happens? Give up all your friends for someone you think you love. She has no other option afterwards: she has to stay with Archie, because who would ever believe it if she said he had raped her?

: 34 :

Harriet stared at the coffee on the table. It would be stone cold by now. She checked her mobile: nothing. She flipped through a copy of the *West Highland News* someone left on the cafe table while she waited.

Morag Munro squeaked the vote in the end by less than a percentage point. Irregularities had been picked up in ballots returned from the Highlands. Vernon Coyle was already calling for a recount but given all that had happened in the last month he was unlikely to get one. There was no public appetite for running the leadership battle again. The local paper talked about the inevitability of Munro as if they had supported her all along. Hailed her success a return to 'grown-up politics', whatever that meant.

According to the paper, Munro was going in hard to woo the soft right of her party: slashing public budgets, talking about tax breaks. Harriet frowned. This probably meant the promise to help keep the mortuary open was long since forgotten, then. A promise made in haste to be left behind as Morag glided into her new role. Harriet was not surprised, but she was still disappointed.

Harriet checked her mobile again. Maybe she should get a fresh coffee? Or ask them to warm this one up? Lucy had not been at the meeting in the church hall today, but Harriet was not expecting to see her there. She had applied for the mortuary assistant job. It made sense. She had studied nursing after all. Maybe having a daily schedule and responsibilities would be good for her recovery, instead of teaching the occasional yoga class.

Harriet was shocked to realise she had already started thinking of Iain in the past tense. But it was true, he was not going to reapply for the role he already had, not at such a reduced rate and with no job security. He made some comments about moving back to Glasgow, but she thought that was unlikely. He had been away for so long. There was always the international work if he wanted it, mass graves and airline crashes. But that would be trying to go back to the past too. More likely he would become one of the area's countless unemployed men, the ones set adrift when their work dissolved. Waiting for industry that was never going to come back.

She was surprised to realise she would miss him. Harriet had known a large number of mortuary assistants over the years and their personalities were often as cold as the bodies. Iain had not immediately been to her taste, but over time she realised he was as competent as any she had met, and then more so – possibly the best she had ever worked with. In spite of his attitude she had grown fond of him. They had started at loggerheads but the last few weeks it felt as if a truce was evolving. Maybe it was her recovery. Maybe he had got used to her, too.

She glanced at her phone. Lucy's interview would have been short if it went badly, but even if it went well, it should have been over at least an hour ago. Harriet was itching to know how it went. She looked up expectantly every time the cafe door opened. Only clutches of damp tourists seeking a brief respite from the spring drizzle. Other customers had been and gone in the time she had been waiting. She hoped nothing was wrong.

Harriet took a deep breath and phoned the work landline. Iain answered on the ninth ring. 'Dead zone,' he said. 'If it's chilled, we're thrilled. How may I direct your inquiry?'

'Iain, can you please not answer the phone that way?' Harriet said. So much for their truce. 'It could have been anyone ringing.'

'But it wasn't, was it. There's a new technology from thirty years ago, kids on the street call it caller ID, you might want to look into it,' Iain deadpanned. 'What can I do you for, Professor?'

'Just following up on this morning's interview,' she said. 'How did it go?'

'Oh, the Kosovan. She was a little odd.'

'Really?' Harriet was surprised. 'I would have thought you two would get on like a house on fire.' A thirty-ish goth chick with a war zone upbringing sounded like exactly Iain's cup of tea. 'Was there a problem with her qualifications?'

'It wasn't her CV,' Iain said. 'Frankly, that all looks in order, and she has the basic anatomical knowledge. Not that the job specification asked for all that much anyway. It doesn't matter. A few weeks' training and she would probably get on fine.'

'Well, that's a relief,' Harriet said. She was not too concerned if Iain hadn't liked her – he would not be working alongside her for long.

'Yeah,' Iain said, his voice uncertain. 'Well, when I asked about her background, she was cagey.'

'How so?'

'Nothing definite, just my Spidey sense,' Iain said. 'She said a couple of place names, and they didn't match up with the geography when I was there. I got an odd feeling from her. I couldn't put my finger on it, exactly. Like she was not quite the person on her CV, if that makes sense.'

'Oh, Iain,' Harriet said. She hoped his gruff and confronta-tional manner had not put Lucy off. 'Some people are terrible in interviews. You shouldn't be so hard on her.' Harriet had always had the opposite problem: she interviewed well, but managed to leave a trail of dissatisfied colleagues behind wherever she went. 'Anyway, she was very young at the time of the war. We all know how memory can get screwed up by that level of trauma so young.'

'Mmm, if you say so,' Iain said. There was something else, it was clear from his voice, but he didn't expand.

'So did she just leave?' Harriet asked.

'Leave? Oh, we had a cuppa then she took off. She's been gone ages. Let herself out.'

'Ah.' Harriet looked sadly at the cold coffee opposite her. Lucy could have met her but didn't, for some reason. 'Thanks for the update, Iain. Are you staying late?'

'Nah, nothing here. I'm feeling a bit off. Thought I'd chill in the flat in case anything comes through the shutters this arvo,' he said. 'But I'll lock up the regular time.'

Harriet sighed. So she had been stood up. No, she reminded herself – this was a meeting, not a date. It didn't mean anything. She and Lucy were just friends. Lucy wasn't even her sponsor! Harriet had a girlfriend. She shouldn't try to read so much into it.

Maybe Lucy hadn't come because she was nervous. Worried that Harriet would have talked to Iain to find out how it had gone behind her back. Harriet bit her lip. That would have put her off, if she had been in Lucy's shoes.

The mobile chirruped, and Harriet answered without looking. 'Hey! Don't worry about being late, I'm still here—'

'Late to what?' Fiona's voice. Harriet nearly dropped the handset.

'Nothing, I . . . nothing. Iain had to go out on personal business, I answered without looking – assumed it was him.'

'It sounds like you're out somewhere.'

'Oh, yes, yes,' Harriet stammered. 'I went for a coffee. Just for half an hour. I'm going back to the office now.' She laughed, the sound high and false to her own ears.

'Fine, whatever,' Fiona said. 'As you're in town, would you mind popping by the station? I have something here you need to see.'

'Is it important?' Harriet said, checking as the cafe door opened again and a new bunch of people came in. No Lucy. 'If Iain gets back before I do . . .'

'It's important, Harriet,' Fiona said. Her voice had a new edge to it. 'Can't talk about it on the phone. Get over here quick as you can.'

'There, there he is.' Fiona twirled the shuttle knob on the video machine, winding the CCTV back several frames. The paused frame showed Archie Lyndon at the petrol station on the roundabout nearest to where the body had been found. He drove to a pump, emerged from the car on his own, then went into the shop.

The camera had recorded still images only, at the rate of one every three seconds, from the forecourt. Most of the cameras were inside keeping tabs on the shop shelves and the register. The camera housing must have been damaged, perhaps in a storm, because the pictures were at an odd angle and partially obscured in a corner. Archie was only discernible if you knew who he was by the registration plate on his Audi.

'I guess that answers that question. You must be pleased to have found it.' Harriet's shoulders sagged. 'Well done. You got your man. I don't know why you felt you had to show this to me, though.'

'For this. Hold on,' Fiona said. She twirled the shuttlebus and the frames lurched forward again. Several minutes later, the same man came out of the shop. He walked over to his car jerkily, the slow frame rate causing jumps between each captured image. Someone in a duffel coat was behind him.

'There's another person with him,' Harriet said.

'Exactly,' Fiona said. 'I haven't told Alistair yet. But you had a hunch, and it turns out, you were right. Lyndon being arrested isn't the full story.' Fiona shuttled through the images again. 'The two of them didn't arrive together, but they left together. He hasn't mentioned an accomplice before now. Apart from his plea, the police have been able to get nothing out of him. Nothing.'

'They have the ID on the body,' Harriet reminded her.

'True, but without a confession or third-party evidence? They don't know for certain that he killed her. All they can say is her body was in his car. As long as he says nothing, it's all circumstantial. Until now.' Fiona grinned. 'This person could be the key. I would have missed this if we hadn't come back to the videos.'

Guilt rose in Harriet's chest. She had got Fiona wrong, so wrong. All these weeks she had been thinking badly of her, flirting with someone else. Because that was what she had been doing with Lucy all this time. She could see it now for what it was. Meanwhile her girlfriend was quietly trying to prove that Harriet's instincts were right.

Harriet felt like a heel. She reached out and touched Fiona's hand. 'You are incredible,' she said. 'Thank you. Thank you for believing me.'

'The other person's hood is up, and I can't make out a face,' Fiona said, and reversed the last few images to let them play again. 'Except here.' She paused the video. A half-scan of a frame hung on the screen. 'It's not much, but it's something. We can put the image out in local media and see if anything comes in. It might open this case right back up.'

The breath caught in Harriet's throat. It might not have been enough of a face for a stranger to ID the person, but she was sure she recognised that arched brow, the flick of dark hair across a familiar cheekbone.

Fiona did not notice Harriet's reaction. 'No one knows about the second person yet, apart of course from Lyndon. It's definitely not the victim, and from the timing, the body was probably still in his car.' She shuttled forward again, showing the Audi waiting to turn out, then driving in the direction of the industrial estate. 'The sooner we can get these images out to all police forces, the sooner we can make an ID and bring them in for questioning.'

Harriet gulped. 'That's . . . wonderful,' she said, her voice flat.

Fiona beamed. 'I would not have bothered if you hadn't been so worried about this case. You did the right thing. I should have listened to you from the start, and I'm sorry.'

'Don't apologise,' Harriet squeaked.

Fiona looked at her curiously. 'Is everything OK? You look unwell.'

'Sorry, work issues on my mind.' She took a deep breath and tried to pull herself together. 'I . . . I'm really glad for you.' She smiled in what she hoped was a supportive way, picked up her bag, and edged towards the door.

'Are you off?' Fiona said. 'I thought we might go for a drink or a bite to eat, have a little celebration.' Her face dropped. 'I thought you would be happy.'

'I am,' Harriet said. 'I am. It means a lot to me, that you listened to what I had to say. I just need to get back to the office for something I forgot, so I'll see you at yours later.'

: 35 :

Denise watched Sandra put the finishing touches to her makeup. Billy and Buster made their excuses after the women checked in. They had a place nearby, apparently. Denise was surprised. She hadn't imagined the pair of crooks kept a Highland getaway somewhere, but then people always did surprise you. Whoever was meant to get in touch with them had yet to make contact. Billy reluctantly gave Sandra her phone back and warned that he would be keeping an eye on things. Of this, Denise had no doubt.

She wanted to know where they were and who they were trying to find, but decided to focus on the escort side first. She should get some names and contacts out of Sandra. She could work on the rest of it later.

Even staying overnight in adjacent rooms, she had not yet seen Sandra anything less than fully clothed and at least partially made-up. 'This is not how I woke up,' she said, catching Denise's eye in the mirror. 'But it's how I look now.' She was preparing for a booking: six hundred pounds for three hours, an outcall at a nearby hotel.

'I'm sorry, the booking specified solo.' Sandra shrugged. 'It was firm about that much.'

Denise was relieved not to have to go along. The thought was starting to crawl under her skin and itch. They had taken a few snaps to update her profile when they arrived, but those did not pique any interest. Probably because she had insisted on all the photos showing her only from the neck down. The punters didn't like that, according to Sandra. They were afraid of getting someone other than who they booked, a bait-and-switch. 'Not that it matters when you're ordering up women on the internet anyway,' she shrugged. 'But they like a face.'

'Next time,' Denise said. 'I don't think I'm ready to take that step yet.' She remembered the pictures of Miri in the Nazi uniform. Had she ever imagined the whole world would see them someday?

Sandra smiled. 'See how you get on this time before you start making any plans,' she said. Denise had to admit she was probably right. 'Anyway. This is where I will be,' she said, and handed over a slip of paper with appointment details. It was the country club on the north side of Cameron Bridge, a complex that boasted a pool and gym but looked, from the side that faced out, like a neglected 1950s holiday park.

'It's a new client. I'll text you when I arrive. Give it fifteen minutes after the booking ends – if you haven't heard from me by then, something is wrong.'

Denise stared at the address as if the loops of ink on paper held some deeper significance. Was it Sandra who killed Miri? Over some clients and a little bit of money? She closed her eyes. She didn't know who to trust, what to believe. Denise had made a promise. She would find out the truth, not fall at the first hurdle.

'Fifteen minutes late, I ring the police. OK,' Denise said. Sandra screwed up her face, about to scold her. 'I'm joking!' Denise said. 'If I don't hear from you fifteen minutes after it's over, I'll call Billy. And then what?'

'Sit tight until you hear back. If you don't hear back at all? Pack up and go home. Don't even think about going to anyone, trust me.'

'I get why you don't trust the police,' Denise said. 'It's just hard to wrap my head around.'

'You ever hear about Madame Meow in Middlesborough?'

'I don't think so,' Denise said. 'Should I have done?'

'Probably not, it was a few years ago now. Big news at the time for sex workers but probably not to anyone else.' Sandra stood up, turned to the side, admired her trim waist in the mirror, and straightened her suit jacket. 'Nice lady. Early sixties, but well-preserved for a white woman, you know? Ran a massage service out of her home. It was a bungalow in a good neighbourhood – good for Middlesborough, anyway – the whole street knew, no dramas. Until the day someone turned up at the door with a shotgun and robbed her.'

'Oh my God,' Densie said.

'Five thousand pounds in cash, her jewellery, everything. Knocked her around a little bit too. She rang the police, as you do.'

'As you do,' Denise nodded emphatically.

'You know what happened?' Sandra said. 'The po-po turn up, and they don't write down a word of her statement. Her description of the assailant, nothing. No photos. She had a black eye from the break-in and all. You know what they did? They arrested her for running a brothel. For giving handies to pensioners at fifty quid a pop in her spare room. She went to prison for two years. Lost her house. Last I heard she was in a halfway house in Washington, my God.'

'That's terrible,' Denise said. 'Did they ever catch who did it?'

'Catch?' Sandra's eyebrows rose so high they all but disappeared under her fringe. 'Honey, they never even filed a report. The police decide who they want to punish. Man with a shotgun. Armed robbery. Versus a woman standing right in front of them. They couldn't have cared less. Just' – She snapped her fingers. 'Poof. Like the robbery never even happened. For all anyone knows it was one of their own. So as I said – no matter what – never call the police for any reason whatsoever.'

'Got it.' Denise nodded.

Cameron Bridge was not like Denise had imagined. It was nothing like the Sunday night dramas Archie loved. The fabric of the place did have a certain charm: old granite houses, Victorian villas on the road into town. But it had been much neglected since its heyday, left to deteriorate until all that was left were the bare bones of a Highland outpost. She walked past windows for outdoor clothing and charity shops, already closed for the night. The only places open past mid-afternoon were pubs and a mostly empty Chinese restaurant. She considered going in, then decided against it. In a place like this, the owners would surely remember a face like hers, and she wanted as much as possible to go unnoticed.

Already town was almost dark. A cool light emerged from behind the hulking mountains, the glow of the full moon creeping out. The longer days of spring and summer would arrive late here, and then when they did, career wildly into almost twenty-four-hour daylight. She knew the theory of what being so far north did to the length of days. But the noticeable difference between Newcastle and Cameron Bridge surprised her all the same.

With a woollen hat pulled low over her brow she blended in with the few other tourists looking for somewhere to sit down. She walked by a pub that looked friendlier than the others. Less karaoke and locals, more real ales and hillwalkers. The sort of place where a stranger would not be a topic of conversation. The sort of place Miri would have laughed at her for preferring. 'What's the matter, are you afraid of real people?' she would have said. It was a trip they never took, but the ghost of her was everywhere. Denise felt empty with nostalgia for something that had never happened.

She took a pint of mild into a corner and sipped it slowly while she kept an eye on the time. In the local paper she spotted a story about Taynuilt bothy and plans to reopen it. The chill ran over her again. That was Miri's bothy, the one they were going to hike to. The one whose crackling log fire and low roof Miri had described as if she had already been.

Denise looked at her watch and realised it was only two minutes since the last time she looked. Waiting out Sandra's appointment was going to be agonising. Maybe she was going overboard being so concerned. After all, Sandra did this all the time, usually without anyone looking out for her. But Denise didn't want to mess up. She told herself it was a crucial step to building trust. To getting closer to finding out what happened to Miri.

She had learned a bit already. One side of the equation: Miri, possibly on drugs, is dumped during a tour by Sandra, clearing her out of earnings as she goes. Maybe she never went back to Newcastle after that, which would explain why all of her things were still at Lamia House. On the other side: around the time Miri's body turns up, someone who knew Billy – and quite possibly Archie – was in Cameron Bridge, something to do with a gun deal.

Now all she had to do was figure out what happened between those two points. To fill in the blanks. A simple enough question, but she had the feeling the answer was not going to be so easy.

A woman in the corner laughed. Deep and throaty, and for a moment it sounded like Miri's laugh, though of course it wasn't. Her group were wearing damp outer layers and looked as if they had come straight from a day climbing the Ben. The laughing woman took off a fleece hat and unwound a tightly curled coil of blonde hair. She was tall, even taller than Denise, and a much younger man kept a possessive arm around her waist.

It should have been her and Miri driving up together, listening to Darwin's old tapes and laughing as funny places names came and went on the road signs: Pulpit Rock, Bridge of Orchy, Rest and Be Thankful. Not an uncomfortable ride in an old Mercedes with three people she barely knew. Miri would have known the right pub to go to, the one with the strangest people and the most local character. And Denise would have been a little braver with her, a little wilder, a little more the person she wanted to be and less of the one she didn't.

Maybe Miri hadn't been holding her back from real life, but showing her how to live it. Together, they had been perfect. Together, Denise could forget about what happened to Darwin, because if Miri could pick herself up and start over again after what her family had done, how could she not do the same? But all the time she had let Miri lead her, drinking deeply of her joy in life, of her laughter and her spirit, Denise had neglected to give anything back. She could have tempered Miri's reckless nature, lent her some of her own caution. Not much. But a little, and she might still be alive.

She should have stopped what happened from happening. She should have gone round, told Miri how she felt. She should have turned up at the door of Lamia House and stayed there until Miri took her in. She would have loved her and her love would have changed everything. She could have prevented her from doing this to herself, from ending up like a piece of rubbish in a skip in Cameron Bridge.

In a small, rational corner of her mind was a voice telling Denise this was not true. Miri was a grown-up who had made her choices, and so had Denise. There is no such thing as saving someone with love. But the heart wants what it wants, and right now she wanted nothing more than for Miri to be alive. Even if only to say goodbye.

'It's 2016. You know what to do,' a gruff voice intoned, before the beep. Billy's phone was still going to voicemail. Denise switched back and forth between dialling his number and dialling Sandra's as she walked up and down the hallways of the country club, frantically trying to find room 1312.

Sandra hadn't phoned at the end of her session. No one had. Fifteen minutes later, still no call. Denise hesitated before calling Sandra – was she being paranoid, because it was her first time? But as soon as the other woman's phone went to voicemail, she started to panic in earnest. When she couldn't reach Billy either, she flagged down the one taxi idling outside Tesco on the high street and had her drive her up to the country club. She chucked twenty at the surprised driver and told her to keep the change even though it was only a two-mile journey. She couldn't wait, not while Sandra could be in danger, not even a minute longer.

Inside, the hotel had the kind of out-of-date décor that its outside had suggested. Violently patterned carpets were worn down to threadbare paths where countless people had trod the same floors. The carpets sprawled out across a warren of annexes where the hotel had added new wings and extensions over the years. Gold-framed prints hung on the walls at intervals, the same three over and over. A stag glowering on a hillside in the mist, a snow-capped mountain above a loch, a bearded man playing the bagpipe with the wind rippling the edge of his kilt. In another context they might have been a knowing nod to kitsch. Here, they were perfectly serious.

The hotel was nearly empty. In spite of the early season coaches starting to come into town, hauling oldfurs up and down the Highlands, few if any had elected to stop here. The air in the hotel had that quality of somewhere that had lain unoccupied for a long time. Not mildew, or even dirt, but a flowery scent of stale, unmoving rooms long since cleaned and left empty. If she hadn't passed the receptionist at the front who pointed her in the direction of the room she was looking for – not the exact number, even she knew not to be too specific, not to arouse suspicion in hotel staff – she would have thought the place deserted.

Denise rounded an unpromising corner into a hallway that she was sure she had tried, her heart beating in her throat. Stag, mountain, piper. Stag, mountain, piper. Finally she spotted it. 1312.

She put her ear to the door. There was no sound inside. In a fraction of a second her mind went through every terrible possibility. If Sandra was missing, and Billy wasn't answering, perhaps she had been kidnapped and he was in there, injured or worse. Or maybe they were both in there dead. What if it was all an elaborate cover, and Billy and Sandra put two and two together, and they had ditched her? Maybe the police had ambushed Sandra, and they were inside now, waiting for Denise to come in so they could arrest her too. There was only one thing for it. Denise gulped, balled her hand in a fist, knocked on the door.

At the lightest tap the door swung open into an empty room.

Not just empty, or even deserted, but untouched like the rest of the hotel. As still as a tomb. Denise stepped inside. It was a standard issue double bedroom, nothing unusual or even out of place: untouched in fact. The bed was still made up as if no one had been there. She checked behind the door, but no one was there, and no one was in the bathroom either. Every towel was folded and on the rack where a maid must have left it, perhaps days before. The toilet roll was folded in a little downward-pointing V, unused.

The wardrobe was empty. Nothing in the drawers except a Bible. She tapped her mobile to bring it back to life. There was phone reception, full bars. Anyone could have called her from there if they wanted to. She rang both numbers again in case the phones were in the room, but there was no sound, and both went to voicemail again. 'Hey – it's me. Hope I didn't miss you,' Denise said, leaving a message on each one this time but not her name, trying to sound as casual as she could. In case someone else listened to it later.

What now? *Never call the police. For any reason whatsoever.* The only backup option, Billy, was also missing. It was then Denise saw the piece of paper on the pillow. A piece of A4 resting on a white pillowcase. It was folded in thirds, as if it had come out of an envelope. She picked it up gingerly and unfolded the crisp leaf, the thin edges of paper only just perched on the tips of her fingers. A few handwritten sentences, carefully printed in black ink.

Come to 25 Loch Glen Road. Immediately. Bring your friend, I have the goods.

Denise drew a sharp breath. She turned the paper over, but there was nothing else. There was nothing else in the room, no indication – apart from the unlocked door – that anyone had been in it at all. Perhaps there had been an envelope, and if there had been an envelope, money; otherwise why would

Sandra consider following the mysterious directions? If she had been stood up, she would have phoned Denise, or come straight back.

Sandra was right: if someone was going to kill her, she was probably already dead. Notifying the police now wouldn't have an effect either way. Except to alert them to Denise's existence, and launch a cascade of questions about who she was and why they were there together. She could leave, but without Billy and Buster, she would have to organise a train or a bus, and it was already dark. The last one of either that could get her back to Newcastle the same night would have left a long time ago. And then what? Forget any of this had ever happened? She would have been going back on her promise to Miri.

She could go to the address and . . . she didn't know what. Rescue them? Save the day? It was a ridiculous thought, the kind of thing Archie would do, or try to do before ducking out at the last moment. Denise took a deep breath. She would go; what else was there? She could be brave. No, more than that – she had to be brave. Nobody else was going to help them.

: 36 :

The large rectangular building at the end of the glen was strictly functional, concrete sided, with a corrugated metal roof. The trees surrounding the fenced yard bent in the breeze, leaves rustling as an owl took to flight.

Billy took his foot off the pedal, switched off the headlights, and let the Mercedes coast the last few metres into the open gate. 'The fuck is this place?' Buster asked from where he was hunched down in the back seat.

'Some kind of warehouse, from the look of it,' Sandra said.

'Nah,' Billy said, and pointed at the yellow shuttered doors at one end of the building. They were set accordion-style, like two garage doors mounted on their sides. 'That's where the hearses go in and out. This is the morgue.'

Sandra shook her head emphatically. 'I am not going in there.'

'You got no choice, sugar,' Billy said. Places charged with handling the final remains of the dead were seldom cheery, but this one seemed especially desolate. The rising moon cast an eerie glow over them. 'First, the note was for you. It would be exceedingly bad form for you to not at least turn up. Second, I still don't know that you aren't in on this. So until we've established who is doing what to who, you are going to stay within my sight, thank you very much.'

'To whom,' Buster piped up from the back.

'Huh?' Billy said.

'To whom.' There was a dull click and then a snap as he ejected an empty magazine from his Glock and loaded a full one. 'Not who. Object of the preposition.' Metal chimed against metal as he pulled the slide and chambered a round.

'Thanks for the lesson, Mister Rogers,' Billy said sarcastic-ally. 'I hope your night vision is as good as your grammar, because already I can't see shit and we haven't even left the car.'

'We can't go in there,' Sandra said, and laid her hand on Billy's shoulder. 'It's a trap.'

Billy shrugged. 'Yes. It's an obvious trap. But then, I always think everything could be a trap. That is why I am still alive.' He glanced at Sandra's large designer handbag. 'Is that your work kit?' he asked. She nodded. 'Anything useful in there, weapon-wise?'

'Not unless I get close enough to attach electrodes to some-one's testicles,' she said. 'My methods of torture are perhaps a bit more close-range than you might be used to.'

'I'll keep it in mind,' he said. 'If everyone's ready, then let's do this.'

The trio crept across the hardstanding. There were no cars, no lights, no sign anyone was there apart from them. Buster went ahead, Glock at the ready, and scanned the surround-ing area. Someone could already be in the building. The only window on the facing side was on the first floor, probably an office. Billy hung back behind Sandra. Her high heels dug into the damp gravel surface. As they reached a regular door on the side opposite the accordion shutters, there was a click. Sandra let out a sharp, short screech.

'Motion detector,' Billy said. 'Calm down.' He looked up. 'Someone's taken out the light.'

'Could have burned out,' Buster suggested. 'Not like people are dying to get in here, you know?'

'Ha fucking ha.' There was a buzzer by the front door, the kind that came connected to a camera and a monitor inside, activated by ringing the bell. 'We're going in. You stay outside and watch the door.'

'Why don't we send the armed guy first?' Sandra said. 'If they have guns in there.'

'I bet the guns aren't here,' Billy said. 'That would be, how do you say it? A schoolboy error. No. You don't bring the goods to the meeting. They want to talk, not shoot.'

She narrowed her eyes. 'Nuh-uh. They're going to shoot us as soon as we walk in there,' she said. 'I'm staying outside.'

'If they wanted to shoot you, they would have done it at the hotel,' Billy said. 'Made it look like another call girl killing.' He registered the foul look on Sandra's face. 'Hey, I'm only saying that's how the media would report it. And how the police would see it. What's that cop saying about prostitute murders? "No Humans Involved." Nah, they brought us here because they want something else.'

Sandra frowned. 'This place is depressing.'

'Jesus, woman. It's a morgue, not Butlins.' Billy nodded at Buster. Buster nodded back and stuck his thumb over the camera lens. He pressed the call button.

The door buzzed open. Billy walked in first, checked the area to either side of the door. Inside was a narrow entryway illuminated by a small red LED. He held up his hand, signalling to Buster that it looked clear. Then he motioned for Sandra to follow. He pulled the door behind them and when he did, turned to see Sandra slump to the ground unconscious. The door locked as it closed. Then a whoosh like a soft breath went past his ear, and Billy hit the tiles.

Denise ran into the street. She looked up and down both ways. Now what? The nearest taxi rank was back in town, two miles away. She could hitchhike to the Loch Glen roundabout. But it might be ages until someone even stopped, and even if she did get a lift, then what? The map on her mobile showed the address on the note was another mile from there. Snagging a lift was one thing; asking a stranger to make a potentially lethal side trip up a dead end road quite another.

She was about to go inside again when she spotted a bicycle leaning against an otherwise empty rack. She checked to make sure no one could see her from the front door – the pushbike probably belonged to the guy at reception – and apologised to no one in particular for what she was about to do. She swung a leg over the crossbar, pumped the brakes once to test them, and took off in the direction of Loch Glen Road.

Harriet Hitchin pulled into the car park at the mortuary to find an unfamiliar vehicle there. A battered black Mercedes, N-reg.

It wasn't Iain's. He had a Vectra that sounded like it was dragging its exhaust over the ground when he drove. Which he usually didn't. She had been by his house and by the pub and there was no sign of him. There was only one place he could be. Could the car be Lucy's? She put her hand on the bonnet of the Merc. The engine was still warm.

'Hello?' she said into the darkness. The only answer was the rustle of leaves in the trees.

Harriet tried the office phone while she fumbled her keychain for the front door. Iain wasn't answering, but he was probably holed up in the flat with a couple of tins of Tennent's and the television volume turned up to eleven.

She needed to talk to him about Lucy. If he had a copy of her job application, then she could get her address, talk to her before Fiona found her. The CCTV footage back at the station looked incriminating, but Harriet was sure there must be a logical explanation. Maybe that man had offered her a lift. Or knew her from somewhere else. That had to be it. Whatever was going on, there was no way Lucy could be mixed up in the Goldstein murder.

A pushbike skidded to a stop on the gravel behind her. Harriet turned to see a Chinese girl with a woolen hat pulled low on her head, her hair loose and tangled below her shoulders. 'Are you lost?' Harriet said. Tourists sometimes came up this way after a wrong turn, mistaking the glen road for the road to the Ben. 'It's the left hand fork after the roundabout. About half a mile back up the same road, I'm afraid.' She spoke slowly, drawing pictures in the air with her hands, uncertain if the woman understood.

The young woman shook her head. 'I'm not lost,' she said.

'And I speak English, yeah?' She had a distinct London accent.

'You know this is the mortuary?' Harriet asked.

The woman shook her head. She winkled a crunched-up bit of paper out of her trouser pocket. '25 Loch Glen Road?' she read.

'That's what it says,' Harriet said, and gestured at a metal sign just inside the fence. To be fair, it was almost twenty years old, covered in mildew, and difficult to read even in daylight, much less in the dark.

'Is this from you?' the woman said, and waved the paper.

'I can hardly be expected to read that from here.' Harriet sighed and walked over. She plucked the paper from the woman's hand. It took a few seconds of squinting before the letters swam into focus. 'My God, what the . . . ? No, this isn't mine. I don't know what on earth would give you that idea.' She folded the note and handed it back to the woman. 'I am Doctor Harriet Hitchin. I'm the forensic pathologist; this is where I work.'

The woman looked doubtfully at her. 'Bit late to be coming to work,' she said.

'Yes, well,' Harriet said. 'Not that it matters to you, but one of my co-workers is still here and I need to speak to him on an urgent matter.' She had no reason to appease this stranger, but the information did seem to have a softening effect.

'I'm looking for some friends of mine.'

'Right,' Harriet nodded. She waited for an explanation but there was none. 'Well, it's been a pleasure chatting with you. Now if you don't mind—'

'Wait, don't shut the door.' The woman jumped off the bike. It clattered to the ground but she made no effort to retrieve it. 'You have to let me in. My friends are inside.' She pointed to the car. 'This belongs to them. This might sound crazy, but I think someone might be holding them hostage.'

Harriet paused. It wasn't the strangest thing she had ever heard. It wasn't even the strangest thing she had heard that day. 'I'm sure you'll find your friends have wandered off somewhere without letting you know, and you're entirely mistaken.' She spoke slowly and calmly, so as not to provoke the stranger into any rash actions. 'I'm afraid I can't just let you inside. Now if you would please leave, or else I will have to ring the po—'

A sharp crack like lightning split the night. The deafening sound rattled the metal roof of the morgue and both women flinched. A flock of starlings took off from the trees nearby. 'What on earth was that?' Harriet said, but as soon as the words left her mouth she knew it had been a gunshot.

'Fuck!' Denise grabbed Harriet's arm. 'Open that door! Now! We might already be too late.'

The floor was cold. Sandra's first instinct was to try to move, but her hands were tied. She tried to call for help, but there was something shoved in her mouth and a gag tied round her head. A warm mass was behind her. A body. She made a noise, and got a familiar gruff one in return. She must be tied to Billy.

It looked like they were alone. A row of stainless steel tables rose from the tiles along the centre of the space. By each was a riser with water taps. Three tables, and on each table, an empty body bag. She shuddered. She had never been inside a morgue before, and the thought of what must go on here every day was chilling. By twisting her head she could see a wall of cold storage lockers. The room smelled of industrial cleaner, floor polish, and something else. Something disturbingly meaty.

How long had they been there? Ten minutes? Twenty? Her left arm, the one on the floor, sang with pins and needles. A headache was blooming in her temples. She felt hungover. The side of Sandra's neck still throbbed. Was it a tranquiliser dart that had been used on her? She couldn't remember hearing or seeing anything or anyone – she couldn't remember anything, in fact, past when they were at the door and Buster rang the bell.

Buster. Where was he now? Billy had told him to stay outside and wait for a signal. He had no way of knowing they were tied up in here.

Billy started moving his body back and forth, trying, she supposed, to shuffle them to the side of the room. Sandra let herself be dragged a few inches before joining in. Their bodies moved almost in sync, his narrow back straining against her. With the friction of the rope on her wrists and ankles, it felt almost like sex. Well, she had been keeping those muscles supple for decades. Who could have known they would be so useful in an emergency?

Billy kicked his legs on the floor, almost like pedalling, until they were turned around with her body furthest from the entrance and his blocking her. From the new angle she could just see a sliver of the door they came through. There was a flicker in the shadow that might have been someone, or might have been her eyes playing tricks on her.

Then the unmistakable sound of a magazine being shoved into a pistol.

Was this it? Was this how it all ended? Sandra had, from time to time, felt a shudder of her own mortality. A client once, in her early and stupid days, who nearly went too far with a strangulation scene. That was when she went off subbing for good. A brief but violent marriage. A wave of adrenaline pumped into her body and a cold sweat beaded her brow. This was not the death she had imagined, drugged and tied up on a floor, in a morgue with a near-stranger. She thought she would go down fighting.

She closed her eyes. 'The Lord helps those who help themselves,' her mother used to say. 'But don't expect him to turn up for your victory lap either.' What does he do when you can't help yourself? She had lived her life never wanting to find out. It had been a long time since she had ever prayed for anything. Now, she prayed frantically for something, anything to save her.

'Oh, don't go back to sleep,' a voice teased from the edge of the room. Sandra stiffened. She knew that voice. But from where? 'It's been ages waiting for the two of you to wake up.' The shadow took shape as it stepped over the low barrier by the door and into the room.

A young woman with choppy black hair smiled down at Sandra. 'You can't imagine how good it is to see you again,' she purred. 'It's been a long time.' The woman craned her neck to get a look at both of them. 'And Seminole Billy,' she said. 'The more the merrier, I suppose.' A smile played on the edge of her lips. She raised a large chromed gun to shoulder height and aimed.

The bullet pierced Sandra's body before she had time to register the sound of the gunshot. The pain, when it came, was so intense that she blacked out instantly.

It took a moment for Denise's eyes to adjust. She peered from the dark of the entryway into the relative brightness of the mortuary. 'They're in here,' she rasped.

'Who is?' Harriet whispered.

Denise shook her head and held up a hand to keep Harriet back. In front of her was a rack of lab coats. Below it, a row of white wellington boots lined up on the floor. A low wall separated where she was standing from the rest of the room.

The entryway opened into the main autopsy theatre. The lights there were switched on, bright. Opposite this was another doorway hung with plastic strips. 'Where does the other doorway go?' she whispered.

'The locker room,' Harriet said.

On the far side of the mortuary were three figures. One standing up, two on the floor. Sandra and Billy down, and there was a growing puddle of what appeared to be blood.

Harriet fumbled in the doorway and knocked over a pair of boots. The standing woman turned. 'Is someone there?' she said to the darkened doorway. A lilting, playful voice though.

A voice Denise recognised.

'Lucy!' Harriet stepped over the barrier into the bright light of the suite. The thin woman turned fully now. Denise saw the gun before Harriet did. 'My goodness, am I pleased to see you here. I've been trying to get in contact with Iain, and he said you were last—' Harriet stopped suddenly as she clocked the pistol in the other woman's grip.

Denise's heart skipped several beats. The name Harriet had said was one she did not recognise. The hair was different. The body that she remembered as shapely was thin now, almost skeletal. The skin, once opal-pale and translucent, was darker, hidden under layers of fake tan. But there was no mistaking her face. It was a set of features carved on Denise's brain. She would have known that woman anywhere.

It was Miri. She was alive. And she was holding a gun and standing over Sandra's crumpled and bleeding body.

: 38 :

A dark patch of blood spread across Sandra's jacket. 'I don't know what's going on here, but that woman needs to get to a hospital,' Harriet said, and ran across the room. 'Quickly!'

'Not so fast,' Miri said. Her hands locked on the pistol grip, her right thumb curled around the heel of her left hand. Her finger shifted from where it was resting on the slide down to the trigger. The pathologist froze. Miri rested her eyes on Denise's face. 'So it is you. I tried my best to keep you out of this, you know.'

'You know each other?' Harriet's eyes flicked from Miri to Denise and back again.

'You could say that,' Denise said. 'We used to be friends.'

'I'm the past now, am I?' Miri said. Her opal eyes danced with amusement.

'Everyone thought you were dead, Miri.' She looked so different and yet, in many ways, the same: the same thin upper lip that curved like a spoon, the same icy glint in her eyes. She had dyed her hair black, and had tattoos now – Denise noticed where a line on one hand met a star on the other when she cradled the gun.

'What's going on, Lucy?' Harriet's voice trembled. 'Why does she keep calling you that?'

'I don't know who you think this is, but she's Miri Goldstein,' Denise said. 'Famously found dead in Cameron Bridge, perhaps more famously engaged by Lionel Brant for some very specific sex fantasies.'

'No, you're wrong,' Harriet said. 'That can't be right. I

autopsied Miriam Goldstein, right there—' Harriet pointed at the second steel table in the room. 'She was dead. The ID was rock solid, there was no mistake.' Harriet's voice shook. 'They had fingerprints. They matched her mother's RNA! This can't be right.' She looked at Miri now, eyes wide. 'It's some sort of trick they're trying to pull on you, Lucy, some kind of lie. Don't go along with these . . . these *criminals* . . .'

Miri sighed in exasperation. 'No, she's right. My name is not Lucy, and she knows me as Miri.'

Harriet muttered to herself. 'I did not make a mistake, I was sober that day. You're a yoga teacher, not a sex worker. Your name is Lucy. You were born in Kosovo, you came here as a refugee. I remember it, I rem—'

'Oh, shut up, you old sop,' Miri snapped. 'You autopsied Miriam Goldstein. I am not Miriam Goldstein.'

Harriet shook her head. 'No. If you're Miriam and you're still alive, then who was the body?'

'The body was Miriam Goldstein. The caretaker of Lamia House.' Miri sighed. 'Messed up girl, she really was. Never quite got over running away from her family's destiny for her. It was sad,' she said. 'We met at a homeless shelter when she was a student. She had such potential. She could have been so much more than she was. She hanged herself from the chandelier on the first floor landing in the end.'

'She kept the body in the house,' Denise said. Now it made sense. She remembered her weak candle barely lighting the far reaches of the cellar during the party at Lamia House. The boxes, the suitcases, and a claw-footed bath. The bath, covered with plastic sheets and full of sand. The bath that would have had to be emptied before the house's rightful owners moved back to Newcastle. No wonder living so close to her family had not seemed to trouble Miri too much: they were not her family in Gateshead. And when she was done with Miriam, she slipped out of that identity like a snake shedding its skin.

Harriet stopped sniffling. 'Lucy, please put the gun down. I will call the police, they'll take these people away for breaking and entering, for harassing you . . .'

Miri swung the barrel of the gun squarely in Harriet's direction. 'Call the cops and it will be the last thing you do, bitch,' she said.

'Come on, please,' Denise said as calmly as she could. 'At least let us untie them. Sandra needs medical attention. Let Harriet have a look at her. None of us are armed, we just want to make sure she's OK.'

Miri laughed. That rich, full throated laugh, identical to how Denise remembered it. The sound chilled her. 'Go on then,' she said. Denise dove forward and tried to prise the bonds apart. Her fingers, cold, slipped in the blood-slick rope. It felt like an eternity before she could get the knot apart. Billy sat up, rubbing his wrists and shaking his hands to restore his circulation. He watched Denise and Harriet tend to Sandra's wound while he took off his gag, applying pressure to her shoulder, freeing her mouth, and slapping her cheeks to try to wake her up.

'Hiya, Billy,' Miri said. 'You're looking old.'

'Augustine. Always a pleasure to see you,' he said. 'Almost as much as it is not to.' He stood slowly, unbending his rusty knees, keeping a keen eye on the gun barrel that Miri raised in direct proportion to his posture. 'I guess worrying about my twenty thousand may have given me an extra wrinkle or two.'

'Your twenty thousand?' Miri smirked. 'Ah, no. Possession is nine tenths of the law. And when you're operating outside the law? It's ten tenths.'

Denise looked from one to the other. The guns had gone from Billy to Miri to Archie, that much she could put together herself. If that was the case, then Sandra's involvement was nothing more than a red herring. A convenient address for Miri to cover her activities, Sandra a convenient fall guy to go down if anyone else unravelled what was going on. 'Miri, put the gun down,' Denise said. She took a step forward. 'You don't have to do this . . .'

'I told you to shut up!' Miri pointed the gun at the ceiling and fired another round. There was a sharp crack as the tiles shattered, raining asbestos fragments on the floor. Denise raised her arms above her head. Her ears rang from the blast. She watched Billy's eyes follow the path of the shell casing that fell from the gun, hit the ground by Miri's foot, and roll some small distance away.

The sound seemed to dislodge something in Sandra and her eyelids fluttered open. Harriet struggled to pull her up into a sitting position, still trying to keep pressure on the wound in her shoulder. Sandra's skin was dull and ashen, but her eyes were alert as she took in what was happening. Harriet looked back at Miri. 'Please,' she said. 'You have to call an ambulance. She needs medical attention as soon as possible.'

'Like hell,' Miri said. 'But, thank you for waking her up. This bitch deserves to be fully aware when I kill her for real.'

Sandra gurgled, a wounded sound in her throat. Harriet put her arms around her. 'Calm down,' Billy said. He held up both hands, palms out, in a gesture of surrender. 'Tell us what you want.'

Miri rolled her eyes. 'Isn't it obvious? I want to finish the job Denise's boyfriend started the day he agreed to give me and a corpse a lift to Scotland. I want to tie up the loose ends. The loose ends being, namely, you' – She pointed the gun at Sandra's inert body still on the ground as Harriet struggled to administer basic first aid – 'and you.' She pointed it at Billy.

'Sure, sure.' Billy nodded. 'I get that. Hell, in your shoes, I would probably do the same thing. Shit, I should have known you weren't really French, Augustine's not even European. I'm assuming you borrowed the name off the saint.'

'You always were better read than you look,' Miri said. 'But then you'd kind of have to be.'

'Thanks,' Billy said. 'So I'm guessing whoever Lucy is, she's an identity that's about to be vacated as well.'

'Died in an immigration removal centre in 2002,' Miri said.

'Yeah.' Billy nodded. 'You hold all the cards here. None of us knows who you really are. You have the money. You have a gun, and I guess you've probably set up whatever you're gonna do next, your next identity or whatever. So who you gonna shoot first?'

Miri blinked, and turned left. The gun was pointing at Harriet, still hunched over Sandra on the floor. 'Left to right, I guess. Three body bags, three bodies. The doctor, the dominatrix, and you.'

Billy nodded at Denise. 'And her?'

'I'll take her hostage, just because.'

Billy shrugged. 'Go on, then,' he said. 'Get rid of the doc, anyway. None of us is going to stop you.'

'What do you mean?' Harriet looked up from Sandra's limp form, panic in her eyes.

'No, it's fine, we don't need you,' Billy said to Harriet, whose mouth fell open, incredulous. He looked at the floor and seemed to contemplate something there. Looked up, and hitched one side of his blade-thin mouth in a kind of smile. 'But she ain't gonna shoot you anyway.'

'The hell I'm not,' Miri said, and gripped the pistol tighter.

'The hell indeed,' Billy said. 'See, there's something you didn't think about. Something, I guess, you couldn't be expected to know.'

Irritation flickered across Miri's face. She took the bait. 'What's that?'

Billy chuckled his dry chuckle. 'Well, I probably shouldn't be telling you this. But you know what they say, honour among thieves and all that. And if I'm being honest? I admire the way you've planned this out. I hate to see a good plan go to waste. The thing is, though, next round you fire out of that gun right there.' He held up his hand and pointed at her, his index finger straight and his thumb up as if mocking the shape of the gun itself. 'It's going to be a misfire.'

'Bullshit,' Miri said. Her hands on the pistol twitched and the whites of her knuckles showed. 'I don't believe you.'

'That's fine. You don't got to believe me.' Billy shrugged. 'Because it's true either way. See, what you have there is a Kimber

1911. Single action pistol. Stainless steel, chromed. A pretty good choice for a small woman. Perfect, in fact. I remember the day I pointed it out to you, suggested you should get one.' He turned to Denise, Harriet and Sandra to explain. 'People think girls should carry small pistols, to keep in their handbags. But how you fire the gun is more important than how you hide it. The truth is that a big gun absorbs a lot more of the kickback, which is better for a chick. To fire, that is. Not to hold. Yeah, it's heavy, and yeah, maybe you do a lot of yoga and whatever but it'll be starting to get difficult to hold up now . . .'

'You're just trying to kill time,' Miri said. But Billy wasn't wrong; Denise could see her narrow shoulders starting to shake as they tired of holding the weapon in front of her.

'Maybe I am. Maybe,' Billy drawled. 'It's definitely the kind of thing I would do. Try to manipulate you and all. I mean you never struck me as a natural-born killer. A criminal and a sneak, sure. Sometimes a junkie. But not a killer. Wouldn't you agree?' He looked at Denise, who was too dumbfounded to answer. 'Anyway. Yeah, it's a good gun for women. Great accuracy, too. Once it's broken in, that is. The problem is, that gun is not broken in. I should know – I'm the one who procured it for the Major in the first place, and I'm the one who passed it on to you.'

'Not broken in? What does that mean?' Harriet asked.

'I said, shut up,' Miri snapped. 'Was he talking to you?'

Billy looked over his shoulder at Harriet, nodded, and turned back to Miri. 'That's a good question, doc, a real good question. See, a gun needs to be fired hot to get the parts working together right. We're talking about going down to the range with a hundred rounds, maybe more. Getting it so the metal heats up and expands, then cools down and shrinks back again. Makes the action a bit better. A bit smoother. If you don't do it, no matter how many times you use that gun, it's not broken in. And every shot you take when it's not broken in is getting you closer to a misfire.'

'How do you know I didn't?' Miri sneered.

'All right, Exhibit A. I saw you aim for that woman's head, but hit her in the shoulder,' he said. 'You're still jerking off target even at close range. A lot of folks do that early on. They're thinking about the recoil, not the shot. Hundreds of range rounds would have trained that reaction out of you. If you'd bothered to do them.

'But that's only the start.' No one spoke. Billy paused, looked at his nails, then pointed to a spot on the ground. 'Exhibit B. The shot you fired, see how close the casing ejected?' The metal cylinder was barely a foot from Miri's shoe. 'It should have flown further than that. The closer they get to you, the closer you are to a misfire. That one practically went down your shirt. Bet it stung too.'

'Bullshit,' Miri said. But she shrugged her shoulder, and Denise could see Billy was right – there was a tiny pink mark where the hot casing had kissed her skin.

'Exhibit C. You got little hands,' Billy continued. 'So when you were loading up that magazine, every round gets tougher to press in. You got, what, about six rounds in there? Seven? In a magazine that can hold ten.'

'Six,' Miri said.

Billy nodded. 'As I thought. I get it, you don't need more than that today, and anyway, your fingers get real tired pushing them in on a spring that is brand new. But the fewer rounds you get in, the less that spring gets itself broken in too, and it's making the misfire all the more likely. So here's what I think. You've shot two. Number three's not going to fire.'

Miri gulped, but her eyes narrowed. 'Keep talking, old man,' she said. 'Nothing you say is going to change the way this goes down.'

'OK, OK.' Billy raised his hands in a gesture of surrender. 'As I said, you hold all the cards. I'd be concerned, is all. Real concerned.' Billy's eyes flicked up as if he spotted something in the doorway behind Miri. Only for a second, and when Denise looked, there was nothing there.

Miri smiled and shook her head. 'Nice try,' she said. 'You

had me going for a minute. It even sounded as if you knew what you were talking about. But I've had this gun for weeks now. If anyone should be concerned, it's you.' Miri trained her eye on the sights.

'Concerned, sure,' Billy said. 'Or maybe not. You know, I never did meet a left-eyed shooter who was any good at firing right-handed. You're a southpaw. I drew those marks you got tattooed on your hands now, when I showed you how to fire a gun. But I also told you that unless you trained your right eye to lead, a right-handed grip was never going to work out.'

Denise drew in a sharp breath. Billy was right – Miri was left-handed. She remembered her long white fingers dipping in ice water to sign her name on a bared back in Lamia House. Maybe he wasn't bluffing after all.

'What you think is not going to matter either way in a couple of seconds, is it?' Miri swivelled; she was aiming for him now. She checked her aim and prepared to pull the trigger. Billy looked at her, expressionless. 'Not when that thought, and the rest of your brain, are about to become part of the back wall.'

There was a rustle of plastic behind her. Miri turned to see what was going on in time to spot Buster emerging from behind the curtain. His Glock looked like a toy gun in his bear paw grip. 'Drop the gun,' he growled.

'Fuck you.' Miri spun back around to Billy's unblinking face and pulled the trigger.

: 39 :

The click echoed in the room. Harriet screamed and cowered. Then, nothing. No deafening shot, tearing into soft flesh. No metallic ring of the spent casing hitting the floor. A misfire.

Harriet lifted her head first, looked around. 'What happened?' she said to no one in particular.

Denise was ready. She lunged forward and tackled Miri. For a moment both of them were on the ground. The Kimber spun across the floor towards Buster, who picked it up and opened the slide to eject the misfired bullet. He pocketed the round and tucked the gun down the back of his jeans.

Denise tried to keep hold of Miri, but the other woman was faster and stronger than she remembered. She soon broke free and ran out of the front door. Denise hauled herself up on her feet and gave chase.

Harriet shook Sandra, whose eyes were starting to close again. Slowly she edged her out of her jacket. The patient's face contorted in pain as Harriet peeled the sleeves off of her arms but raised no noise higher than a whimper. The silk of the lacy camisole underneath was slippery with blood.

'That was incredible,' Harriet said, looking at Billy. 'How did you know the gun would do that?'

'I didn't,' he said. 'It was a long shot. But she didn't know that. How's the patient?'

The wound was smaller than Harriet expected. She put her ear to her chest and listened to Sandra's breathing; it was erratic but normal, no whistling or gurgling. Her lung had not been hit. The amount of blood looked dramatic but was hardly a gusher; the subclavian artery had been missed too. The slump in her shoulder told Harriet the woman's clavicle was certainly broken, probably in several places from the force of the bullet straining the collarbone.

'Can you do anything for her, doc?' Billy asked.

Harriet bit her lip. 'This is not my area of expertise,' she said. 'She's not going to die here, not anytime soon, but we need to get her to the A&E.' She pointed at Sandra's back. 'There's no exit wound. The bullet is still in there and it needs to come out or she could die of infection. And her shoulder will need to be set, probably with surgery . . .'

'No fucking way are we calling anyone,' Buster said. 'You fix her up here, end of story.'

Harriet looked at his glowering face. She could refuse; there was every possibility her intervention would do the patient more harm than good. The Cameron Bridge hospital was only a few miles away. It was underfunded and understaffed, but still had an A&E. They would doubtless be better prepared to handle a wound like this than she ever could be.

He must have been watching her weigh up the options, because Seminole Billy cracked the knuckles of both hands. It was clear they did not want any more people involved in what was going on than already were. And her knowledge, while not perfect, was better than nothing – certainly better than they could do on their own if they chose not to take the injured woman to hospital. With luck, Harriet might be able to stabilise her and they would seek help later. Certainly it didn't seem the two men were going to give her many options. 'I can't do anything about the bone,' she said. 'But I can try to retrieve the bullet and stop the bleeding.'

'Then fucking get on with it already.'

The three of them lifted Sandra onto one of the steel mortuary workstations. The bleeding started again now that direct pressure was off the wound. Harriet unwound a length of gauze from a large spindle, tied a tourniquet, and advised Billy how to

255

keep the pressure on while she rolled up her sleeves, washed and powdered her hands, and put on a thick pair of rubber gloves. Sandra closed her eyes and sobbed softly as Harriet probed the shoulder with her finger.

'No painkillers?' she moaned.

Harriet shook her head. 'My patients don't usually need them,' she quipped, then felt guilty for joking. 'Sorry. Gallows humour.'

While Billy looked after the slowing blood flow, Harriet turned a tap on the autopsy station. She cleaned around the wound from the short hose they normally used to flush waste out of the guts at post-mortems. There were no surgical disinfectants to hand, nothing that could go on living flesh, anyway. Another thing they usually did not need in the mortuary. Water and some industrial soap were all she had. Red, then pink bubbles gurgled down the drain at the end of the tilted platform. She glanced up at Buster. 'I need you to hold her down. As firmly as you can. This is going to feel worse coming out than it did going in.'

Harriet unwrapped a post-mortem scalpel blade and slotted it into a steel handle. With the scalpel in one hand and a pair of disposable plastic forceps in the other, she probed the edge of the wound. She cut a bit into the skin on either side, as neatly as she could manage, to widen the hole enough to explore further. The first inch of plastic disappeared into the flesh. Harriet gripped the forceps tighter and cut again so she could go further. Sandra's shoulder twitched but she was weak with pain and Buster kept her firmly held.

Harriet took a deep breath. The bullet had gone deeper than she thought. The scapula could be fractured as well. She was going to need to cut even more. She felt bad for Sandra. Her work was not comparable to a surgeon's or even to a GP's. Her patients underwent surgeries they never got back up from again. Once evidence was catalogued, it hardly mattered how the pieces went back together.

Harriet could barely remember the last time she practiced

medicine on anyone living. Probably during her student years, when they had to select placements. She had known from the start she wanted to be in Forensic Pathology, but they were meant to diversify, so she did six weeks in general obstetrics and the same in a GUM clinic. Those mainly involved administering antibiotics and being on the business end of a speculum. She once assisted in a delivery using the ventouse, a sort of plunger-cum-hoover that extracted a misaligned baby from the birth canal and left a deep red mark on the child's head. The closest she had ever come to A&E or proper surgery were a few prosections she performed for the Biomedical Sciences department, demonstrating dissection techniques to first-years in order to earn some money during term time. Even then the patients – such as they were – had all been dead.

'Well, what are you waiting for?' Billy snapped. 'Get to it.'

'Right. Yes,' Harriet said. She tried to remember what little ballistics she had read in textbooks or seen at conference presentations over the years. Gunshot wounds were uncommon enough when she started working and even more rare in the decades since the handgun ban. How she approached the removal would depend on what was happening under the surface. It could be straightforward or the bullet could have bloomed into a mushroom-shaped popcorn of shrapnel inside the body. She looked at Buster. 'Is it a hollow point or a full metal jacket?' she said.

He checked the magazine in the Kimber. 'FMJ,' Buster confirmed. 'Range rounds.'

That was a good start. Finding it, however, was more difficult; a higher power round that did not expand on impact would have travelled further into the body. Harriet's forceps disappeared almost completely until the tip of her finger was pressing against the skin. Finally, she met a firm resistance, an edge of metal. It was not near Sandra's lung, and though taking it out might cause more bleeding and tearing of tissue, it was not life-threatening. She readjusted her fingers on the green plastic and gripped again. Wiggling her hand back and forth in tiny movements, the metal began slowly to dislodge.

Sandra passed out for the rest of the procedure.

Harriet stitched the wound with a large S-shaped needle, sharp on both sides and curved like a fishing hook without the barb. The waxed, heavy thread, dark brown and normally used for closing up bodies after an autopsy, would certainly scar. But that was the least of anyone's concerns. Sandra's breath was deep and even now. She was asleep and Harriet hoped for her sake it would be a long one. She looked at the faces of the men standing on the other side of the table. Her heart clutched; she remembered what she had come back to work to do. 'Has anyone seen Iain?' she said.

'That white man in the back?' Buster said. 'He's passed out on the bed with a Tennent's. Dead to the world. Looks like somebody drugged his skinny arse.'

'Augustine, no doubt,' Billy harrumphed. 'We're out a shit ton of money if we don't go after that bitch.'

'You mean this money?' Buster pulled a purple hemp shoulder bag from under his jacket.

Billy grabbed it and looked inside. It wasn't everything, but it was enough to cover their stake. 'Where the hell did you get this?'

'She left it in the locker room.' He watched Billy rifle through the rest of the bag. 'I already looked,' Buster said. 'There's nothing else in there but some makeup and shit. No ID.'

'Thanks, man,' Billy said. He withdrew a fat wad of fifties, tucked it in his jacket, and threw the bag on the floor. 'Good work. Now let's finish this off and get gone.' His gaze fell on Harriet. 'Buster, you know what to do.' The tall man retrieved his Glock and aimed it at the pathologist.

Harriet gulped. She had never been on the business end of a gun before, but now it was the second time in one day. In spite of seeing her fair share of deaths over the course of her career, she was hardly familiar with firearms at all. That mattered little.

She knew that the instinctive fear that swept her now, the goose pimples rising on her skin, the flush of blood to her cheeks, was due to her sympathetic nervous system preparing her to run. She also knew that even if she did run, she had no chance of outpacing this man. There were only two exits. The shutters, which he blocked, and the front door that still swung open, on the other side of the low barrier. She would have to slow down to get over it, and she had no doubt both his motivation and his fitness far outstripped hers.

She knew what the right thing to do was. The right thing would be to raise the alarm. She needed to call Fiona, wake up Iain in the flat, and try to get this lot hauled over to Blair Mhor for breaking and entering and goodness knows what else. Her right hand strayed to her pocket and found the mobile there.

'Don't even think about it,' Buster growled. Harriet, panicked, dropped it to the floor. 'Get against the wall,' he said, and gestured to the cabinets by the handwash station. Harriet walked backwards until she was up against the cupboards.

'So I shoot her,' Buster said. 'Then what?'

'The obvious,' Billy said. 'Where better to get rid of a body than in a morgue? Clean it up, stick her in a bag in the back of the cooler. No doubt the same thing Augustine was planning to do with us. And you know, she was probably on to something. In a cowtown like this it'll be weeks before the Keystone Cops even figure out where she is.'

'You can't do that,' Harriet said. 'I came to the mortuary straight from the police station. They showed me a CCTV video with Lucy – with Augustine on it. If I don't turn up soon, this is the first place they'll look for me.'

'Like hell,' Billy said, but something seemed to give him pause.

'Why were you at the police station anyway?' Buster said.

'Because I was the reason they were looking for anyone else at all,' she said. 'I knew there was something wrong about the arrest in Newcastle. Something about it didn't feel right. The police weren't going to keep investigating, but I wouldn't let it go. That was how they found a CCTV image with Lucy and the man who was arrested. Time stamped the same day the body was dumped.'

'Shit,' Buster said and turned to Billy. 'She's right. This is the first place they'll come looking.'

'So what?' he shrugged. 'No camera, no problem. We'll be long gone.'

'Please,' Harriet said. 'Please.' The word felt strange in her mouth. She had never begged to save herself. Not when the tribunal in Leeds found her guilty of professional misconduct, not when her partner there walked out on her less than a month later. 'Don't shoot me. I won't tell them anything. I won't.'

The media would come sniffing as soon as it was revealed that Miri Goldstein was not, in fact, dead. Or that she was, but the person whose Cheshire Cat smile peeked out from under a Nazi uniform cap on the front pages of all the newspapers was not Miri Goldstein after all. There would be questions the police would want answered. And the press would want to know how they could have got it so wrong.

More to the point, they would want to know how the pathologist had got it so wrong. And Dr Harriet Hitchin, formerly professor, formerly of Leeds University, formerly a respected Home Office pathologist with a publication record founded almost entirely on sloppy records and unverifiable data, would be even more firmly in their crosshairs than she was now in Buster's.

'Please. Listen to me. Everyone leaves here,' Harriet said. 'Separately. We leave Iain in the flat. He'll wake up later and assume he fell asleep after drinking too much.'

Seminole Billy blinked his strange pale eyes, shook his head. 'No way, lady,' he said. 'You're a witness. And if there's one thing me and Buster never do, it's leave witnesses.'

'Please,' Harriet said. As long as she was talking, they were not shooting. Maybe she had a chance. 'I'm as culpable as any of you. More so. I'm the one who befriended Lucy – or whatever you want to call her. If not for me, she never would have been in here, we wouldn't all be here now. It's my fault.' Her stomach lurched, an acidic squeeze jumped into the back of her throat. 'I won't grass on you because I can't. If the press find out, my life is worthless. I'd probably be arrested. I'd be struck off, lose my job, everything I have. I would be ruined.'

'Fuck that shit,' Buster said. 'I know how this goes. You tell us one thing and as soon as we're out of the door you do another. Yeah, they might arrest you. So what? When the dust clears, it's the establishment bitch who walks away clean.'

'Think what you want,' Harriet said. She was babbling now, unable to stop the words pouring out of her mouth. 'But you have to believe me. Please. I'll stay here until you're gone. Whether you trust me not to call the police is one thing. If you kill me, the time you spend covering it up is time you could have spent getting away. The police station at Blair Mhor is five minutes away. I mean . . . I don't know any of you. I wouldn't even know how to start giving them descriptions if I wanted to.'

Harriet closed her eyes. A hard lump formed in her throat. So this is how it ends then, she thought. She waited.

And waited. And nothing happened.

'She's probably right,' Billy said. Harriet opened her eyes to see Buster nod assent. 'Let's get out before the crap really does hit the fan.'

Buster lifted Sandra off the table while Billy took charge of the gun, keeping its malevolent, unblinking eye trained on Harriet until they left. The front door slammed shut behind them.

Harriet fell back to her knees. Her head rested on the cold linoleum floor of the mortuary. One of the fluorescent lights flickered, the metallic ping of a bulb about to give out. She would have cried if she had any tears. Those had been wrung out of her back in Leeds, over many sleepless nights and even more empty bottles. She had nothing left. There was only the desolate certainty that by letting them walk out she had saved herself, and her career such as it was, by the skin of her teeth. And the even greater certainty that she could never talk to Fiona again.

: 40 :

The damp ground rose steeply behind the mortuary. Denise could barely see the trees in the thick dark night, much less Miri in front of her. The sound of her crashing through branches and bracken gave her a general direction though, and she followed it.

Her shoes sank in the moss and leaves. After a few minutes of struggling the woods gave way to a broad, rocky hillside, empty of trees. The moonlight offered some vision: Miri was about fifty metres in front of her.

Instead of wet forest floor underfoot there were now lumpy hummocks of grass and heather on the exposed side of the hill. Denise was forced to slow down. The pitch here was not only sharply steeper, but it was also difficult to tell, each time she stepped down, whether her foot would land on solid ground or a furrow between two rocks. She was a runner, yes, but no fell runner. She looked up to see Miri silhouetted by the full moon. To her surprise, the distance between them was growing.

At the next crest of the hill Miri turned a sharp left. Denise reached the spot almost a minute later. Here, there was a walkers' path, paved with stone and gravel. She paused a moment to catch her breath, letting the searing pain in her lungs subside. On a flat surface like this one she would be more likely to close the gap between them. She was fast enough, but – more importantly – she had endurance.

What she did not have was any knowledge of where this route went. Miri was probably going to a place she knew, but where was that? She checked the mobile still in her pocket but there was no reception. Denise only dimly remembered the Ordnance Survey maps of the area they used to examine, planning the hiking trip that never happened.

Then it dawned on her. They were less than a kilometre from Taynuilt bothy.

Denise squinted. She could not see Miri on the path now, past where it dipped beyond a stony outcrop of boulders that shone dark silver in the moonlight. But if she was right about their location, from here the elevation dropped until it reached the sea. Taynuilt was on a clearing only a few feet higher than the mean high water springs mark. There would be a burn and a pebbled beach, and then the bothy itself – an abandoned stalker's cottage. She started jogging in that direction. There was enough light that she could see what might have been the ridgeline of a corrugated metal roof. She started to pick up speed.

After about ten minutes the bothy came into full view. Miri was gone from the path, probably inside. A candle flickered in the cottage's small window. She stepped over a ford of stones that had been strewn across the burn and felt the icy snowmelt filling her boots.

The bothy sat close to the water, exactly how it was placed on the map, close to the seaweed tide lines. A black RIB was tied to a rock and floated just offshore. It bobbed in the gentle wavelets. The cottage's low stone walls were scarcely higher than Denise's head and most of the pointing had come away. The metal roof was held to the structure with lengths of twisted wire stretched to boulders on the ground. On one side the roof was intact, but on the other, rust was making headway on some of the panels. Signs posted on and around the building warned of danger and forbade anyone to enter. The front door was ajar. Denise hesitated a moment before nudging it with her toe.

The door swung open into a spartan room. There was a sleeping platform along one wall, up to the old fireplace at the end. On the opposite wall, a stripped wooden table and single plastic chair sat under the window. The small flame of a votive candle flickered when Denise walked in.

Miri looked up from where she was crouched over a rucksack. She shoved the last of her drybags into the bag and closed it up.

'Took you long enough,' she said. Miri stood up and slung the pack over one shoulder. 'I thought you were fitter than that.'

Denise's heart was still pounding, her breath coming in short gasps. She didn't know if it was because of the physical effort of running up the hill, or something else. 'I'm not going with you,' she panted. 'Miri – this is wrong. This is all wrong.'

Miri tilted her head. The dyed black hair made her green eyes look especially vivid. 'What's wrong?'

'You know what,' she said. 'This was not how we planned this to happen. Not at all.'

'I told you I was coming back for you,' Miri said. 'I kept my promise, didn't I?'

Denise's face grew hot. 'Not like this!' she said. She took a ragged breath and tried to collect herself. 'Not like this.'

Miri walked towards Denise and slid her arms around her waist. 'I didn't want to trouble you with the details, darling.' Her warm breath in Denise's ear made the hairs on her arms stand up. 'You have to trust me. This way was for the best.'

'This was not what you said was going to happen. You said you had something to sell in Cameron Bridge, you found us a place to stay. I thought—' A sob wrenched her chest. 'I really thought that you were dead.'

Miri frowned, and pulled back slightly. 'Oh, honey,' she said. 'I just thought if you knew how I was going to do it, Archie might find out. And he would have ruined everything for us, and we would never be together.' She tried to pull Denise closer again, but Denise twisted away from her grip.

She had been stupid, so stupid. Miri had seen her on the Haymarket that day, and she had walked away, pretended not to know who Denise was when she called her name. But an hour later she sent a text – *meet me at the path* – and Denise had known exactly where she meant.

Miri had told her, she realised now, everything she wanted to hear. That she had to cut contact with Denise all those years ago, that someone had been after her but wasn't now. That she had a plan, that they could be together. That she just had to sit tight and wait, and soon, Newcastle and Archie and the dull life Denise had resigned herself to would be a thing of the past.

Miri had looked so beautiful then, standing on the Waggon-way, the last afternoon light glinting red in her hair. It had been as if no time had passed. Denise could see now that she had fallen for a lie because she wanted so badly for it to be true. And the realisation made her angry. It made her furious.

'A man killed himself because of you!' she shouted. 'Another man is in jail for a murder he didn't commit.' Denise paced the floor. 'I mourned you, Miri. I mourned you like – like that family in Gateshead who believe their daughter was a call girl. Who think she only just died.'

'Baby, please.' Miri's face contorted with something that might have been amusement. 'A man killed himself because he was lying to himself, his family, and the world,' Miri said. 'Even if Lionel Brant had never met me, that would still have been the case. Do you really think I was the first sex worker he met? I'm not responsible for someone else's conscience. Or for their inability to handle the inevitable when it all comes out.'

'And Archie?'

Miri crossed her arms over her chest and looked Denise up and down. 'So you are still taking out Archie's trash, then, like a good little girlfriend.'

Denise bristled. 'Well,' she said. 'You are alive, so he was right when he said he didn't kill you.'

Miri shook her head sadly. 'You are incredible. You came all the way up here to clear that man's name? After everything he did to you.'

Denise gulped. 'I came because of you,' she said. 'I know he isn't perfect.' No one was perfect. That still didn't excuse the things he really had done, to her or to Miri.

Miri laughed, a short sharp honk. 'You always were the master of understatement. He lied to you, he abused you, he cheated on you for years . . .'

'Not that it's any of your business, but I kicked him out the night he was arrested. I want us to be together, but this is too much. I don't want anyone else to get hurt. If he gets done for something, it shouldn't be for something he didn't do.'

'Something he didn't do, now there's an interesting concept,' Miri said. 'Let me tell you what he did do. He got in contact with me about a year ago. Tried to make a booking through my site. I tried to block his messages, because who needs that kind of creep in their lives? But he wouldn't give up. He kept starting new accounts. He found my number. Then, those two down there, Billy and Buster, put the word out that they had a gun collection they needed rid of.' She smiled, the tilting of her lips so familiar to Denise. 'And then I happened to run into you that day in town . . .'

'And that's when you decided I was worth having in your life again,' Denise said bitterly. 'Because you needed a fall guy in case Archie didn't work out.'

Miri ignored this. 'Your Archie, he's been working both sides as an investigator for the Revenue for extra money. Men like him always do. But you knew, didn't you? Because you're not as dumb as you pretend to be. There's no way he could live the lifestyle he wants, not even on your money.' She didn't wait for Denise to answer. 'When I told him about the guns, he jumped at the chance to sell them through dodgy contacts he'd made in the car boots.'

Denise's head swam. The black threads were coming back, rushing almost, like a seaweed-strewn tide, like a tsunami. She steadied herself on the back of the chair and felt as if she might be sick.

Miri continued. 'He sold them, and took his cut of the money. You know what he did with that cash? He took Josie on holiday abroad. Not you, her. That's how much your seven years meant to him. His car was the dead drop – where he left the money for me and Billy. There is practically no security at those long-term car parks. You'd be surprised. Anyway. He bragged about the whole thing to me – told me how, even all these years later, you were still as clueless as you'd been when he met you. He was going to propose to her on that holiday, did you know that?'

'No. You're lying.' And yet, Denise knew it must have been true. The ring was never for her. Archie had not been waiting for the right moment to propose to her, because she would never be Good Denise. He had been planning to give it to someone else all along.

'You should be thanking me,' Miri said. 'I did it all to save you from him.'

Denise narrowed her eyes. 'Dumping a corpse to help me?'

'I had to get rid of Miriam's body anyway,' Miri shrigged. 'Bella and Alan were coming back, so there was no way I could stay in Lamia House. They thought they were corresponding with her all that time, not me. And it would have gone off without a hitch too, only he couldn't control his temper, could he? Him and Josie had a bust-up, he comes back a day early and finds me at the car with the body. Awkward as fuck. I told him he needed to help me get rid of it. Told him if he ever breathed a word about it the guys I got the guns from would be down on him. Which I guess is why he's still sitting in a cell staying shtum. And would you believe, he was the one who suggested Cameron Bridge. I didn't even have to make up a story to get it here.'

Denise looked at the bare stone and dirt floor. Her face burned. She had bought the fantasy and it turned out to be horror.

Miri reached forward and put her hands on Denise's shoulders. 'I am sorry,' she said. 'I should have let you know what was going on.' She paused. 'When did you figure out I was alive?'

'I had an inkling,' Denise said. 'But I didn't know for certain until I saw the note on the bed in the hotel today.' The school-girl lettering, she knew it well. The precise loops and peaks of black ink that told her exactly whose hand had written those words. The only thing Miri had never been able to change: her sinister hands.

'Sweetie, honey.' Miri started rubbing Denise's shoulders. She stiffened but did not pull away this time. 'I always thought you could be so much more than you are now. What does it take to make you see that? I seduced your boyfriend – right in front of you! – and you couldn't see what he was. I seduced you. Tell me, what does it take? What does it take to break through that mask you wear, so you can see the woman you really are?'

Denise started shaking. She knew that every word Miri was saying was true, but that did not make it easier to hear. Even if a snake tells the truth it is still a snake.

A pain started to crush her chest like a belt tightening. She could run back over the hill, try to find reception, and call the police. But then what? She could not force Miri to do anything, what point would there be? Miri, whoever she was, would never confirm the story. There was a real Miriam Goldstein and she was dead. Everyone involved, from the police to the politicians, wanted someone to pay for this, and for it to be wrapped up quickly.

Archie should not have been the person arrested. If Miri disappeared there would be nothing to prove she wasn't the girl whose remains had lain in a bin in Cameron Bridge. Denise would look insane if she tried to claim otherwise. The realisation hit her that Archie had not been the only one to use her. There had been no murder, no one in danger apart from the people Miri decided to put there. No one to save. Miri was a mirror facing on to another mirror, a person Denise did not even know.

'Let him rot, Denise. You know in your heart he isn't worth any of this.' Miri put a finger under her chin and looked deep into her eyes. 'Come with me,' she said. Her voice was as low as a cat's purr. 'It can still be like we planned. I miss you.'

Denise's eyelids fluttered. 'I can't. I . . . I don't even know who you are,' she said.

'You already know everything you need to know.' They stood there, still. A breeze came from over the hill. It blew the door open, ruffled the sleeping embers in the fireplace back to life. 'Come with me,' Miri said, and picked up her bag again. 'The rest of the world is just on the other side of this door.'

It would be so easy. Denise wanted to follow. She wanted it like she had wanted nothing else.

She could not deny the warm stirring Miri's words aroused. Then what? How would they live, like vagrants or princesses? Or both? Going from one crumbling bothy to another, picking up the skin of someone else's life and wearing it as if it was her own. She could never go back to her house again. Never speak to her family again. Nothing would be worth that, nothing would replace that, no fine fluffy down of a warm bed or table glistening with Michelin-star feasts could be enough to leave behind everything she had ever been and everything she was. She knew in that instant that she loved Miri. And she knew, had always known, that love was not enough.

Denise turned away from Miri. Tears fell onto the dry pine tabletop. She heard footsteps going towards the door. 'Now or never, Denise,' she said. 'It's your decision. It always has been.' She waited in the open door a minute or two. Then all Denise heard were her footsteps heading to the pebbled beach, the chug of the engine as the throttle opened and the boat motored away.

: **41** :

Denise went to the Cameron Bridge station, where the lights were on and the doors were open all night. She dared not go back to her hotel. She tried to sleep but the metal seats were hard and cold, and even if they had not been, it was doubtful she could have stopped her swirling thoughts long enough to drop off. In such a small town someone must have seen something, reported some unusual activity to the police. And if not, anyone who was in the mortuary could tell the police at any time, send them sifting through CCTV footage and forensic evidence until the trail finally led to her door. Surely it couldn't be so easy. Someone would tell.

By the time the sun lightened the sky Denise realised that if anyone was going to tell, it was going to be her. She worried a smooth oval stone in her pocket, a pebble from the beach at Taynuilt. No, it was too crazy. There was nothing to be gained and a lot for her to lose if she told anyone what had happened that night.

And perhaps she had enjoyed it. A little bit.

Slow-moving attendants opened the tourist information kiosk at seven a.m. Denise bought a ticket in cash for the first coach going south. The bus was busy, students on summer break. Rucksacks took up most of the space between aisles. In her muddy trousers and boots she blended in.

The landscape outside the window unspooled like a film: the narrow gorge and steep peaks of Glencoe, the long, barren expanse of Rannoch Moor. At stops along the way, laughing groups of hikers disembarked for trails and pubs, and new passengers replaced them. Rain settled on the green and grey of the mountains, smeared everything until it looked like an oil painting. Perhaps that was what Miri liked best about the place.

At every stop fewer and fewer people were on the coach. Old ladies with blue hair and boxy waterproofs chatted about their grandchildren down south. Backpacking couples watched videos on their phones. A lone man sprawled across two seats, snoring loudly. No one noticed her.

She went through her mobile, erasing as much of her call history as she could. Sandra's number and Billy's. When the signal reappeared she logged in to the escort sites and deleted her profile. She checked the news, but Miri's death and Archie's arrest were buried in regional pages now. Even Lionel Brant barely rated a mention. The headlines were all about the new opposition leader, Morag Munro, and her debut performance at Prime Minister's Questions.

When the coach changed in Edinburgh, Denise was seized by a momentary desire to get on the bus going back north. She stopped herself. Miri – wherever she was – was long gone. Denise had to go back to Newcastle. She had her house, alone. She had her job, if they let her back after her leave of absence.

Then there was Archie. If she never told him what she knew then that would be it. Maybe his solicitor would push him to plead guilty. It was as good as done. She had not saved him. And Miri. It turned out Miri had never needed saving after all.

She waited for the crushing feeling in her chest to return. But something new seemed to have replaced the black threads. A slender beam of silvery light, slippery and warm and smelling of vanilla. *He'll get what he deserves*, it said, and her heart fluttered with excitement. It was a voice she recognised. *You can't save everyone. Just get on and live*, it whispered in familiar tones. She didn't want to put a name to it though – not yet.

Denise spent the last leg of the journey looking at the listing for Lamia House on estate agent websites. It was already under offer. She swiped through photos that showed rooms stripped of furniture, but she still recognised them: the tiled bathroom, the papered toilet room. The bedrooms on the first floor, the attic rooms. The William Morris room.

The Paratas would never know that their housesitter's body had lain, dead in a bathtub filled with sand, in their basement for years. Denise remembered the odd, musty smell of leather down there, the tomb-like sensation of being under the house in the near dark. It would be better if the Paratas did not find out about that. Or the truth about a woman who had for years pretended to be someone they knew.

A month later she went to see Miriam Goldstein's grave. It was in a cemetery south of the river, a twenty minute Metro journey from Wallsend. Denise emerged into sunshine and walked through a neighbourhood where her knee-length skirt felt suddenly revealing and men in flat, wide-brimmed hats crossed the street to avoid meeting her on the pavement.

The grave was in the far corner of the cemetery. She was briefly surprised to see that it existed at all. She thought the Goldsteins had sat shiva for their daughter years ago. But then, she reminded herself, the real Miriam was not dead to her parents, not when Denise knew Miri. They never had a funeral for her until they knew she really was dead.

A bird's call rattled from the bushes on the edge of the cemetery. 'Nightjar,' Denise said to no one in particular. Where was her Miri now? When she imagined her, she pictured a woman in sunglasses on a private jet. Or slinking across a dance floor, clubbing until dawn in Ibiza. Lamia had, after all, been the mythological mistress of Zeus. It would take more than a misfire in Cameron Bridge to make someone like that give up her taste for high adventure.

The white headstone that rose from the earth slender and pale. Most of the writing was in Hebrew but Miriam Goldstein's name was also in English. Denise looked around. No one else was nearby. She took the stone from Taynuilt out of her pocket, felt its smooth cool face briefly, then placed it next to the other stones on top of the monument that the family must have put there.

On the way out of the cemetery, Denise's phone rang. She checked the screen, and answered it with a smile. It turned out Jack from her master's course had remembered her after all that time. Wasn't it shocking what happened to Miri? It was unbelievable, she said. He said he was coming to Newcastle soon for a job interview, would she like to meet up for coffee?

She'd love that, she said. She really would.

EPILOGUE

When she dreams, she dreams of a time when it seemed no one mattered in the world except the two of them. Other people were figments of their imagination, unreal. Even their own parents. She dreams of the forts they made out of sheets and pillows, an entire world to get lost in.

She dreams of the food her grandmother used to make. The pan-fried dumplings joined together by a lacy crisp of rice flour, served whole so the twins could break them apart with their small, greedy hands. The pungent and spiced papaya shredded and bruised in a tall, tube-shaped pestle and mortar. The tiny pots of pastes, the writing on the labels a language they cannot read.

She dreams of Darwin coming back. Things will be the way they were before. Before the scholarship, before the tsunami. Before even the pool. Inside the cool, white cotton walls that rippled when they laughed.

When she wakes and looks in the mirror she sees a face that is like his and unlike his. The long features that look somehow slightly wrong on her, but refined and classic on him. The beauty of his face, a beauty she knew before they were even born and which no longer exists. With time the memory of that face becomes less strong. It is swallowed by her own living reflection. She will get older and he never will. It becomes so painful to look at that one day, she stops. She decides she will never look in a mirror again.

Until the night she meets the woman in the green velvet dress.

ACKNOWLEDGMENTS

Maggie McNeill

Sarah Brown

Laura Gerrard and Genevieve Narey

Patrick Walsh and Michael Burton

Jimmy Creed

Luke Martin, John Rickards, and Russel D McLean